The Entropy of Knowledge

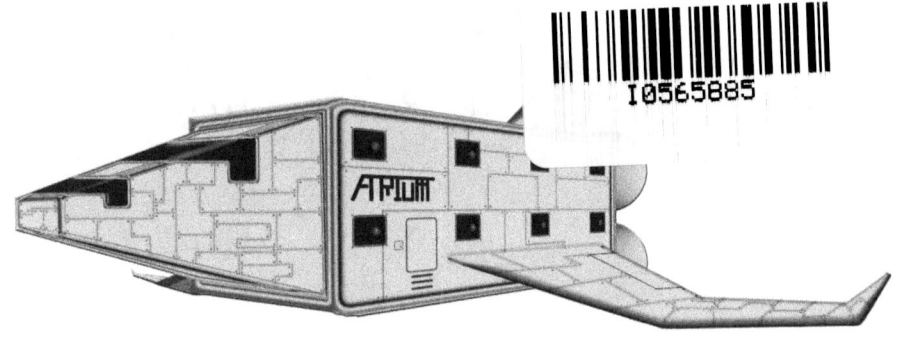

Mark Dellandre
and Britton Learnard

DIVERTIR
PUBLISHING
Salem, NH

The Entropy of Knowledge

Mark Dellandre and Britton Learnard

Images from https://openclipart.org and https://pixabay.com

Published by Divertir Publishing LLC
PO Box 232
North Salem, NH 03073
http://www.divertirpublishing.com/

ISBN-13: 978-1-938888-21-2
ISBN-10: 1-938888-21-9

Library of Congress Control Number: 2018954215

Printed in the United States of America

Acknowledgements

Mark Dellandre:

No piece of work is ever written in a vacuum. There are always people to thank for their hard work along the way. This book is no exception.

My friends and family who have supported me along the way, I owe a tremendous deal of thanks. Especially Dominic and Natalia, who accepted my crazy nonsense without batting an eye. And Amber, who I wrote my first story for a long time ago, and who made me feel like maybe I could be an author someday. That day has come.

Two people who deserve a great deal of praise are Ken and Heather. Ken took a big chance with our manuscript and really gave us the break we needed. Everything you will read is because he took that chance. Heather, on the other hand, really gave me a lot of great tips and taught me how to write. Maybe someday I'll take her advice.

Britton Learnard:

As I sit here and write this acknowledgment I cannot help but feel surreal considering the chain of events that led me here. **The Entropy of Knowledge** had its genesis as a conversation that Mark and I had about merging black holes when I was blitheringly drunk. From the ether of my delirium, and Mark's audacity, a dare was made between us to craft a story that was both funny and intelligent: something we will never know because we've read this book so many times.

From here I would like to thank my parents. My mother, who would read stories like James and the Giant Peach at a young age, and gave me a great appreciation for books, reading, and eventually writing. My father who instilled in me the virtues of knowledge and learning as we paged through his collection of atlases and encyclopedias (of which he insists he can look up something faster than I can find it on Google. Joke's on you Dad).

I would be remiss as an author of Science Fiction if I were not to tip my hat to the author who made me fall in love with the subject, the late Arthur C. Clarke. I was given a choice by an English teacher to read either Catcher in the Rye by J. D. Salinger or Clarke's Childhood's End. Thankfully I chose the latter and was gripped by the science fiction bug indefinitely.

Lastly, I would like to thank our editor Heather Meeks for providing some great ideas as well as some invaluable help on making our story much better, and, let's be honest, coherent. I cannot finish this without also thanking Ken Tupper for taking the time to read our manuscript and managing to see a polished gem hidden within a piece of ore...or at least a shiny rock. Yeah. Managing to see a shiny rock.

Contents

Prologue

WITHIN THE VASTNESS of empty space that exists between the planets of a solar system, there is typically not a lot of traffic. Yet that didn't stop Sophie from screaming into Lester's ears every five minutes about watching where he was going. "You're going to kill us!" the little old lady shouted at her red-faced husband.

"I'm not going to kill anyone!" he reiterated for the thousandth time. "We're not even within a light year of a single thing out here." He gestured to the inky blackness outside the window.

"Keep your hands on the wheel!" Sophie screeched, shaking him by his shoulders. "You're going to hit a comet."

"I might just if you don't unhand me this second, woman!"

Lester and Sophie had been married for 62 long years. They lived full lives, worked hard, made a boatload of money in their time together, and were now leaving their solar system to retire in a warmer part of the galaxy. Maybe somewhere down true south. Sophie was tired of living in a place with two suns, and Lester was tired of listening to her complain, so they crammed their worldly possessions into their little space coupe and set out for the cosmos.

Space travel was rare these days, unless someone had a lot of money like them. The technology was hard to come across for most folks, and even worse, the people who owned space ships didn't have a clue how to operate them. Lester once heard on the AM/XM radio that some planets in his solar system didn't even know what space travel was. Apparently, his wife never forgot this little fact.

"That's why I still think you should stop and ask someone at the next planet for directions," Sophie said. "We might not see another living soul out here for the rest of the trip!"

"We didn't need any directions to get here. We don't need any now!"

"We didn't need directions because Marshall was driving, not you. You couldn't find your way out of a plastic bag!"

Lester felt his cheeks warm under his straw hat. He gripped the crème leather wheel even tighter. She would *never* let him live that plastic bag episode down, would she?

"Look." Sophie stuck her withered finger right past Lester's bulbous nose to point out the window. "That sign there says this is the last planet with a Bob Deans for the next three light years. Let's stop, Lester!"

1

The old man glanced at the faded metallic sign floating just outside the window. It was so caked with ice that he could barely make out the restaurant's logo: a breakfast sandwich wearing overalls. He scoffed, looking forward again.

"We don't need to stop. We're making good time."

"But I'm hungry!"

Lester nodded to the glove compartment in front of his wife. "We have plenty of dehydrated food in there. It should last us a decade."

"I don't like any of that stuff. I want scrambled eggs from Bob Deans! And maybe you could ask somebody there for directions."

"If you bring up directions one more time, just ONE MORE TIME, I'm going to plow this baby into the nearest quasar! You better believe it!"

Sophie shrank away and pulled a gumdrop from her pocketbook. "Now, Lester, there's no need to get so upset. If you don't want to stop at Bob Deans, then we don't have to stop at Bob Deans. But when we're months down the road, and you get a craving for some of Bob Deans' home cooked scrambled eggs, don't come crying to me!"

He could hear her false teeth flapping as she chewed, making his blood boil. "I won't get a craving for their scrambled eggs! I don't even *like* their scrambled eggs!"

"What are you talking about; you love Bob Deans' scrambled eggs."

"They're always gritty. I can do without them."

The sound of her chewing got louder. "Maybe this time they won't be. Oh, let's stop anyway. Please."

Before Lester had a chance to respond or make any more wild threats, a massive ship materialized in front of them. It was huge, sleek, and resembled a giant egg. The coupe screeched to a halt.

"Would you look at that," Lester said, catching his breath. "They came out of their warp drive right in front of us. That was a close one."

"They could have killed us!" Sophie clutched her flowery pillbox hat in panic. "I bet they don't even have insurance. You should give them a piece of your mind."

"I wonder what a ship like that is doing in our neck of the woods," Lester went on, ignoring his wife as he so often did. "That there is an invasion ship. Haven't seen one of those in years."

"You've never seen one before; quit lying." Sophie threw down her tiny pocketbook and turned on the dashboard radio. She held the mouthpiece to her lips and spun the rotary dial until she reached the colossal ship's frequency.

"You listen here, now," she shouted into the mouthpiece. "You better watch where you're going! What's the matter with you? There are decent people

2

out here, you know! So, mind your manners!" She slammed the mouthpiece back on its cradle with an air of finality.

A small compartment opened on the bottom of the egg-shaped ship. A laser turret popped out, blasted the coupe to dust, and retracted back inside. It didn't pay the destroyed vehicle the slightest bit of attention after that.

After all, it had a planet to invade.

Section I

Chapter α

BABYLON BRIGGS WOKE up in his humble room on the morning of his sixteenth birthday. The light of the twin suns shone through the solitary window, bright and warm. His eyes fluttered open, and a wide grin spread across his narrow face. With an excited start, he swung his legs over the side of his straw-stuffed mattress and bounced out of bed. Today wasn't just any other run-of-the-mill birthday. Today was the day he became an adult.

His father, or Papa Briggs as he was sometimes called, was cooking breakfast in the kitchen. He was a thin, middle-aged man with pointed slippers and a tuft of bright blue hair atop his head. The hair wasn't his natural color; it was an occupational necessity.

Papa Briggs worked as the under-jester to the Duke of the province. That meant he was lowest man in the jester hierarchy, and a source of ridicule in the village. Even the manure boys scoffed at him behind their wagons of dung. Sometimes, even Papa Briggs could be caught scoffing at himself in a mirror. All his life he worked towards being the head jester, but try as he might, he couldn't seem to figure out what to do or what color to dye his hair to be promoted. The only person who didn't look down upon his father was Babylon, who saw the daffy old man as the only family he had left in the world.

"Good morning, Son," his father said, with a cheerful jig.

"Good morning, Dad." Babylon yawned. "What's for breakfast?"

"Oh, the usual," the kindly old man said with a smile. "Barley cakes."

Babylon looked into the dingy pot which sizzled on the wood stove and immediately regretted it. The grains inside crackled, giving off an all-too-familiar pungent odor. He rolled his eyes.

"Aw, come on, Dad," he sighed. "Today's going to be important for me. I was hoping for a nice, big breakfast. Or at least one I can keep down 'til lunch."

"Well, I was going to cook up some chicken, but darn it if old Clucky hasn't been clinging to life these last few days." Papa Briggs shot a dirty look at the chicken in its pen outside the window.

Babylon and his father sat and ate their unfortunate breakfast in silence. He was more than ready to get the day started. Today was going to be the biggest day of his whole life. Today he would undergo his Rite of Passage.

Every year, all the children who had recently turned sixteen would endure the village's Rite of Passage. It was one of their oldest traditions and dated back to the origins of the town. To be considered true adults, the sixteen-year-old boys and girls would journey to the mysterious Mount Trespass and bring back means to protect their families from invaders and the dangerous wildlife that lurked around the village. It used to be a solemn task fraught with all kinds of peril, but nowadays, it was more of an annual celebration.

Over the decades, the children encountered fewer and fewer hardships, and when they did return home, there wasn't really a need to protect their families because most of the dangerous wildlife had moved on to better, tastier villages. The others in town regarded the Rite as an obligation, but Babylon viewed it as the single most important event in his life. He wanted nothing more than to become an adult. To become a man.

When he finished his breakfast, his father stood from his seat and jigged over to the wooden cabinet by the stove. He opened the dilapidated doors and pulled something out, a goofy grin on his face the whole time.

"I have a little present for you," Papa Briggs said. "I hope it aids you on your journey today." He laid a small, shoddily wrapped package on the table.

"Aw, pop, you shouldn't have," Babylon said, starting to grin himself.

"Happy birthday." His father pulled him into a hug.

Babylon tore the wrapping off the gift to reveal an old wooden box. He opened it, and inside was a small dagger made of solid steel. He held up his new toy, so it glinted in the sunlight. It certainly wasn't a weapon that could kill any vicious animals from the woods, but it would certainly do the job on smaller ones, like Clucky.

"Wow." His mouth hung agape. "Thanks, Dad."

"You're welcome, Son. Just make sure you're careful when you play with it," he said, staring at the dagger. "You know, that thing's been in our family for a long time. My dad gave it to me, and his dad gave it to him, and his father stole it from a farmer. I think now is as good a time as any to pass it down to you."

Babylon slipped his gift into his belt and stood. "Now I really can't wait for this journey to begin."

"Whoa, slow down there." His father laughed. "You still have a while yet before the Duke gets here. In fact, there are a couple of chores I need you to do around here. Remember, the whole point of becoming an adult is to care for your family."

Babylon's face fell. He couldn't believe he would have to do chores today. "You're right, Dad," he sighed. "What do you need me to do?"

"For starters, we need to replace our living room wall. It burned down last night."

"Again? How did it happen this time?"

8

Papa Briggs's eyes darted around. "Well, I was practicing a new trick for the Duke's arrival, and I…well, I guess I haven't really gotten the hang of it yet."

"A new trick?"

"Oh, yeah! I think the Duke's going to love it. I spit fire into the air like a monster. I got the spitting part down, I got the fire part down, but somewhere in between, things just get out of hand. Here, let me show you…"

A few dramatic minutes later, Babylon stepped out of his house onto the dirt road with a task at hand: find wood and straw to replace the wall in the living room and the new smoldering hole in the kitchen.

His village was simple, perhaps too simple. It wasn't a place that put a lot of stock in things like education or common sense, opting instead to focus on more inane fancies, such as rock burying, or dancing, or rock dancing. The residents were a friendly enough group, but Babylon always felt out of place. It was something he couldn't describe, but somewhere in the back of his mind, he knew he just didn't belong.

He walked along the dirt road, passing by primitive houses, huts, and lean-tos the residents called home. Some folks had poorly constructed wooden fences with mangy dogs in front of their dwellings. Others had better looking dogs but no fences. The poorest of the lot had neither. Babylon was content to just have a cozy home with a smug chicken hobbling around.

People stopped to wave hello as he walked by, an ax slung over his shoulder. Some said, "Happy birthday," and a few wished him luck on his upcoming Rite. He strode through the village with a smile on his face. He whistled a jaunty little tune, thinking nothing could dampen his bright mood today. Nothing whatsoever.

"Well, well, well," a gruff voice called from behind him. "If it isn't little Babylon Briggs."

He gulped. He didn't need to see the man to know it was Sheriff Kudgle. He spun around; his happiness vanishing within seconds. "Good morning, sheriff," he said, with practiced politesse. "How are you today?"

"I'm fine boy, just fine," the burly man said, with a sneer. "Say, didn't you turn sixteen today?"

"Yes, I did."

"That means you'll be undergoing the Rite of Passage, then?"

Babylon held his head high. "Yes, I will."

Sheriff Kudgle rubbed his copious chin in thought. Finally, he spit on the ground and gave Babylon a sharp smile. "You know, I just realized it's been a long time since somebody got hurt during the Rite. Too long, if you ask me."

The thought made him uneasy. He wasn't sure if the sheriff's words were a threat.

9

"I do hope you come back safe and sound," Kudgle said. He sauntered away with a joyless laugh.

Sheriff Kudgle hated him; that he was sure of. The sheriff didn't really like anybody, but he seemed to especially hate the Briggs. Maybe it was because, as a proud man of the law, he looked down on a title as low as under-jester. Maybe because as children, Babylon's father and Kudgle were constantly at odds. Or maybe his hatred started when Papa Briggs accidentally burned Kudgle's house down. Whatever the reason, the sheriff held contempt for them and made sure to remind them of it whenever he could.

Babylon tried to forget the ugly encounter as he followed the dirt road that ran through the village and into the forest. This was not his first time rebuilding a section of his home, so he knew where there was an abundance of wood, sticks, and grass deep inside. With his ax in hand, he strolled into the thicket.

The immediate part of the forest had already been harvested for wood, mostly by Babylon. He was one of the few people in town that could use an ax properly. A lot of the other villagers tried chopping trees down with the wrong end, or got their tongues stuck to the blade when it was cold. He ventured deep into the woods. The suns, which shined down so fiercely in the village, were blotted out by the increasing density of the treetops. Before long, the whole area was so dark he could barely see.

Just a little farther, he told himself. *Just a few more yards and I'll find something.*

Finally, he thought he spotted an easy answer to his problem: a felled tree in the middle of a clearing. It was an old dried out husk, but its branches and trunk still looked useable. For a fleeting moment, he considered just dragging the whole thing back to his house. That way, his father could burn the house down for weeks.

When he tried to lift the trunk to check its weight, something scurried inside the husk. He peered into the darkness and was surprised to see a small furry chipmunk step out. Then a cuddly squirrel. And finally, an adorable, little badger. His first thought was that this was the perfect chance to try out his new dagger. Maybe he could get that hot breakfast after all. But one look at the cuddly critters, with their chubby cheeks and razor teeth, melted his heart. He couldn't bring himself to kill these cute, meatless animals.

"Come on, get out of here," he said, trying to shoo the animals away so he could chop up the tree. But the animals wouldn't leave. Instead, they just looked at him with their furry faces in a way that seemed to plead with him not to take their home. As he looked deep into their adorable crimson eyes, he knew he couldn't go through with it.

"Don't worry, little fellas," he said, looking at each of them. "I won't take your house. But maybe I could just take some of its branches?"

10

He readied his ax, but the animals stared at him sadly. He could almost hear their tiny words. *Those branches are part of our home,* they seemed to say. *If you take them, we won't have enough room for everybody.*

He paused for a moment, weighing his options. Finally, he groaned and set his ax down. He couldn't take the branches either. In desperation, he went for a few sticks that were loosely scattered around the base of the tree, giving them a questioning look. The animals just shook their heads. Dejected, he continued further into the forest.

It took a few more minutes, but he finally found another tree that boasted better branches, with much uglier animals living inside it. He surveyed his surroundings. He'd never ventured this deep into the woods before. He was a little worried he might be too close to the Forbidden Zone.

The Forbidden Zone was a large area on the other side of the forest. It was thought to be another, bigger village that existed long before his was founded. Rumors said it was the remnants of a technologically advanced civilization. The Royal Family condemned it centuries ago because no one had ever gone inside and come back. But the greatest simple minds in the village claimed the place contained magical weapons and mystical secrets. It was a tantalizing concept. Everybody was curious to see what wonders lie within, but no one was brave enough to enter.

Babylon was afraid of the Forbidden Zone as well. He'd heard stories of it since he was a child and, like everyone else, the fear was ingrained in him. He resolved right then and there to never travel any further into the forest. He even decided to mark the tree he was about to carve up, so he would never go past it in the future.

It took a little while, but he was finally able to dig the letter "B" into the trunk with his dagger. B for Babylon! Although, most of the bark fell off during the process, so it looked more like a big splotch than an actual letter, but it was close enough. He looked over his handiwork with pride. And as a bonus, some twigs and loose branches fell off the tree while he was working, so there was a fair amount of wood to gather. He smiled.

Before long, his arms were full. He was just about to turn back when something caught his eye. A thin stream of light from the suns glinted off something on the ground a few feet away.

He dropped his bundle on the grass and hurried toward the shiny object, immediately forgetting about his decision to never venture past the tree. He picked the object up and looked it over. It was rectangular, metallic, and flipped open at the top. He studied it intently. It was unlike anything he'd ever seen before. Equal parts bewitching and sophisticated, like a magical item he didn't have the authority to wield.

11

He opened it, and inside was a small circular wheel. Gripped by a frenzy of discovery, he spun the wheel. Once, twice, three times. It made a pleasant clicking noise and released an unpleasant, burning odor. He spun it one more time, and it sparked into a flame. Excitement jolted through his body. He had made fire in his hand. It was incredible. Most of the time, fire was made in his village with sticks or houses, and even then, there was a bit of luck involved. But now, Babylon held in his hands a device that could make fire at will; a power that not even the Duke's mightiest alchemists wielded.

He turned the flame off and then on again to make sure it worked consistently. It did! Then he lit a few objects in the woods to make sure it was actual fire. It was! He'd made the discovery of a lifetime. Part of him wanted to venture into the forest even farther, to see what other treasures he could find, but his deep-rooted fear got the best of him.

I should quit while I'm ahead, he thought. *No point risking my life, especially when I already found something so great. I should just head home.*

And head home he did, the new fire-maker in his pocket, a bundle of sticks in his arms, and a song in his heart. When he arrived at his house, he was practically jumping up and down in excitement.

"Dad," he shouted, bursting through the door. "Look at what I found!"

"Is it another goat?" Papa Briggs frowned. "Because we have enough of those already."

"No, it's a magical device that makes fire."

Babylon held out the metal rectangle. His father grabbed it and looked it over carefully. Try as he might, the old man couldn't quite get it to work, no matter how many times he yelled at it or tried to sip it.

He shook his head. "It's made of metal, Son. It will never make fire."

"No, watch," Babylon said. He grabbed the device and flicked it on in one quick motion. The older man recoiled. His father gazed at him the same way he gazed at suspected witches.

"How did you come by such a magical object?" he asked, inching towards his pitchfork.

"Well, I was gathering wood, and I guess I got a little too close to the Forbidden Zone—"

"YOU WENT INTO THE FORBIDDEN ZONE?"

"No, Dad, I was only on the edge of it. I was too afraid to go any further."

His father's face relaxed. "Thank goodness. Don't scare me like that. We have enough problems in this village without you risking your life. Now hand over that fire-maker."

Babylon hesitated before doing as he was told. "But doesn't it make you wonder what other treasures are in there?"

12

"The only thing that awaits you in that terrible place is death. We'll discuss this no further."

His face fell. "All right, Dad. I won't go into the Forbidden Zone again."

"YOU WENT INTO THE FORBIDDEN ZONE?"

Babylon got to work repairing the house while his father sat inside, trying his hardest to start the fire-maker. He looked out past the village, into the forest. He was afraid of the dangers that lay on the other side of the thicket, but he also couldn't deny a needle of curiosity. It was all he could do to focus on the task at hand and not to think about the wonderful treasures waiting for him inside the Forbidden Zone.

Chapter β

TIME SEEMED TO drag on forever. Babylon did everything he could to keep himself busy, but it was no use. He was too excited to sleep and too giddy for chores. When he practiced swordsmanship with his instructor, Nails, he was so distracted by the upcoming Rite that he broke two wooden practice swords and three wooden practice bears.

"Come on, Babylon," Nails said, as he picked up another splintered hilt. "What's gotten into you today?"

Babylon waved him off and stared out the window, not paying attention. Finally, the suns reached their zeniths, heralding midday. That meant only one thing to him and the residents of the town: the Duke would arrive soon.

Every year, the Duke visited the village to honor all those about to participate in the Rite of Passage by giving a grand speech. It was one of the biggest events of the year, and everybody got excited about it. The men always walked the streets holding shovels and hammers to demonstrate their productivity, and the women wore their most provocative tunics in the hopes of catching the Duke's eye.

Before long, an eager crowd had gathered in the village square to await the arrival of their royal leader. Some swapped stories of their own Rites of Passage, others gossiped about their uglier, and therefore less important, neighbors, and Sheriff Kudgle kept order with his new beating stick. A few merchants even set up stands in the middle of the road to sell newer, sportier rocks. Papa Briggs stood off to the side of the throng with the fire-maker in hand and a grin on his face. Babylon worried he might try to debut his dangerous new trick. A frenzy of excitement gripped the town, but none of the villagers were as excited as the four young men standing front and center at the head of the masses.

First and foremost, was Babylon. He felt he was the most excited of the bunch. He rocked back and forth from foot to foot in anticipation. The closer the Rite came, the slower time seemed to move.

"Good luck out there," a feminine voice whispered into his ear.

He turned for a quick peek. His neighbor Emmunda stood there. She had a beautiful pear-shaped face and long hair the color of a radish. She wore a plain gray dress, over which hung a fine white apron with crimson splotches. As the daughter of the butcher, this was not uncommon attire. Emmunda's parents had owned the butchery for years, though in that time Babylon never saw them hunt animals, and the vagrants they invited over for dinner would seldom leave.

"Thanks, Emmunda," he said, his voice coming out at a higher pitch than he'd meant. "I'll come back safe."

With a smile, she slithered back into the crowd. Babylon breathed a hearty sigh as he watched her leave. He really liked Emmunda and planned to finally ask her out on a date after he returned from Mount Trespass as a real man. This made the Rite of Passage an extra special event in his life and did nothing to calm his nerves.

When she was gone, he grinned and nudged his best friend, Moot Fabrin. Moot gave him an absent-minded nod. He was busy scanning the crowd, probably looking for his family.

Babylon spotted Moot's father, Foxx Fabrin, in the middle of the road, loudly hawking his patented Wonder Dirt. According to him, it was the cure-all the villagers had been searching for. Foxx was an extravagant showman, and Moot was no different. Moot was always spinning a yarn to anybody who would listen about all the monsters he'd fought and the exotic places he'd visited, whether they were true or not. Usually, Babylon wasn't taken in by these stories, but most of the villagers would lend an ear to his tales. After all, nobody who'd slayed all those werewolves and murderous leprechauns could possibly be a liar.

Next to Moot was Stump Muffkin. Whereas most of the villagers were thin due to constant physical exertion and lack of a proper diet, Stump was ridiculously overweight. Because Mr. and Mrs. Muffkin ran the town bakery, they were more financially secure than the rest of the villagers. They always made sure to stuff their son with three or four meals a day, plus desserts. Stump never seemed to be given any chores, either. Instead, he spent his days lying around playing with his action sticks and eating junk. As a matter of fact, in the ten minutes they'd been standing at the front of the crowd, Stump had already consumed an entire rack of pork and a few handfuls of Wonder Dirt.

Stump's best and probably only friend stood to his left. He was, by far, Babylon's least favorite person in the entire universe. He was short, arrogant, and mean-spirited, with a thin face that made even the nicest donkeys angry. Nobody in the village could stand the kid, but they were obligated to like him because his father was the sheriff.

"Stand up straight, Flint," Kudgle said, with a hand on Flint's shoulder. "The Duke will be here soon. Let him see how proud you are. After all, you are *my* son."

"I always stand up straight, pop. You know that," Flint said, a smug smile on his face. "Unlike some of these lowlifes." He shot a nasty look in Babylon's direction.

16

Every word registered like needles in his head. It was all he could do to keep himself from running over there and smacking Flint in his arrogant Flint face. He wanted to do it so bad, in front of everybody, in front of Emmunda. He bit his tongue and firmly planted his feet, like he had so many times in the past. Before he could give in to temptation, the crowd roared with excitement. The Duke's procession approached the village entrance.

The Duke was a tall, middle-aged man who was well-adorned in all the fineries the Royal Family could provide. He came into town on a litter carried by a group of peasants who themselves were carried by a group of peons. He was eating grapes from a vine that was carried on a second smaller litter.

The throng of people wiped the dirt and bugs off their clothing and out of their teeth as their leader approached. They straightened their spines, obviously hoping to catch the Duke's attention for even a fraction of a second.

With a small cloud of dust, the litter came to an abrupt halt in front of the crowd. The peasants and peons took a tired, sweaty breath before stooping down on all fours to form a human pyramid next to the litter. The Duke yawned and strolled down the human staircase.

An awed hush fell over the people as the Duke put a hand to his purple-stained lips and cleared his throat. "Good day to each and every one of you," the Duke said, in a loud booming voice.

Everybody started talking to each other at once. "Did you hear that?" a few of them whispered. "He said good day to me."

The Royal Family's representative waited for everybody to quiet down before continuing. "Another year has passed, and that means it's time, once again, for the village of Pending's Rite of Passage."

More townsfolk chatted amongst themselves. Apparently, "Pending" didn't sound right to them. A couple wondered out loud if the Duke was in the right place.

"Before I send these brave young warriors on their journey," the Duke said, with a perfect smile that revealed a row of purple teeth. "I'm going to regale you all with a little history on the Rite of Passage."

Before the Duke could even finish his sentence, the crowd groaned. He told the same story every year, even the years no one had turned sixteen. Villagers began shuffling their feet in anticipated boredom. Even Babylon was bored. His gaze drifted to things that were more interesting; a rock, and then a stone, and then a rock that looked like a stone.

"The Rite of Passage has been held for decades, before you were all born," the Duke began. "Even before the oldest member of Pending was born."

The oldest member of Pending, Gramps Feffermeyer, swooned when the Duke said this.

17

"In fact, my very own grandfather used to give this very same speech before he sent his own bold heroes off to Mount Trespass. It's one of our oldest and proudest traditions. According to legend, the first Rite was held hundreds of years ago, well after the older towns had fallen. A group of men and women journeyed out into the dangerous territory to get much needed supplies and weapons for their families. Today, I am proud to say, the new men and women of this village will carry on this tradition." He paused for dramatic effect. A few people applauded weakly, while others nudged their neighbors awake. "Now, let's see who will be honoring us today."

The Duke pulled out a long scroll. "First on my list is...Moot Fabrin. Step forward and face the crowd."

Moot bowed before the Duke and spun around to smile at everyone. There was a smattering of applause and a few awkward coughs.

"Next is Stump Muffkin."

Stump did the same routine as Moot, but slower and drawing louder coughs from the crowd.

"Babylon Briggs."

Babylon stepped forward, and the crowd clapped with a little more enthusiasm. He stood with his chest puffed out next to Moot. This was the happiest moment of his life.

"Flint Kudgle."

The crowd hooted, hollered, and cheered with smiles that looked more anxious than joyful. Sheriff Kudgle gave them all a warning look, and the residents applauded with even more enthusiasm. A few people in the front row hollered so loudly, they passed out. Flint strutted next to the rest of the boys, the smirk on his face growing larger and larger with every clap, roar, and wail. He faced his supposed fans and blew them kisses.

After the noise had died down, the Duke finished his speech. "And now for the final name on our list." The crowd murmured. Babylon looked up and down the row. There were only four people standing there. Not five. He couldn't count too high, but he could at least count to five.

The Duke cleared his throat. "Emmunda Remmundo."

Babylon peeked behind him, where Emmunda was staring off into the distance, her finger in her nose.

She looked around at the faces staring at her and shrugged her shoulders. "What?" she asked.

"You're sixteen, right?" the Duke asked, annoyance clear in his voice. "You're doing the Rite of Passage."

"Ooh!" Emmunda clapped her hands and stepped forward, knocking Moot out of the way.

Babylon stared at her from the corner of his eye. "You never told me you were sixteen," he whispered, trying to hide his excitement.

"I am?" she said, then popped her finger back in her nose.

The Duke pursed his lips and continued, "These five brave heroes will leave this village as mere children, but upon their return from Mount Trespass, they will be adults. Each of them has earned your esteem. Best of luck!"

Once again, the crowd burst forth in a fit of applause. Babylon and the others waved goodbye to their families and headed out. The Duke climbed up his peasants onto his litter and followed them to the exit. Babylon glanced back to see the Duke reclining in his chair with his eyes closed and his purple tongue hanging out. He wondered if the Duke actually did any work besides giving the Rite of Passage speech.

Moot nudged him. "Are you ready?" he asked, with a flickering smile.

Mount Trespass towered over the grassy plains, its summit piercing the sky. "Yes."

§ § §

Only fifteen yards from the village gate and Flint Kudgle was already testing Babylon's patience. His incessant bragging and smug demeanor were one thing, but the way he talked down to the rest of them was just too much. He acted like he was the star of the whole expedition, and anybody else journeying with him existed for the sole purpose of making his trip easier. Of course, they all acted that way, but Babylon just didn't like Flint.

"This is going to be a dangerous trip," Babylon would say. "We should travel together and take breaks every couple of hours so we don't overexert ourselves."

"Are you kidding me," Flint would interrupt. "This journey is a piece of cake. I could do it on my hands. If you babies need breaks, you can take them, but don't expect me to wait for you."

"I'm with you, Flint," Stump would say between mouthfuls of nuts. Moot wouldn't say a word to back Babylon up, and Emmunda would be staring off at the suns. This was the framework for most of their conversations. Eventually, Babylon gave up trying to make small talk and instead trekked forward in silence.

Before long, they came to a fork in the trail. The right path was serene and lush with grassy slopes, while the left one was desolate and rocky. Of course, they had conflicting opinions about which path to take.

"I say we go left," Flint said.

"I don't know," Babylon said. "To get to Mount Trespass, I know we have to cross the river. And that doesn't look river-ish to me. The right path has greener grass, and there are more birds."

19

"Birds drink air, not water." Flint scowled at him. "That's how they fly, stupid. My gut is telling me to go left, so I'm going left."

"But, listen," Babylon said. "I hear water flowing to the right. It must be the river."

"I'm with my buddy," Stump said. "He's the son of the sheriff. He knows what he's talking about."

A smug smile spread across Flint's narrow face. "Thank you."

Babylon sighed. "Emmunda, what do you think?"

"You're Babylon."

Flint laughed. "It looks like we're going left," he said, as he started walking down the path. The others followed him, leaving Babylon alone. With another louder sigh, he followed the group the wrong way.

It took a few hours and a couple of rest stops before they reached their destination. Flint bragged the whole way, and Emmunda described how her family removed bones and hair from the meat they sold. Finally, they stood at the banks of the river. The rapid water splashed at their feet, soaking their burlap socks. Flint smirked when they got there, as if he had been right all along. Babylon looked around and had a feeling the group had walked in a circle. In fact, from the river bank, he could see the fork in the road. He mentioned this to the group, but no one seemed to care.

"You're just jealous because I knew the way and you didn't," Flint said.

"That's not it at all. *I* knew the way here. I would have gotten us to the river a long time ago if we'd gone my way."

"Oh, so you're saying you can find your way to Mount Trespass faster than I can?"

"Probably, but we're all on the same team. I don't think we should make it a competition."

Flint was silent for a second, and then his face lit up. "Hey, I have an idea. Let's make a competition out of this."

"What?"

"You heard me. We'll split up. Me and Stump will go our way, you and the—" he snickered, "—rest of the ladies can go yours."

"Who are you calling a lady?" Emmunda said, grimacing and rolling up the sleeves of her dress.

Flint laughed out loud, and so did Stump. Moot did too because, apparently, he didn't get the joke.

"Whoever reaches Mount Trespass first," Flint said, "will be the winner, and therefore the best person ever. What do you say?"

Babylon rubbed the back of his neck. "I don't know. We should probably stick together—"

"Let's sweeten the deal. Whoever gets there first gets to ask Emmunda out on a date."

Emmunda's grimace turned into a smile. "Ooh, I hope *I* win." She clapped her hands and danced from foot to foot.

Babylon felt his face warm. "You're on!"

"Good, it's settled," Flint said. He ran to the riverbank with Stump in tow. "See you losers at the top!"

Babylon started forward with Moot and Emmunda on either side.

"It's okay," Moot said. "I'm an expert adventurer. This will be a breeze."

"Well, our first problem is getting across this river safely. Flint will have the same problem, too. So, I think we should…" He lost his train of thought as Flint and Stump glided across the turbulent water in a canoe, whose side had the sheriff's crest etched into it. It was Kudgle's personal paddling canoe that was used whenever the sheriff needed to beat people on the other side of the river.

"They're cheating!" Moot cried. "That's not fair."

Flint waved his oar at them and laughed. "Good luck staying dry, losers!"

Babylon clenched his jaw. "Let's swim across," he said in haste. "We won't be too far behind them."

"I can't swim." Moot said.

"What do you mean you can't swim? You said you battled three mermaids last year."

"Yeah, on *land*!"

Flint and Stump dismounted on the opposite bank. Babylon contemplated leaving the others behind and just swimming across himself, but he forced the idea out of his head. To him, the Rite of Passage was about becoming a man. What kind of man left behind friends in need?

"Okay, we'll think of a way across."

The group split up to search for anything useful. They reconvened a few minutes later with armfuls of sticks, rocks, and leaves. Emmunda, apparently confused about the assignment, pulled an assortment of objects from beneath her apron, including a butcher's knife and a vagrant's hat.

"How about we make a bridge with these sticks?" Babylon said, pushing Emmunda's gear to the side. "Then we could just walk across."

"Yeah, that's a good idea," Moot said. "I was just about to suggest that."

Unfortunately, building a bridge across a rapid river is easier said than done. Every time they laid a stick in the water, it was quickly washed downstream. They'd watch it go with their hands on their hips, frustrated at their rotten luck. Then they would do it all over again, with similar results. Before long, they were almost out of sticks, and hadn't gotten very far on their bridge's foundation.

"I'll go look for more branches, stronger ones this time," Babylon said. "You two wait here and try to think of another way across."

It took a while for him to find any sticks he considered strong enough. He had to venture away from the river into the surrounding forest before he found anything worthwhile. By the time he returned with an armful of thick branches, the suns in the sky were starting to sink. They would run out of light soon, and they were still stuck on their first obstacle.

He dropped his load when he noticed Moot hunched over Emmunda's legs. "What are you doing?" he asked, shoving him aside.

Moot stood with a smile and showed him the giant fern leaves he had tied to her feet with the twine from his shoes. "During winter, people use snow shoes to travel through the snow. So, I made river shoes to travel through the river!"

"But why are they on Emmunda's feet?"

"I asked her to volunteer to see how they worked."

She smiled and waved. "How about a hug for luck?" she asked.

Babylon's heart raced as he wrapped his arms around her. It was the best moment of his life. Of course, it was undercut by Emmunda rubbing his muscles and saying how much meat she could get out of him. After that, he pulled away, not sure if he was excited or scared.

Moot guided Emmunda into the river, her steps strained by the awkward river shoes. As soon as she took one step off the bank, they realized the flaw in the plan: rivers aren't as solid as snow. It was a small problem, granted, but it certainly had a big effect on the outcome. The shoes, and subsequently Emmunda, sank below the water like a dimwitted rock.

Panic gripped Babylon. "Emmunda?" he called. "Are you okay?"

She didn't come up, and every attempt to fish her out was thwarted by the murkiness of the water. After twenty minutes of trying and failing, Moot suggested they move on.

"We can't leave her!" Babylon said.

"But we're running out of light. We need to get across now. Who knows, maybe we'll find her on the other side."

He perked up. "Do you really think so?"

Moot just shrugged his shoulders.

"In that case, I think I have a solution to our problem."

"It better be a good one." Moot said.

"Trust me. I'm sure you'll like it."

That's how Babylon found himself pulling Moot across the river on a raft made from sticks and twine. He swam with all his might, a piece of twine attached to the raft held between his teeth. Moot just laid there, hands around the branches, complaining about his queasy stomach, and asking Babylon to slow down.

22

Finally, when his strength was just about gone, Babylon reached the other side. He fell onto the muddy bank, panting and sweating. Seconds later, Moot crumpled next to him, panting just as much and sweating even harder. "Well," Moot said, between gulps of air. "It wasn't easy, but we finally made it."

"Yeah, but there's still no sign of Emmunda."

Just then, bubbles started bursting on the surface of the river. The water parted, and a pear-shaped head covered by damp, radish-colored hair popped out. It was Emmunda. She walked clumsily onto the bank, the river shoes still tied to her feet.

"You made it!" Babylon bolted to her and wrapped his arms around her waist. "Are you okay?"

She took the river shoes off. "Okay, your turn," she said, holding them out for Babylon.

Moot pierced the air with a whistle. "Come on, lovebirds," he said. "We have to catch up to Flint. Let's go!"

Emotionally and physically exhausted, Babylon half walked, half crawled away from the river to the trail that led to the plains. He was still gasping, but Moot insisted they continue moving and that rest was for the weak. After a few minutes of labored movements, Babylon finally gave in and collapsed in front of a wooden hut.

"What are you doing?" Moot asked, eyebrows raised. "We're wasting time."

"Just five minutes," he gasped.

"Sounds like you need more than that," a voice called from inside the hut. A man walked out dressed in a black cloak. He looked at them and continued to speak in a low, slick voice. "If you need to keep your energy up, you might want to consider buying my strength tonic. It'll make you run faster, last longer, and smell stronger than you ever thought possible."

Emmunda's eyes lit up. "Ooh! Do you have it in cherry?"

The man smiled. "No!"

"Hold on," Babylon said, putting a hand up. "First, did you see two other guys come down this path? One is fat and the other looks like a complete jerk."

The man rubbed his chin. "Yes," he said. "Those two boys passed through here a few hours ago. They bought many of my wares. But I still have plenty of fabulous items for sale." He turned to Emmunda. "How would you like a few of my wake-up pills? They're guaranteed to keep you up all night."

Emmunda offered her river shoes in trade, but the salesman told her he already had plenty of those in stock.

Babylon brought the others into a huddle. "Did you hear that? Flint and Stump are ahead of us by hours. We'll never catch up to them now."

"Of course, you can," the man said, standing in the huddle next to them.

23

"With my patented wing shoes. If you put them on, you can fly over every obstacle you come across!" He held up a pair of old, cracked leather shoes with feathers nailed to their sides.

"That's perfect!" Moot said. "We'll take them."

"Great," the salesman said. "What do you have to trade?"

Moot searched around his belt but came up empty. "Aw, my money satchel," he cried. "It must have fallen into the river. There were at least two chickens in there."

"You don't have any goods to trade?" The man's eyes narrowed.

"No," Moot said, "but if you give me the shoes, I can fly back to my house and get you something."

The man wrapped his cloak around his shoulders and slipped back into his wooden hut. He slammed the door shut, and a lock slid into place. A moment later he peeked through the curtains, then quickly closed them. He did this every few seconds until they left.

"Well, I guess that's that." Babylon laughed. "Let's keep going until it gets dark."

"All right. But I really wish I could have gotten those wing shoes. They would have made things a lot easier...for me."

They made it a few more miles before dusk. In the dim light, they tripped over every rock and bush in their path. A few times Emmunda tripped and landed in Babylon's arms. Every time she did, he smiled and his heart pounded in his chest. When Moot did the same thing, Babylon decided it was a good time to stop.

"Hopefully, we'll get an early start tomorrow," he said, as he laid his supplies on the ground.

"Maybe we shouldn't even sleep," Moot said. "It might help us catch up. Heck, I've gone a few days without sleep before. I'll be fine."

"No, we don't want to risk wearing ourselves out so soon. If we don't rest, we could be in serious trouble."

Moot nodded, and then grabbed himself a nice comfy rock to rest his head on. Babylon followed suit and lay in the tall grass. Emmunda, meanwhile, stood staring up at the night sky.

"Look at all those stars," Babylon said to her. "They sure look beautiful out here away from the fires of the village."

She nodded. "Stars are pretty," she said, drool dripping from her mouth.

Moot yawned. "You should have seen the sky when I went to the desert and fought those trolls. The stars were even better."

Babylon stretched his arms over his head. "I wonder if there are other villages out there on those stars. You know, just other people doing different stuff in another place. That would be neat."

24

"Don't be stupid, nobody could live out there. It would be too cold to live on another star."

"I guess you're right. Do you think we'll ever be able to go out there?"

Moot shrugged. "I don't know. Probably not. I can't imagine anyone could ever travel to the stars."

Babylon rolled over to his side. His eyes slipped shut, opened briefly, and then finally closed again. The last thing he saw before drifting off to sleep was a shooting star streaking across the inky black sky.

It was egg-shaped.

Chapter γ

THEY WOKE AT dawn. Well, Babylon woke at dawn; Moot didn't wake up until water was splashed on his face and he was kicked in the ribs. Even then, it took a considerable amount of time before he was ready to move again. When they were finally prepared, had eaten breakfast, and Moot had stopped lying back down and asking for a few more minutes of sleep, they were ready to travel.

"Have you seen Emmunda?" Babylon asked.

Moot yawned. "No. Why don't you look for her while I rest up?"

He surveyed the area. The footprints and felled trees in a line indicated one thing. "She's gone back to the village." He frowned. "I guess the Rite wasn't that important to her."

"What are you going to do?"

He looked back at the path they had taken, then forward to where they were going, then back again. Finally, he let out a sigh. "Emmunda made her decision, and so have I. We keep going. The Rite of Passage is too important." He woke Moot back up and pressed onward.

With the careful rest they'd received, they were able to travel at a brisk pace. And since the suns weren't completely risen yet, the air was still cool and refreshing. They traveled for a few miles before coming to a crossroads. The trail forked into two very contrasting paths. One path led towards the flat and easily traversable plains. The other, as told by its jagged sign and gloomy atmosphere, led to Prospector Woods.

After some careful consideration, Babylon made a decision. "I think we should go through the woods," he said. "We'll be able to make up some lost time."

"Are you sure we want to do that?" Moot gulped. "I heard Prospector Woods is a dangerous place. The crazies live there."

"I think it's worth the risk. The plains go all the way around the woods. It will take too much time. But if we go through the woods, it's a straight shot to Mount Trespass. Besides, I'm positive Flint went through the plains."

"How can you be so sure?"

"He never would have taken such a dangerous route. Especially, with the head start he had. And look at this." He pointed to footprints in the mud. "These tracks and half eaten pieces of cheese lead *away* from the woods."

"Are you positive those are their footprints? They could be anybody's."

27

Babylon squatted and pointed out the different features in the mud. "Look at this set of small prints. They're the same shape as a boot, and we both know Flint wears the same kicking boots as his father. He never takes them off. And these bigger tracks are probably Stump's. See how deep in the mud they are?"

Moot crossed his arms. "What about that last set of prints? Who do *they* belong to?"

Babylon studied the third group of markings. These tracks seemed fresher than the others, and in some places, they overlapped the older ones, as if whoever had made them was following Stump and Flint. Also, they left an unusual impression, as if the shoes weren't made of bound cloth or animal skins. The edges were crisper, more sophisticated.

"Hey, those *are* strange." Babylon's brow furrowed. "I've never seen tracks like that."

"I have!" Moot pointed his thumb at his chest and smiled.

"Well, it doesn't matter. They all lead to the plains. Our only choice is to cut across Prospector Woods. Now, are you coming or not?"

Moot looked from the deep dark woods to the comfort and security of the plains, then back to Babylon. Finally, he threw up his hands. "Whatever," he said. "If we die, though, I'm going to punch you in the face."

They took one final glance at the simple path they were leaving behind, then steeled themselves for the unknown and walked into the woods. They were plunged into darkness as they trekked into the mysterious forest. The natural light of the suns was extinguished by the thick branches and leaves overhead. The air was cold against their skin. The woods were as terrifying as the rumors said they were. More terrifying, even.

After a few minutes, however, the boys couldn't help but notice a conspicuous lack of crazies. They shared a confident glance. Sure, this place looked scary, but so far, that was it. Babylon's fear evaporated. Clearly, the tales of the crazies were just that: tales. The two increased their stride. A few yards farther, they added a spring to their step.

A quarter of the way through the woods, they were joyfully bobbing and singing loud songs about how safe they were. The anxiety they faced moments earlier gave way to oblivious calm. The woods weren't so scary after all. They were actually quite peaceful. In fact, they were starting to like this forest.

That feeling of safety vanished in an instant when something rustled behind a bush up ahead. They froze in their tracks.

"Did you hear that?" Moot jumped back. "It's one of the crazies!"

"Were you even listening to the song? There are no crazies here. We're completely safe. It was probably just a squirrel."

"Maybe it was a crazy squirrel."

They began tiptoeing, listening to the sounds around them while humming much more ominous tunes. They had only taken a few cautious steps before a high-pitched giggle floated between the trees.

"Let's get out of here," Moot whispered.

"Calm down, that was only the wind laughing at us. We have to keep moving forward." Before they could move, a loud whisper came from above them. Babylon took his dagger from his belt and held it with a shaky hand. "Is someone there?" he asked.

There was no reply. For a few long seconds, the boys stood still, waiting in tense anticipation. They looked at each other before continuing.

A gruff voice came from behind them. "Who goes there?"

They spun around, but all that greeted them was eerie nothingness.

"Who said that?" Moot asked, his whole body quivering. Babylon cocked his head. He could barely make out a whispered conversation.

"Don't scare 'em, Brother Jed," one of the invisible voices said. "They might have some stuff on 'em."

"I'm not scaring them, Brother Ned," the other voice said. "I just want to know who they are."

"You don't have to shout like that, is all. At least not until we search 'em."

"I think my voice was at quite an acceptable level!"

After a few more minutes of this bickering back and forth, Babylon grew impatient. "Hey, guys," he said. "Who's out there? Show yourselves."

"Might as well do what he says," Brother Ned said.

"The heck I do," said Brother Jed. "Who's he think he is marchin' into our woods, singin' songs, and givin' orders like that?"

"Now, Brother Jed, you're bein' rude to our guests."

"They ain't no guests of mine."

"All right, fine. Be that way. But you can't very well search 'em for 'stuff' from that bush over there, now can you?"

"Dagnabbit, Brother Ned! You just gave away my hidin' spot!"

"Well, then I guess there's no use hidin' anymore, is there?"

A figure stepped out from behind a large tree. He was a grizzled old man with a long, white beard and a pair of dirty overalls, the back of which held a pickax. The whole ensemble was completed by an oversized hat on top of his gray head. After he stepped into view, the other man popped up from behind a bush wearing identical clothing.

"It's the crazies!" Moot shouted, staring wide-eyed at the men.

"We ain'ts crazy," Brother Jed said, putting his hands up. "We're just hard-working folks like you."

"Is it just you two out here?" Babylon asked.

"Not at all," Brother Ned said. He shouted to the forest, "All right fellas, come on out!"

Similarly dressed prospectors sprung up from all over the woods. Some were hiding in logs, others swung down from branches on ropes, a few peered out from inside hollow trees, and one had been pretending to be a rock the whole time. The whole forest became alive as men scurried into view.

"Welcome to Prospector Woods," Brother Ned said, with a smile.

"Who goes there!" Brother Jed shouted into the boys' faces.

Moot took another step backwards. "No one, we're leaving." He turned to run away, but Babylon grabbed him by his shirt and pulled him back.

"We're from the village. We're doing our Rite of Passage, and we have to get to Mount Trespass. Cutting through these woods is the fastest way."

"You guys wouldn't happen to have any stuff on you, would you?" Brother Jed asked, his beady eyes narrowing.

"'Stuff'?" Moot asked.

Brother Ned leaned in close. "Our group, the whole lotta us, does one thing each and every day," he whispered. "We mine for pretty yellow rocks that are worth lots and lots of money."

"You mean gold?" Babylon asked.

Every head perked up in the forest. A loud commotion rang out as each prospector passed the same word through his lips. "Gold?"

"Did someone say gold?" Brother Jed asked, eyes alight with excitement.

"Shh!" Brother Ned said to everybody. "Quiet down now! False alarm. Nobody's found nothin'!"

All the prospectors groaned. One started crying.

"Did I say something wrong?" Babylon asked.

"We don't say the G-word 'round here," Brother Ned said. "Everybody gets in a tizzy when you do. We call it 'stuff' if we have to talk about it."

"So…" Brother Jed leaned in, scratching at his sweaty neck. "Did you bring any stuff?"

"No, I'm sorry."

Everybody groaned again.

"Well, have you boys ever mined for stuff before?" Brother Ned asked.

Before Babylon could open his mouth, Moot shouted, "I have!"

"Did you ever find any?" Brother Jed grabbed the boy by his shoulders and gave him a hearty shake.

Moot put on a big smile. "Yup, lots of times."

Suddenly, everybody was Moot's best friend. The men gathered around, surveying him, asking him questions, and touching his face. They wanted to know everything they could about their new champion.

"You, my boy, are comin' with us to the stream," Brother Jed hollered. "We're finally going to finds us some stuff!"

Babylon watched in bewilderment as the crazies lifted Moot onto their shoulders and led him away, hooting and cheering. Moot beamed from his newfound popularity. When the dust settled, Babylon found himself alone with Brother Ned.

"Well, while your friend is busy, I might as well get you a hot meal," he said, leading Babylon through the woods.

They walked along the dark path in silence. The further they went, the more Prospector Woods lived up to its name. Babylon couldn't take a step without spotting someone searching for gold. They rooted around the ground, panned in the stream running through the center of the woods, and searched in each other's hair. A small group of men had drilled holes into trees and inserted spigots. They sobbed when all that came out was worthless amber.

They came to a clearing crowded with tents and campfires. Babylon guessed this was where the tired prospectors slept after a long day of disappointment and failure. The smaller tents circled a larger tent, which stood proudly in the middle.

"That's our town hall." Brother Ned pointed. "It's where we meet to have great feasts and talk about town issues. Most of which are minin' related."

Ned slipped into the large tent, beckoning for Babylon to join him. Before Babylon followed him inside, he looked at the stream where Moot was panning for gold. He didn't look as happy as he did a few minutes ago. Likewise, some of the prospectors seemed to be losing their patience with him. They were prodding him with sticks and making rude hand gestures.

Babylon couldn't help but chuckle as he stepped into the tent. Inside, there was a great table with rusted pots and pans. A few bent and dirty metal plates were scattered across the floor, some with crumbs still on them. In the back of the tent, a cauldron was boiling over a fire with some sort of strange creature stewing inside. He couldn't tell what the animal was, but he could see part of its trunk sticking out of the scalding water.

"Take a seat," Brother Ned said. Babylon looked around and noticed chairs of all different shapes and sizes. Most of them were wooden, while others were just chair-shaped piles of dirt and bones. One in particular, at the head of the table, caught his eye. It was metal and sported two big wheels on its sides. He ran a hand over its shiny surface and let out an impressed whistle.

"This is nice," he said. "How did you make something like this?"

"Can you keep a secret?" Brother Ned whispered, gaze shifting around the empty tent.

"No."

"I found it in the Forbidden Zone."

Babylon's eyes widened. "The Forbidden Zone? You went there?"

"I went there a while ago with a few of the boys. We were hoping we might find some…" he looked around again. "Well, you know."

"What?"

"G-O-L-D," Brother Ned whispered.

"Oh. Did you?"

"Unfortunately, not. We lost a few good men, too. But we did find one or two little things. That chair bein' one of 'em. Boy, I tell you, that ancient city sure knew how to live."

Babylon walked to the front of the chair and was about to sit down and take a load off, when the prospector shouted.

"What's the matter?" Babylon asked, butt hovering just above the seat.

"You can't sit there," Brother Ned cried. "That there chair is only for our mayor to be sittin' in."

He stood. "Oh, I'm sorry. Which one of you guys is the mayor?"

"I'm the mayor," a voice said. A man walked into the tent with a flask in his hand. "I'm Brother Zedd, ruler of these parts."

Brother Zedd looked a lot like the other prospectors, but something about his appearance made him seem more mature than the rest. His beard was a little longer, his hair a little grayer, and his pickax a little shinier. There was no doubt about it. This man was in charge.

"Hello, Mr. Brother Zedd." Babylon said. "I'm Babylon Briggs. Me and my friend Moot are on our way to Mount Trespass and—"

"Another villager?" Brother Zedd shook his head. "We've had a lot of your kind today."

"What do you mean?"

"We had a young lady in here earlier today. She said she would cook us breakfast."

"Emmunda?" His eyes lit up. "Was it Emmunda?"

"I couldn't tell you. We kicked her out when she tried to stuff Brother Ned into the pot. Right, Brother Ned?"

Brother Ned lowered his head. "I was in the pot."

Babylon looked from bearded face to bearded face. A long, uncomfortable silence followed—one he tried to break, but lost his nerve and cleared his throat instead—then the mayor clapped his hands together and stomped his feet.

"Anybody else hungry?" he asked, then rang a bell that hung above the table. Almost immediately, the room filled with grizzled hungry miners. They all took seats as Brother Ned put on a set of apron overalls and served them stew from the boiling cauldron. The prospectors began their feast, talking excitedly.

32

"Ooh, I think today's the day we finally find something," one of them said, with his mouth full of tusk. "I can feel it in m'bones."

"Hopefully, that kid is as good as he claims to be," another one said.

"You know, I thought I found some stuff last night," someone else replied. "Turns out it was just a boil that needed lancing."

"I think I found something!" a man shouted at the end of the table. His shaking hand held a small yellow nugget on one of its fingers. "This is it. Gold!"

Excitement shot through the table. The prospectors exchanged words of congratulations. "Where did you find it?" a few of them asked.

"My ear!" the man said. He took a small bite out of the soft nugget and his expression fell. "Nope, that wasn't gold. Sorry."

"I would kill everybody in the entire world for some precious gold," Brother Jed said, under his breath.

There was a moment of silence before Babylon asked, "Have any of you guys ever found gold before?"

"Gold?" everybody shouted at once, jumping up and hollering until Brother Zedd rang the bell to silence them.

"What did I tell you about saying that word?" Brother Ned said, stomping on his own hat.

Babylon looked around the table as the prospectors sat down, muttering to themselves.

"I would sleep with my own wife for just one taste of sweet, sweet gold." Brother Jed's face turned sour.

"Poor old fool doesn't know what he's saying," Brother Ned said, shaking his head.

"I'm sorry," Babylon said, staring at the crowd. "I only meant to ask if anybody here has found any...'stuff' yet? Ever?"

"Well," Brother Zedd said, "so far we haven't found anything in these woods. But I truly believe there's some here. And if your friend is half as good at finding the stuff as he says he is, then today is going to be a great day for Prospector Woods. Now, you were asking about a safe passage to Mount Trespass earlier. Well, I think the best way for you to go is—"

Just then, a miner burst in, shoving Moot in front of him with a stick. "These boys is liars!" he said.

"Take it easy, Brother Ed. What's wrong?" the mayor asked.

"This boy told us he was an expert at findin' the stuff. But it turns out he's never even seen it before." An angry grumble traveled around the table. The prospectors narrowed their eyes at Babylon and Moot.

"The durn fool even thought my pickax was a lollipop," he said. "He's a phony! They both are!"

At this, the grizzled men started flinging hats and shouting out suggestions of what should be done with the boys. One by one, each person offered a proposal that became more grim and gruesome as it went down the table. Beatings, stabbings, and canings were all popular ideas. Then someone mentioned a hanging was in order. Everybody else nodded. That was an idea all of them could get behind. The angry crowd gathered around them and someone tied a noose together.

"Run!" Babylon shouted, bolting out of the tent. Moot followed behind, trying his best to keep up.

The boys sprinted to the edge of the woods. Babylon had to stop a few times so Moot could catch up. Once or twice, he even gave Moot a head start, only to pass him moments later. All the while the dangerous prospectors were behind them, some of them with their pickaxes lit up like torches. There were even a few miners who had missed the announcement at lunch but went along with the crowd because everybody else was doing it.

After a foot race that seemed to stretch on forever, Babylon and Moot finally made their way out of the forest and into the open space of the plains. Brother Zedd put a hand up to stop his men. "This is the edge of our territory," he said. He shouted to the boys, "Don't come around these parts again." The prospectors, glum with defeat, turned around and headed home. After all, the day was young, and there was still gold to pan for.

"That was too close," Babylon said, between heavy breaths.

"Yeah," Moot gasped. "But I still feel like I could have taken them on."

Babylon surveyed the area. They were no longer on the path. He had no idea where they were or how far they'd gone. Then he caught sight of something that caused him to shout in excitement. Moot looked around for a few seconds, then he shouted too.

Less than half a mile ahead was the base of Mount Trespass.

Chapter Δ

THEY SPRINTED ALONG the grassy plains toward the mountain. Babylon couldn't believe their good fortune. The detour through the woods saved them so much time, they might even beat Flint and Stump. With each hurried step, the soft dirt became harder and rockier. The ground sloped upwards, making Babylon's legs burn. His lungs ached for air, and his heart slammed against his chest. Still, he was doing better than Moot, who was doubled over and wheezing. Babylon stopped running and craned his neck up to see the top. There was a lot of ground to cover yet, but he was so close to his goal that he could almost taste it. He didn't taste it, though. Didn't even try. It probably tasted like rocks, anyway.

The climb was slow, and the hard ground was tough on their feet. Loose stones made the terrain dangerous and unpredictable. A few times, Moot slipped and fell onto his stomach. Once he slid all the way to the bottom, and Babylon had to wait for him to climb back up. In all that time, Babylon saw no sign of Flint or Stump.

Eventually, they began making faster progress. It wasn't that Moot was learning from his mistakes; rather, Babylon tied a rope around their waists so he could pull Moot along. Moot seemed to enjoy having the freedom to fall without regret, and practiced falling as much as he could, much to Babylon's frustration.

About halfway up the mountain, voices began echoing off the cliff side. "Did you hear that?" Babylon asked Moot, who was asleep behind him. "I think that's Flint."

As soon as Babylon climbed over the next ledge, dragging Moot's snoring body behind him, he spotted Flint and Stump.

Stump was sitting on a rock while Flint stood with his arms crossed, yelling at him. "Hurry up, you fat oaf," Flint said. "We'll never reach the top if you keep stopping."

"I'm sorry," Stump said, breathing hard. "I need a handful of butter every now and then to recharge my body. You know that."

"But you just ate a handful of butter. You've been eating one every ten feet."

"I know, this mountain is really hard on me," he said. As if to emphasize his statement, he pulled out another handful of butter from his pocket.

Flint threw his hands up. He turned, his eyes narrowing on Babylon and

Moot. "Well, well, well." He sneered. "Little Babylon Briggs finally made it to Mount Trespass?" He pointed to Moot, who was now wide awake. "And what's this? Are you guys rope buddies now?" Flint shot a glance at Stump and nudged him on the shoulder.

"Joke all you want," Babylon said. "At least *we* didn't squander a huge lead. One that you got by cheating."

"Yeah, by cheating," his rope buddy said, before hiding behind his shoulder.

Flint chuckled. "I take every advantage I can; that's what makes me a winner. And if it wasn't for lazy bones here, I would've already reached the top." He kicked Stump in the shin. Stump yelped and cursed at Flint, but with a mouthful of butter all that came out was a garbled mess.

"Why thank you, Stump," Flint said.

"Too bad you went through the plains," Babylon said, with a smirk. "If you went through Prospector Woods, like we did, then you would have beaten us for sure."

"Yeah, for sure," Moot said, from under Babylon's shirt.

"You guys went through Prospector Woods?" Stump's mouth dropped open, splattering food onto the ground. "Did you meet any of the crazies?"

"They didn't go through Prospector Woods, stupid." Flint shook his head. "They followed us the whole way here."

Babylon stared at Flint, confused. "What are you talking about? This is the first time we've seen you since the river."

"Yeah, right. I don't believe that for a second. I could hear you behind us."

Babylon remembered the third set of footprints in the mud from before. "Wait, did you actually *see* who was following you?"

"I'm looking at him right now." Flint laughed. "I heard you behind us every step of the way. Following us in the plains, raiding our camp at night, tagging Stump's ear—you did it all."

Stump turned his head and displayed the tag on his ear. It had "Plumpus Ignoramus" printed on it.

Babylon looked around. Whoever was following Flint was probably still around, watching them now. "We'd better move," he said.

"I decide who gets to move and when," Flint yelled.

"Listen, I think the guy that's tracking you is still here," Babylon whispered. "And I think he might be from the…" He looked around again. "The Forbidden Zone."

Flint's face paled. A rock clattered down the mountain and the boys jumped. From around the bend, a familiar radish-colored head bobbed into view.

"Emmunda!" Babylon cried.

"Is this Mount Trespass?" she asked.

He wrapped his arms around her. "What happened to you?"

She grinned. "I saw a turkey!"

"Oh, that's right. You come from a family of butchers. I guess you know a lot about animal meat."

"Animal meat?"

Flint stepped between them. "Now's not the time for this," he said. "We're still being watched. It's time to move." Together again, they hurried up the mountain as fast as they could. It wasn't long before they reached the top and stood before a building. It was old, worn-down, and displayed a dilapidated sign that read, in peeling red letters, TRESPASS. Babylon looked at the others, and one at a time they went through the open door.

Babylon once asked the villagers what Mount Trespass was before it became part of the Rite. Some said it was the center of the former civilization, while others told him to get lost. Papa Briggs told him it was something called Manifest Destiny. Now he was in the building and could find out for himself. There were scrapped remnants scattered all over the ground. The floor was made of some sort of material arranged into squares, not the typical wood or straw. There were several large rooms that looked like they were built for an army of people. The place clearly wasn't a house, but people did live here at one time.

"Look at the size of this place," Moot whispered.

"This place is bigger than our vagrant paddock," Emmunda said.

"Let's not waste any time," Babylon said. "We should get what we need and go before that stalker catches up with us."

There was a general murmur of agreement amongst the others.

"Now, the most important thing is to stick together and—"

Flint rolled his eyes. "That's stupid. If we want to get out of here quickly, we should all split, find a weapon, and then meet back here."

There was another murmur of agreement. They shuffled off in different directions, leaving Babylon alone staring at their backs. After a few seconds, he shook his head and walked around the area, searching for scrap metal.

Stump was the first one to find something, or, rather, the first to settle for something. He walked a few feet and bumped into an old, rusty drum. It was big, unwieldy, and ultimately useless for defense, but Stump seemed content. He laid it on its side and sat on it.

Babylon went into the nearest room and found Moot. There was a thin leather bed in the center and charts with giant letters along the walls. Moot was searching through drawers and cabinets when he entered. "Any luck?"

"No," Moot said. "These knives are too small, and these bottles are filled with pills and not weapons." He kicked a bag of liquid across the room, and it splattered against a pair of plastic crutches. Moot let out a gasp. "That's it!"

37

"What?"

"These!" He picked the crutches up and displayed them to Babylon. "I don't think there's anything else in here. You might as well try somewhere else."

Babylon walked out into the hall and bumped into Flint.

"Watch where you're going, loser," Flint said. He had a thick lead pipe in his hand and used it to bash holes into the walls and ceiling. "Gotta find a weapon," Babylon heard Flint mutter as he disappeared around the corner.

Babylon peeked into a room across the hall. There were rusted cans of food and faded cookbooks on dilapidated shelves. A kitchen. Sure, the stove wasn't wood burning, like the one back home, and the spoons didn't have holes in them, but it was a kitchen nonetheless. He sighed. Every possible piece of scrap had already been cleared out. Skillets, pots, pans, forks, knives, spoons, plates, and even the literal kitchen sink had been taken away by previous generations. All that remained were empty cabinets and cupboards.

"Hurry up," Flint shouted, his voice dripping with scorn. "Everyone else is ready to go. What's taking you so long?"

Babylon brushed the comment off and stepped into the sleeping quarters. There was a long stretch of beds against the wall with lockers hanging open next to them. This area also looked like it was picked clean. He thought about trying to take one of the steel bed frames but realized he didn't have the tools to dismantle it, nor the strength to carry it.

"You're not going to find anything in there," Flint said from the doorway.

Babylon scowled. He was determined to find something in the sleeping quarters. He didn't care if he had to rip the bed apart; he would find something and rub it in Flint's arrogant face. He walked up and down the aisle, desperately looking for anything. Most of the things he found on the floor were useless, like tattered clothes, slippers, and the occasional pillow.

Then something caught his eye. There was a strange object peeking out from under one of the beds. He hurriedly pulled it out and looked it over, only to be disappointed by a long wooden box. There was no metal in wood. Everybody knew that. Even Stump. He started to return the box when something shifted inside it. His curiosity piqued, he remembered boxes sometimes contained things inside of them, like the time he found that white stick in a box at the cemetery.

He gave the wooden box a little shake. There was definitely something moving around in there. He tried to open it, but it had rusty hinges and latches that wouldn't come loose. Determined, and maybe a little bit desperate, he lifted the box above his head and threw it to the ground. The wood exploded into a thousand splinters, and something heavy clattered to the floor.

He picked it up. It was large and made of cold heavy metal. There was an inscription on the side: Model LZ-57 Assault Rifle. He couldn't believe his good luck. He held in his hands the best thing he could have found. Now, it was his turn to brag. He ran out to join his teammates.

"Wow." Moot's jaw dropped. "That's awesome."

"Thank you." Babylon smiled. "I think it's a pretty good find, if I do say so myself."

Emmunda rubbed the barrel. "Cool," she said, staring him in the eyes for an uncomfortable period of time.

He gulped. "What did you get?" She held up a large rock and grinned. Her hungry gaze made his heart race faster.

Stump came over to ruin the moment. He ran his hand over the sleek steel, though he didn't make as much eye contact. "Man, that's neat," he said. "Good job."

Babylon looked at Flint. "It looks like there was something in there, after all. What did you find?"

Flint held up a lead pipe, and then stared at Babylon's weapon. "You should give that to me," he said. "As the sheriff's son, I'm the only one who could possibly use something like that."

"Dream on, Flint," Babylon said. "I found it, fair and square."

"That's because you looked in the bedroom. If I went down there, I would have found it. Now, hand it over."

"No way!"

"It wasn't a request," Flint said. "Give it to me."

"You aren't going to get it, so back off."

"Oh, I'll get it." Flint lifted his pipe. "One way or another, it'll be mine."

Babylon felt a grin spread across his face. He had been waiting for a moment like this for a long time. "Bring it!"

And bring it he did. Flint swung his weapon down with tremendous force.

Without a second to think, Babylon grabbed his rifle with both hands and took the brunt of the force with the weapon's barrel. The rifle weathered the blow easily, but the soft inferior metal of the lead pipe dented upon impact. Flint screamed with rage and reared back to swing again. Babylon surged forward and shoved him down with the butt of his weapon.

Flint's eyes widened. He stood and took a shaky step forward. "Stay back, Stump," he said. "I got this."

Stump, however, was busy watching a resident caterpillar inch up the nearby wall. Moot, on the other hand, hopped from foot to foot, making suggestions for other places to hit Flint, and Emmunda cheered loudly.

"Go, Babylon," she said. "Beat him! Kill him! Eat him!"

Flint took another wild swing, which Babylon dodged. He returned the favor with a swipe at Flint's hands. Flint brought his pipe up, but as soon as the rifle struck the lead weapon, it bent and flew out of the boy's hands. It skidded

39

across the floor, coming to a halt on the opposite side of the room. Flint stood there weaponless.

Flint balled his hands into fists. "I don't need a crummy pipe to beat you!"

Flint lunged at him, but before he could make contact, the building started to rattle. They looked at each other in a panic, their battle abandoned. Babylon had no idea what was going on; it felt like the whole planet was being torn apart beneath their feet. Bits of the ceiling fell to the ground, and furniture danced around the room.

Babylon ran to a nearby window and saw something impossible: a small, metallic pod blasting off next to the building, only a few feet from the window. He watched, mouth agape, as it flew through the sky and disappeared into the clouds. After it vanished, the rumbling stopped, and everything went quiet.

"What the heck was that?" Flint asked, his face ashen.

"It looked like an egg," Babylon cried. "A flying metal egg!"

Hearing that, Stump's ears pricked up. "An egg you say?" He licked his lips.

"I've never even heard of something like that," Flint said.

"I have." Moot pointed to his chest with his thumbs. "It was probably just a gremlin egg or something. They're usually pretty big."

"Where did it go?" Emmunda asked, looking out the wrong window.

"It's gone now, whatever it was," Babylon said, as he gazed at the sky.

§ § §

The King stared at the stars and empty space through his window. The foolish planet hovered like a marble just below his warship. He smiled. It wouldn't be long now.

The door opened, and his scout entered.

"Your majesty," he said with a salute. "I've just returned from the planet."

"Yes," the King said. "This I can see."

"I'm ready to give you my full report." The King waited patiently, but his scout just stared at him. He stared at his watch and tapped his foot until the scout continued. "It appears that the air is definitely breathable and will sustain us for as long as we need."

"And the inhabitants?"

"I followed a couple of boys for a little while. They are very similar to us but appear to be much more primitive. The scanner classified them as 'non-threatening.'"

The King cackled. "Perfect," he said. "Luck is on our side. Ready the troops."

Chapter ε

THE JOURNEY HOME passed mostly without incident. Flint tried picking fights with Babylon every now and then, and even tried to steal his assault rifle, but without success. Stump offered to trade his drum and caterpillar with Flint but was brushed off. It was a slow two-day slog through the plains and over the river, especially with Stump stopping every few minutes to rest on top of his rusty drum, but eventually, they arrived home, hungry, dirty, and exhausted.

Babylon expected some sort of fanfare over their return. He thought the town would throw the same party they usually did, or his father would bake him a special barley cake, or at the very least, someone would shake his hand. But, alas, it was not to be. He couldn't really blame the town for their lack of enthusiasm since they were on fire.

"What happened?" he asked nobody, as flames assaulted the rooftops.

"Maybe they're celebrating our return," Moot said.

Babylon stopped to question someone who was running around and screaming with his shoes on fire.

"Hey, Tako. What's going on? What happened?"

"Some fool was playing with something in the windmill," Tako the Troubadour said, as he danced from one flaming foot to the other. "It started a blaze that spread everywhere."

"Who started it? Is everybody all right?" Babylon asked, but Tako only tipped his smoldering hat and ran away screaming.

They walked further into the village, looking for a way to help, or at least another victim to interrogate. Then Papa Briggs ran by with a pail full of water from the well.

"Dad!" Babylon yelled.

Papa Briggs stopped. "You made it back!" he shouted.

"What's going on? How did this fire start?"

His blue hair flopped from side to side as he looked around. He tugged at his collar. "I'm not sure. I think it began in the windmill, but thankfully, nobody got a good look at the guy who started it."

"That's a shame," Babylon said. "I'm just glad you're okay."

"And I'm glad *you're* okay. Did you find something to bring back?"

"I sure did." He displayed the assault rifle.

41

His dad's blue hair stood straight up. "Wow, that's amazing. That may be the best thing anybody's ever brought back."

Flint huffed. "Mine's better."

"I don't think the fire has reached Poxxy's hut yet. Head over there while you can."

"What are you going to do?" Babylon asked.

"I'm helping." Papa Briggs motioned toward the pail. "The firefighters are over there, fanning the fire out. I bet they're thirsty. I'm going to bring them some water." The under-jester took a sip from the pail before running off.

"Let's get to Poxxy's," Babylon said. The others agreed, and they rushed off to the other end of the village.

Poxxy was the best blacksmith in the area. In fact, he was the only black-smith in the area. At one time, there were other aspiring blacksmiths that opened shops, but they all died from mysterious anvil related injuries. Thus, Poxxy had cornered the whole blacksmithing market. He also did wedding cakes but wasn't as infamous for it.

The smith was a tall, older man with a wide frame. His face was scarred from years of flying sparks and from experiments smelting gunpowder. He was crotchety and would have been run out of town years ago if he didn't play such a crucial part in the Rite of Passage. He took each piece of scrap the young men and women found and fashioned them into weapons. Most of the people in town still had the swords and knives from their own Rites; almost all of them were crafted by Poxxy.

They entered the blacksmith's hut one at a time. He was sitting with his back to the door, staring out the window and watching the fire. He chuckled.

"Um, sir?" Babylon asked.

Poxxy spun around and threw a knife at the door frame. Babylon didn't flinch. He had visited Poxxy before.

"How long have you been there?" Poxxy cocked an eyebrow.

"We just got here."

"Oh, good." Poxxy hurriedly stuffed a bottle of champagne and a party streamer into a drawer before approaching them. "What can I do for you?"

"We just returned from Mount Trespass," Flint said, with an arrogant smile. "And we found some pretty good supplies."

"Ah, so you survived the Rite, did you? Come forward. Let me see what you brought for ol' Poxxy."

Stump stepped up first. He handed Poxxy his drum, which had been flattened by his rump. The blacksmith looked at the drum and frowned.

"Yeah, all this rust will surely help things," he said. He shot Stump a dirty look and pointed for him to leave the hut. After that, he called for the next person.

Emmunda stood in front of the blacksmith and held out her rock. "I got this for you!" she said.

Poxxy sputtered. "What am I supposed to do with this?"

"It's a gift."

"Oh." His leathery face lightened. "Why, thank you." He turned around and put it on the shelf next to the other rocks.

Flint barged forward. "I think I've got something good here," he said, handing him his bent pipe.

"Oh, joy, another one of these pipes," Poxxy said. "They always make me woozy when I melt them. This will be a real thrill."

Moot was next. He handed the crutches to the smith with a grin on his face. The old man just looked at him and shook his head. Moot left with a blissfully ignorant smile.

"Next!" the blacksmith said.

Babylon walked forward and handed over the assault rifle. Poxxy looked it over carefully and let out an impressed whistle.

"High grade metal," he said, turning it this way and that. "No rust, no impurities. My young friend, this will make an excellent sword."

Chapter Z

THE NEXT DAY was one of celebration. It was the same celebration they always had whenever they were forced to rebuild their town. Fires, landslides, and hoedowns were common occurrences, so they were used to starting the town over from scratch. They were so used to it, in fact, that instead of fleeing from their obviously cursed land, they turned the disasters into fun-filled events. There were special "rebuilding the village" songs, and even a few games, like the ever-popular Pin the Tail on the Under-Jester.

The people would hammer away with smiles on their faces. Some would laugh uncontrollably while sawing planks of wood. Even Poxxy had a good time, running around with his party hat on and charging outrageous prices for supplies. It was truly a period of joy for everybody, especially for the group that had just returned from the mountain.

On Babylon's very first day as a man, he helped his neighbors lay a foundation for their new home and built replacement tables for the town's market. He really felt like a productive member of the community.

Of course, there were trips into the woods. Lots of trips into the woods. You can't rebuild a town without sticks; don't be stupid. Babylon was invited to join the gathering parties. Since he was one of the most adept navigators, they didn't really have a choice but to bring him along. In turn, he showed them the best places to gather the sturdiest materials, like at the base of trees and in certain shrubs. He also corrected the others if they searched for wood in tar pits or in the mouths of bears. Throughout these trips, he made a conscious decision to keep them away from the tree he had marked. He didn't want some fool to wander into the Forbidden Zone. The last thing they needed now was a village-wide panic.

Overall, the townspeople rebuilt their homes with their usual productivity. By nightfall, everything was back to the status quo, and the village was as peaceful as it had been before. The townsfolk celebrated a job well done with mead and music. As Babylon sat back and watched the singing and dancing, he couldn't help but feel empty. The most important moment of his life had come and gone, and nothing had changed. He still didn't feel like a man.

A large explosion burst from the sky and shook the town. At first, the residents were too busy applying the drunken finishing touches to their homes to notice anything was amiss. They just assumed it was another fire to celebrate.

Only Babylon paid attention to the events transpiring above them. Dozens of metallic egg-shaped pods appeared in the sky out of nowhere. Babylon immediately recognized them as the same type of "gremlin eggs" he'd seen at Mount Trespass. Except now, instead of one, there were dozens.

"Moot! Moot!" Babylon shouted, running to his friend. "Do you see that? It's those same weird things we saw a couple of days ago."

"No, they're not the same. I think these are, uh, meteors," Moot said. "I heard that they look like that."

"Meteors? What are meteors?"

"They're like moon babies. Soon we'll have a few more moons."

The pods circled the town before finally landing on various homes and chicken coops. Their doors opened, and troops clad in black armor stormed out. Without hesitation, they attacked. They blasted fancy weapons, set fires, and stomped on flowers. A few folks were outraged at the intrusion, but most just happily picked up saws and began construction again, humming their rebuilding songs.

"Are you sure those are meteors?" Babylon asked, his body tensing. "'Cause I didn't think moon babies did that."

"Yeah, they do," Moot said, his beady eyes darting back and forth.

The final pod landed on top of the golden statue of the Duke. Its door opened, and a small man stepped out. He was dressed in the same black armor, but his suit had more decorations lining the chest. He had an air of authority, his tiny hands rested on his tiny hips.

"You," Babylon heard him say to one of the soldiers. "Rough up that guy with the party hat."

The army moved through the town, causing damage and mayhem. As soon as they finished with a house or a barn, the villagers would cheer and get to work rebuilding it. Babylon didn't cheer. He stood in place, keeping his hand on the hilt of his sword the whole time. The tiny man pulled out a strange device from his tiny belt. He pushed a button and spoke into it.

"Sir," he said. "This is Lieutenant Stryker. I think these guys are about as conquered as they're going to get. Might as well head on down."

Babylon's heart slammed in his chest. He waited, but nothing happened at first. The man called Lieutenant Stryker put the strange device back in his belt and started terrorizing the community with the others. There was a noticeable lack of effort at this point. It seemed the soldiers were tired of terrorizing people that weren't being terrorized and moved on to shop at the marketplace. One or two even helped rebuild the houses they had knocked down earlier.

A terrible screech erupted from above. A strange object broke through the clouds in a stream of flames and descended towards the town. It was another pod, just like the others, except made of solid gold. Tethered to its front were two green, scaly, winged creatures that breathed fire.

A few of the more interested townsfolk panicked, but everybody else was too preoccupied with their repairs to notice. The pod did a few loops in the air before landing with a flourish to scattered applause by the townsfolk. Seconds passed. Babylon studied the golden pod, his pulse racing. Only fate could have sent such invaders to his town at the same time he became a man.

The pod's hatch opened. Out stepped a tall, thin, mean-looking man. He was dressed in a regal green and purple robe, under which he wore a green and purple vest. One hand was bare, while the other was covered with a black leather glove. The only contrast on his impeccable outfit was the bright yellow box strapped across his back. The man cleared his throat.

Babylon drew his sword.

§ § §

The king cleared his throat again, louder this time. He wanted the attention of this foolish village but wasn't getting it. He coughed as loud as he could to signify he meant business. One of his soldiers handed him a lozenge, which he waved away. "Greetings, fools!" he shouted. "I am your conqueror! Bow before me!"

He waited a few seconds to see if anybody bowed, but no one did. He unleashed a terrifying scowl to see if that would get the ball rolling. It didn't. A few soldiers bowed uncertainly, but that was it.

"My name is King Dragons!" he yelled. "I am from the planet Dragons."

Nobody seemed to notice the king screaming in the town square. Dragons felt a little offended by this. "And these magnificent creatures that you see behind me," he continued louder, motioning toward the green, scaly animals, "are dragons!"

There was a palpable silence before one or two people looked up from what they were doing.

"Who are you?" asked a villager.

"Once again, my name is King Dragons!" he yelled, having lost some of his energy.

"What's a dragon?" another villager asked.

"T—these are dragons," the king said, and made an even more exaggerated gesture toward the beasts.

"But you said you were Dragons," the first villager said, in an accusing tone.

"Yes, I am King Dragons, these animals are just—"

"You can't be the King Dragon, you don't even have scales! You're fibbing!"

47

Dragons' jaw dropped. This was not going as smoothly as he had hoped. "Does anybody have any other questions?" he asked, with a sigh. "Ones that don't pertain to my name?"

"How do they fly?" a child asked, before his father hushed him.

"Ah! Good question." Dragons tossed the kid a lollipop. "As luck would have it, they can fly anywhere. Even through the dark recesses of space." After he finished his sentence, the machinery on his back began to hum slightly, as if in response to his comment.

"What do you want?" a boy holding a sword asked.

"Your puny planet!" he said, letting out a long, menacing cackle. A few more people started to take notice of him now, especially since he was standing on top of the jailhouse they were trying to rebuild.

"Do you mind?" a villager said, hands on his hips.

"I'm terribly sorry." Dragons stepped out of the way. Then he realized what he was doing and stepped back in the way. "Wait a minute, no! I'm taking this planet from you, and there's nothing you can do about it!"

The villager crossed his arms but didn't press the issue any further.

Lieutenant Stryker stepped forward. "Sir, what are your orders?"

"Destroy this insignificant town!"

Stryker rubbed his neck. "Well, we uh…kind of already tried that."

"Don't argue with me, just do it!"

"Yes, sir." Stryker shook his head and gave the order to the army.

The soldiers moved back around the town, resetting fire to buildings, breaking tools, and tearing down foundations. Dragons cackled again as the destruction unfolded in front of him. After a few seconds, his menacing laugh turned into a mean-spirited giggle, and then into an alarmed chuckle. Everything his men were doing to destroy the village was being immediately negated by the townsfolk. It was hypnotic. The soldiers and villagers entered a rhythm and, eventually, became a sort of assembly line. One man would knock something down, then the man to his left would move in to rebuild it. This spectacle continued for a few minutes before Dragons started to question his process.

"What's going on here?" he asked himself. "These people aren't being defeated. They're only being mildly inconvenienced."

As more time passed, the soldiers and townsfolk began to work as a team. If a soldier wasn't doing a good enough job at breaking somebody's furniture, one of the stronger villager would give him a hand. In return, a few of the armed men started learning a few of the lyrics to the "Rebuilding Song." When the troops started lining up for some of the fun and games, the king knew that something was seriously amiss.

"This is ridiculous." He sighed. "Did they rebuild the apothecary already?

I just saw that thing go down!" He watched, his forehead starting to pound. "How can it be so? They build without hammers. They plunge without plungers. They paint without brushes, rollers, or sponges!" He puzzled on the situation for a little while longer before he finally came up with an idea.

"Soldiers!" he screamed out at the top of his lungs, interrupting a conga line. "We're switching gears. These puny villagers, feeble as they may be, are also extremely efficient. We might be able to use that to our advantage! So, stop wasting time on destruction. Let's try a different strategy: enslavement."

The soldiers let out a groan. Just as quickly as they had made friends, they were now going to lose them. They began attacking the townsfolk with sticks and blunt objects and bound them with ropes and twine. This seemed to get everybody's attention. They couldn't rebuild their homes if they were tied up, even though some of them tried. After a few minutes of beatings, bindings, and stern talking-to's, all eyes were on King Dragons.

"That's better," he said. "I want to make sure I have your undivided attention. I am your new ruler. You will all bow down before me. Then you will assist me in my plans."

There were a few minutes of silence before someone in the back of the crowd spoke up. "Assist you with what?" That person was immediately slapped by one of the guards.

"Don't you *dare* question your leader!" Dragons shouted at him. "But that is a good point. You people have no idea why I'm here or what I want, do you?"

Everybody shook their heads, afraid to answer out loud.

"Well, allow me to explain why I conquered your village. I come from a far away planet. There was once a rare substance on it called Falkorite. This substance is very important to me and is worth more than gold."

"Gold!" one of the bearded villagers erupted, before he was wrestled down by five soldiers.

"Thank you," Dragons told the soldiers. "Yes, this Falkorite is extremely rare and valuable. The problem is, we ran out of it on my home planet. We mined every single bit of it. So, it became necessary to find a new planet that naturally produced Falkorite. And I did. Yours."

The people shifted and muttered to each other. Apparently, they didn't like the fact that their home was full of an expensive substance that they had to give away. They felt that they should at least get some money for the Falkorite.

"Anything you find in our village is property of the Duke!" one brave soul shouted.

"I have easily conquered your town, and I will easily conquer your duke. And let's make one thing clear. Neither I, nor my men, will be mining for anything. You people, with your remarkable efficiency, will be doing all the work for us."

49

The villagers groaned. A few of them argued the situation wasn't fair, no matter how easily conquered they were.

"Starting today," Dragons continued. "You will be burrowing deep into your planet. You will bring me the Falkorite, and once I've collected it all, I will leave you in peace. If you refuse, you will die!"

The residents grumbled, but nobody really argued with the plan. They didn't enjoy mining, but they enjoyed dying even less.

"Are we all in agreement? Good! Let's not waste any more time."

A man in front of the crowd broke free from his bindings and stood up screaming. He had a sword in his hand, which he waved menacingly. "I'll never let you get away with this!" he shouted. His face was contorted into a mask of rage.

Dragons chuckled. "And who might you be?" he asked.

The swordsman tossed his sword from hand to hand. "I'm Nails," he said, grimacing. "Nails Franklin. I'm the best swordsman in town. Prepare to meet your doom." He made a few more cliché threats and tough-guy one-liners while swinging his sword around.

Dragons sighed. "Stop that man, get him back in line."

A group of soldiers blocked Nails path, as did a few brown-nosing members of the village. Nails hacked and slashed his way through all of them with ease until he stood before the king. Dragons smiled and unsheathed his saber with his gloved hand.

"This should be fun," he said. "I haven't had to kill anybody in a while."

Nails took a swing at Dragons' head. The king easily blocked the attack and countered with one of his own. Nails ducked and did a backwards flip, landing next to the windmill. The crowd gave an impressed murmur. This was a pretty good fight, they muttered. Much better than the fight between Nails and that arrogant goat.

"I have the moves *and* the skills," Nails said, with a cocky smile. "Tell your men to leave or you will suffer at my hands."

Dragons laughed and stared at his soldiers, who were gathering around Nails. "Stand down," he said. "I'll take care of this."

"Bring it on!" Nails said, who started doing tricks with his sword, demonstrating remarkable skill. Most of the town had apparently seen his fancy swordsmanship before, so the only ones who were really impressed were the guards. They clapped their hands several times during the presentation.

With a final flourish, the warrior threw his weapon into the air and held out his hand to catch it. This was apparently his "Grand Finale." The villagers kept calling it that at least. Nails did a few times as well. In fact, he wouldn't shut up about how he had done this trick so much that he'd perfected it. But this time was different. The machine strapped to Dragons' back started to beep

50

and whir. The gears, cogs, and spokes moved and vibrated, and buttons on the side lit up in bright colors. Dragons smiled. This was a sensation he was used to, and always found comforting.

Almost immediately, a gust of wind blew through the village. It rustled through his hair and made the tall grass around the windmill lean over. The sword that was flipping around in the air got caught in the gust, knocking it off course. So now, instead of Nails catching it gracefully in his hands, he caught it screaming in his chest.

The villagers watched this in silence. Apparently, they had never seen this part of the act before. A couple of guys nudged each other and said that this Grand Finale was even better than the old one. Nails staggered around crying, bleeding, and trying to pull the sword free from his body. The machine whirred and beeped again. Nails stumbled into the windmill, as astronomical as the odds were—and Dragons knew. They were printed on the readout on the side of his machine: one in a blublatt! —Nails managed to fall on the tiny spot that was the building's one and only structural weakness. As soon as he made contact with this weakness, the whole wall collapsed. Nails peeked up just as the top of the windmill crashed down on him, crushing both him and any chance for a slave rebellion.

When Nails was good and dead, and the machine had stopped its activity, Dragons took a step toward the crowd. "Oh, did I mention?" He paused and let the moment sink into them. "It's impossible to kill me."

They shook their heads, their faces glum. This was apparently news to them. A few said they wished he had mentioned it before Nails died.

Dragons continued, "Now, is there anybody else who wants to fight me?"

The people glanced over at the crumbled windmill and the corpse beneath it. They shook their heads again, more vehemently this time.

He was pleased. "Excellent. Let's get to work."

The soldiers rounded up the villagers and fitted them with mining equipment. Then, they set up a ten-foot fence around the town with barbed wire and armed guards. The simple village had become a prison.

Dragons entered his golden pod. A set of reins rested in front of him and connected to the dragons outside, which allowed him to steer his pod. Next to those reins was a steering wheel, which also steered the pod, but required less skill. He grabbed the reins and shouted "Giddyap!" The dragons' wings beat, and they took off into the sky.

"On Thunder Blitzen, on Puff!" he said, as they flew higher. He stared out the window and watched his obedient slaves become smaller and even more insignificant, until he lost sight of them completely. The blue sky darkened into inky black nothingness.

51

The pod pulled into the landing bay of the warship hovering above the planet. Dragons stepped out, smiled to a few soldiers, and waved his hands in victory. He walked into his private chambers and his smile melted away. He was less confident and more worried. With shaking hands, he tugged at his hair. The strands came out with little resistance.

The door opened, and Lieutenant Stryker walked in. Dragons stiffened.

"Shut that door!" he said. "Quickly!"

Stryker did as he was told, then moved closer. "I think we did well today, sir," he said.

"I agree," Dragons said, as he pulled more hair from his scalp.

"How is the machine holding up?"

"Not well. It's running on fumes. We need that Falkorite soon, or my luck is going to change forever."

"The slaves have been put to work. It's only a matter of time before they find the mineral."

"I hope so," Dragons said, staring at the clump of hair in his gloved hand. "For the time being, I'm going to stay onboard the warship. No point in risking myself needlessly."

"Yes, sir. I'll stay behind on the planet and watch over the slaves. The moment they mine any Falkorite, I'll deliver it to you personally." With that, Lieutenant Stryker marched out of the chambers.

Dragons let the hair fall from his glove to the ground. "Please, hurry," he said to the empty room.

Chapter η

THE NEXT FEW weeks were some of the worst in Babylon's life. The guards spat on him daily, beat him with a variety of objects, and worked him to the brink of collapse. He asked to be transferred to a different slave camp, one that wasn't so physically demanding, but his request was denied.

A typical day for the slaves was rough. First, they would wake with the rising of the suns. Then they were given one cracker for breakfast, followed by a glass of mud. After that, they got to work digging with shovels and pickaxes while guards stood behind them, attacking them for whatever reason they could think of. This would go on until dinnertime, when they would have their feast of boiled mouse and sauerkraut. When darkness fell, they would finally pass out into an exhausted, dreamless sleep. Then the suns would rise, and they would do it all over again.

To make matters worse, the villagers weren't very good at mining. Most of them had never done it before, so they didn't understand the basic principles behind it. A few of the slaves held the shovels upside down or used their teeth instead of pickaxes. Some people tried asking the guards for advice, but they just ended up being beaten.

The worst part about the whole thing, by far, was the death toll. Every day it seemed that somebody died in an accident or at the whim of a guard. And because they were lousy at mining, the shafts suffered constant collapses. People got trapped inside or were crushed instantly, and a whole day's work would be lost. They would have to begin a new shaft a few feet next to the old one. Three or four awful days went by before somebody found something in the ground, but it turned out to be worthless silver, so they had to keep digging.

The women were separated from the men the first week, to keep breeding down. The women seemed to be more pleased with this arrangement than the men. Babylon often watched Emmunda from the barrier fence, longing in his veins. She was beat the hardest by the female guards, but never seemed to notice. In fact, she often asked for better beatings, and soon Stryker assigned her a personal beating guard. Babylon winced every time they struck her. Emmunda usually danced.

Not everyone hated the new slave conditions. The guards loved it. All they needed to do was stand around and keep order while everybody else did the manual labor. It was a pretty sweet deal for them. They bragged about it all the time. Some of the guards really enjoyed being brutal, too. They beat the villagers when they were out of line or when they were in line. It all depended upon the guard's mood. Some complained that the slaves weren't making enough progress. Others complained that the slaves were making too much progress. And still others urged the captives to embrace their slavery. One guard tried to befriend everybody. He was the most hated one of them all.

"Hey, there's my main man, Limpy," Mirthos the guard would say. "And here comes trouble! It's Foxxy, the Foxxster!"

Bottom line, slave life was miserable. They had suffered through droughts, floods, fires, plagues, and unfair tariffs, yet they had always managed to survive and adapt. But this forced labor was just too much.

Babylon was lying on his bed one night, lamenting the misery of being a slave. Mirthos' suggestion that "it is what you make it" was not helping him tonight, especially when the guard kept whispering it to him from the window. He lay on his bed, teetering on the precipice of sleep, trying to think of a way to escape it all when the front door opened. The unmistakable sound of belled shoes crept toward his room.

"Hey, Son," Papa Briggs said, as he jigged past. "I hope I didn't wake you."

"No, I'm not asleep yet."

"I'll leave you alone then, you need your rest."

Babylon closed his eyes and tried to fall asleep. When he opened them again, he saw Papa Briggs smiling down at him.

Babylon jumped. "Are you okay?"

"Just fine."

"You seem happy."

Papa Briggs laughed and slapped his knee. "Yeah, maybe a little bit."

"What could you possibly be happy about?"

The old man opened his mouth and smiled wide, then patted Babylon's head. "Not now, you look tired. I'll tell you in the morning."

Babylon closed his eyes again and rolled onto his side. He struggled valiantly to shut his brain off and relax, but it was very difficult with his father kneeling next to him stifling laughter. Finally, after a few wasted minutes, he rolled back.

"Okay, you might as well tell me why you're in such a good mood."

"All right, if you insist," Papa Briggs squealed. "I've been promoted."

"You've been promoted?" Babylon tried to wrap his head around the statement. "To what?"

"A full-time jester! All my dreams have come true; I'm finally a real jester!"

"How did that happen?"

"The old one died. Apparently, he made Stryker laugh too hard and was beaten to death. This is the happiest day of my life!"

"But aren't you worried he'll do the same to you?" Babylon asked.

"No time to talk now. I need to practice," Papa Briggs said, as he started juggling two balls and a pickax.

Babylon watched a few minutes before interrupting. "Dad, I hate it here."

His father dropped his balls. "What do you mean, 'you hate it here'?" he said. "I'm having the time of my life."

"I'm not. Neither is anybody else. We're being beaten and overworked."

"That's life, Son. Better get used to it."

Babylon crossed his arms and stared up at the ceiling. "I'm thinking of escaping," he said.

"Escaping? Are you crazy? Where would you escape to?"

He scratched his head. "Well, the Duke might be able to free us."

"Oh, well then I have good news for you. The Duke is dead!"

He sat up straight. "What?"

"Yeah, Stryker murdered him," Papa Briggs said, with a smile on his face. "Stryker drinks his tea from the Duke's skull now. So, you don't have to worry about escaping any more, since there's no point."

Babylon's face fell. "Well, then I don't know where I would go, but anywhere has to be better than here. If I escape, at least I won't be a slave anymore."

His father put a warning hand up. "Listen, Son. This is the first time a Briggs has ever held a dignified job in the history of our village. I won't have you running off and jeopardizing that."

"I'm a man now." Babylon stood and met his father's eyes. "If I want to fight back against Dragons and Stryker, it's my right to do so! What's the point of the Rite of Passage if I don't try to protect my home from attackers?"

Papa Briggs put his foot down. "As long as you're living in MY house, and are a slave to OUR king, you will do as you're told! Now, I don't want to hear another word about this ridiculous escaping nonsense!"

Babylon wanted to argue but realized it was futile. His father had never acted so hostile towards him before. He decided it was best not to press the issue any further.

Papa Briggs left, and Babylon lay back down, staring up at the thatched ceiling. He thought about everything he had been through the last few weeks. His father didn't want him to break out, and apparently neither did Mirthos, who kept whispering, "Don't escape. It is what you make it." That night, he came to a decision on what needed to be done. If nobody else would save them, then it was up to him. It was time to become a man.

§§§

The next morning, Babylon came up with a solution. The best way to regain his freedom was to get the whole village to rise up and fight back. There were twice as many slaves as guards. All they needed was a spark to ignite a revolution.

The first few people he talked to were excited about the idea of rebellion. They were as tired of the beatings and shabby conditions as the next guy. And as soon as Babylon planted the seeds of insurrection in their minds, it caught on like wildfire. He whispered phrases like "we're breaking out" and "meet at the windmill" to passersby and watched them spread the message to others. Before long, the phrases came back to him, though garbled— "Weird raking gout," one slave whispered. "Rubber baby buggy bumper," said another— and before long, just about everyone in the village got wind of the plan and was in favor of it. A couple of the guards heard of the plan too, though they seemed a little less enthusiastic about an uprising.

Through the rest of the day, the general attitude was more positive than it had been for weeks. The slaves couldn't wait for the day to end. They smiled while eating their cracker and giggled while being beaten. It was the first time they had something to look forward to in a while.

That night, when dinner was over and there were less guards walking around, the villagers met in the rebuilt windmill. Most of the residents were so excited they showed up before Babylon even got there. When he stepped through the door, there was a loud roar of applause.

"Shh!" Babylon whispered, waving his hands. "We have to be quick. We don't want to get caught. You all know why I called you here, right?"

Everybody nodded. A few of the less popular slaves were in the dark, however, and just showed up because they wanted to have more friends. So, they leaned forward, trying to capture every word being said.

"We're taking back the village," Babylon whispered. "One way or another. I called you here to start an uprising. We outnumber the guards."

"But they have swords and shooty sticks," one of the slaves said.

"We have swords too," Babylon countered.

The slaves looked at each other. Those that hadn't already sold their weapons for snake oil had given them to Stryker. Babylon asked why they didn't lie about being armed, like he did, but they said that would have been rude.

"Okay." Babylon shook his head. "It doesn't matter. We could still fight back if we—"

"Maybe we should try a non-violent approach," someone said. "I say, starting right now, we all go on a hunger strike."

56

There was a roar of approval from the people. They all cheered despite Babylon's protests. Before he could even suggest his plan, the townsfolk scattered back to their homes, some of them chanting "hunger strike" over and over again. Babylon stood flabbergasted in the empty windmill after they'd left. The first meeting of what he dubbed "Project Turmoil" hadn't gone as well as he'd planned. He was hoping for a much more violent approach than what the villagers had decided upon. But he walked home anyway, trying to carry a little hope in his heart. Maybe the hunger strike would work after all.

It didn't.

The next morning, the slaves refused to eat their scraps, and went right to work instead. The guards didn't mind. They barely had to dip into their cracker stockpile. And there was less complaining now that the villagers were starving. They were too hungry to speak. And the physical exertion they were forced to endure sapped the rest of the energy. Then people started dying. That ended the hunger strike as quickly as it had begun. The villagers didn't realize how dangerous starvation was.

Project Turmoil met back in the windmill that night, a little angrier than they were before. They all felt that the whole thing was a bust.

"You're hunger strike plan didn't work out," somebody yelled at Babylon.

"It wasn't my idea," Babylon said. "My idea is much different. I think we should rise up, and—"

"I say we pick a new leader!" another person shouted to applause.

"I can be your leader." Foxx Fabrin stood up.

"Say, I like this new leader." Moot Fabrin nudged the slaves next to him.

"And better yet," Foxx continued, "I have a plan worthy of a new leader."

Everybody cheered. They already seemed to like Foxx better than Babylon and were willing to listen to his plan.

"Young Mr. Briggs was out of his league with his hunger strike idea," Foxx said, sticking his thumbs under his suspenders. "He's young and naïve, and so he thought a diplomatic approach would work." He shook his head. "But my idea is much simpler. I say...we escape."

Cheers went up from the crowd. "I never would have thought of that," a slave whispered to his buddy.

Babylon crossed his arms in his seat as he watched Foxx steal his thunder. Foxx unhooked his thumbs from his suspenders, then jammed them back in. "Now, we have the tools to dig our way out of this place here in our hands. The guards foolishly gave them to us, so we could mine. All we have to do is use them during the nighttime when nobody can see us. We'll work in shifts and dig a hole, right here under the windmill. One that will lead us directly to the outside, where we can make a break for it."

Once again, everybody cheered. The entire group seemed excited to begin the escape tunnel towards freedom. A few people were apparently so excited, that they started digging right then and there with their hands.

"Tomorrow we'll smuggle some tools in here and begin our getaway!" The windmill erupted with cheers for a third time.

§ § §

Making a tunnel wasn't as easy as Foxx promised it would be. After a hard day of digging a hole for King Dragons, the last thing the slaves wanted to do was dig another hole against King Dragons. So, for the first week, digging progressed at a snail's pace. The hole was barely a foot wide, and about three inches deep. They were getting nowhere fast. Foxx decided he needed to motivate the villagers. He and some of the more zealous slaves took a lesson from the guards and began regular beatings. This certainly motivated the workers, but it didn't do much to improve morale. A few villagers even branched off to build a different tunnel to escape from Foxx.

Another problem that nobody had foreseen was the large amount of displaced dirt. It accumulated at an alarming rate and was bound to attract attention from the guards. It was decided that they needed to find some place to stash it. Unfortunately, the only place big enough to hide all that dirt was the mine shaft. So, every night the villagers would haul the dirt into the shaft, and every day, those same villagers would haul the dirt from the shaft back into the tunnel. It was counterproductive, to say the least.

It took a while, but the slaves finally got the hang of tunneling undetected and were beginning to make some progress. They discovered that they could hide the dirt in a variety of places, like behind rocks or under rugs. Things were starting to look up for Project Turmoil. They were digging under the village with relative ease. Unfortunately, that gave rise to a new problem.

Babylon discovered this problem on one of his night's off. He woke to a clinking, clanking, clattering cacophony of scratches and loud voices coming from directly below him. After contemplating on this for a few moments, he realized what was happening. The tunnel wasn't deep enough, and anybody within earshot would hear the obvious sounds of escaping prisoners.

"What's that noise?" Papa Briggs asked, when the noise woke him up as well. "What's going on?"

"It's nothing, Dad," Babylon said. He was still reluctant to tell his father about the escape, especially after his last reaction. "You don't hear anything. Go back to sleep."

"I thought I heard somebody underneath us," he said with a yawn.

"You must have been dreaming," Babylon said, creeping toward his father with a frying pan in his hand. "Please, go back to sleep."

Snores came from the bed, and a feather floated up and down above his father's mouth. Babylon stuffed the frying pan back into the frying pan credenza and breathed a sigh of relief. But, if his dad could hear the slaves in the tunnel, the guards would be able to hear them as well. He was going to have to talk to Foxx before it was too late.

Babylon's fears were justified moments later when the entire guard shack heard the escapees in the ground beneath them. Luckily, the guards were just as incompetent as the slaves and didn't understand what was going on. They tried to rationalize it by saying it was just the planet settling, or that it might be ghosts. Thankfully, none of them considered that it was the slaves, though a few of the soldiers ended up requesting transfers from the haunted village.

The next day, Babylon approached Foxx after breakfast to tell him the bad news. "You have to be quiet in the tunnel or at least make it deeper. I could hear you guys down there last night, and I don't want you to get caught."

"It seems to me," Foxx said, thumbs affixed to his suspenders yet again, "that young Mr. Briggs is still jealous of my tunnel idea. I suppose that means you don't want to be part of the escape tonight?"

"Tonight? Really?" He did some quick addition on his fingers. "How is that possible? I worked a few nights ago and we still had a long way to go."

"The boys work rather fast when they're properly motivated," Foxx said, cracking his knuckles. "I was even thinking of becoming a slave owner when this is all said and done. I feel I have a certain knack for it."

"What time is the escape taking place?"

Foxx smiled. "I knew you'd come back around. Be at the windmill after dinner. We start then."

Later that night, Babylon arrived on time to the tunnel entrance, as did the rest of the villagers. They were all eager to be free from the miserable life of slavery. One by one they filed into the hole, with Foxx leading the way.

"I did some rough estimates," he shouted back to the group. "And, the way I figure it, we only have to dig a little more until we are outside the fence. Shouldn't take us but a few minutes."

Foxx and the others at the front of the tunnel dug as fast as they could, wild and desperate. Liberation was just a few feet away, and it looked like everything was going their way. Even the ground became softer and easier to dig through. Finally, a faint light peeked through the dirt above them

"This is it, boys," Foxx shouted. He ran his fingers over the muddy ground and popped them in his mouth. "I can taste freedom!"

Foxx broke through, sticking his head out of the ground. A few slaves, including Babylon, also stuck their heads through nearby holes. Foxx looked at the others and smiled broadly.

"You dug more holes, eh boys?" Babylon couldn't see, but he was sure that Foxx had jammed his thumbs under his suspenders while he talked.

"I thought you dug these holes," someone said on the other end.

"No," Foxx said. "I guess these holes were pre-dug."

Another head popped out, spraying mud everywhere. "Why would somebody pre-dig holes?"

Babylon shot Foxx a glance, and they shook their heads at the same time. They had dug straight into the latrine.

"I think we may have made a mistake, boys," Foxx said.

Just then, a guard walked into the latrine with a roll of toilet paper tucked under his arm. He spotted the confused, filth-covered faces of the townspeople. For a few moments nobody moved. Both the guard and the slaves were frozen in shock. Then the guard grabbed his club and started beating anything that was sticking out of the ground like a grotesque game of Whack-a-Mole. The villagers scrambled back through their tunnel and out of the windmill.

Naturally, the guards weren't very happy about the escape attempt. They felt betrayed and claimed they were doing a good job as guards. So, as punishment, the breakfast crackers were replaced with clumps of animal fur, and the group picnic was canceled. Foxx was hanged as well. Not by the guards, but by the slaves themselves, who were very upset about the failure, and because they were really looking forward to that picnic. After a few days of hanging, they released him, though he did have rope burns on his wrist for a week.

Ragged and broken, the members of Project Turmoil met the next night and devised one final idea of how to attain their freedom. One of the villagers was struck with the thought of how easy it was for the birds to fly above the guards' heads and out of the village. He asked what would happen if the slaves had wings of their own. Would they be able to fly out just as easily?

Everybody thought that it was a good enough concept to think over. It was better than waiting around for death, at the very least. The only question was how they would get wings.

"Everybody knows that birds fly because of those nifty feathers, right?" Tako the Troubadour said to the crowd.

Most of the slaves murmured in agreement. A couple of people argued that birds drink air to fly but were quickly silenced.

"Well," Tako said. "I say we lure some birds into our village, capture them, and use their feathers to create flying suits. Then we can fly out of here in style."

Overall, the people didn't think it was the greatest plan. Or the most cohesive one. In fact, the general consensus was that the goat could think of a better scheme. But, at this point the slaves were desperate, so they decided to give it a chance.

Unfortunately, the villagers lacked the one crucial item needed to catch a bird: bait. The only thing they could use to lure them was their already meager allotment of food. And that meant sacrificing their rations yet again. The grumbling slaves all donated crumbs to the cause. Tako donated two crumbs, since he was the only one who really believed in his idea. A few slaves donated their collection of bugs and worms as well, but the rest of them claimed they were saving those bugs for the holidays.

Eventually, the bait worked. Birds flew into the village and started picking at the crumbs while the hungry villagers watched, salivating. Tako wrangle a few of them with his bare hands, but most flew off when Stump showed up to eat some of the bait as well.

After a few days of wrangling, Tako said he had enough material to start crafting his flying suit. He sat in the windmill every night with the other slaves. He plucked feathers off the birds and sewed them onto one of his overcoats while the others looked on and gave him helpful hints, like "don't sew them all in one spot" or "take the feathers off the bird first."

He worked all through the week, tossing the de-feathered birds into the trash. When he finished, he held the wing suit up for the others to admire. There was a weak smattering of applause and coughs.

"Fellow slaves," he shouted from the top of the windmill the next day. "Freedom awaits you as it awaits me. Let this be but the first step, or should I say flight, toward liberty."

Babylon stood next the windmill, his heart racing. The others watched on next to him, eating their crackers and holiday bugs. Tako took a step off the windmill. He looked so graceful, with his arms extended and the wind fluttering through his hair. Babylon wasn't watching a man, but a delicate dove taking off from the roof. That grace was lost a few seconds later when he began plummeting straight to the ground, screaming and flailing his arms. His messy crash into the dirt signified the official end of Project Turmoil.

"All right," Babylon said to himself, after witnessing the spectacular failure. "The villagers were no help. I'll just have to get out of this place on my own."

He knelt on the ground and started drawing figures in the dirt with the dagger he kept in his shoe. A guard stopped and asked if that was a weapon in his hand, but Babylon assured him it wasn't, and the guard apologized and kept walking. Moments later, a looming figure blotted out the suns and cast a shadow over him. He expected to see another guard, but what he saw instead was much worse.

61

"What are you doing?" Moot shouted. "Escaping?"

"Shh!" Babylon said. "Keep your voice down."

"If you're breaking out of here, I want to go with you."

"No, I can't take anybody else with me. I have to do this alone. I'm not even telling Emmunda." He looked across the fence where Emmunda's guard beat her while she laughed and danced from foot to foot. "The less people I bring, the lesser the chance of something going wrong."

"When have I ever screwed up? You need me on this. Come on, I thought we were friends."

Babylon stared at Moot for a little bit, watching his lip quiver. "All right," he finally said. "You're in. Just don't tell anybody else."

"I won't. I promise."

Within three minutes, two more people interrupted Babylon's planning in the dirt: Flint and Stump. "Moot tells me you're escaping," Flint said.

Babylon glared at Moot for a second before saying, "Well, he's lying. I'm not escaping. It's impossible to escape this place."

"I don't believe you." Flint scoffed. "And since we're also tired of being here, that means we're coming with you as well."

Babylon stood, and locked eyes with the Sheriff's son. "Even if I was breaking out, the last people I would do it with are you two."

Flint laughed. "You don't seem to understand. Either we come with you, or we go to the nearest guard and tell him what you're planning."

Babylon clenched his jaw. He knew Flint wasn't lying. He was trapped. He would have to take them along, whether he liked it or not. "Fine," he spat. "But no one else can come along. I think I have a plan that might work, but you guys have to keep silent the whole time and let me do the talking."

The young men all nodded in agreement.

"All right, then," Babylon said, picking up his sword.

"When does the escape take place?" Flint asked.

"Right now."

§ § §

"Hey," Babylon said, as he and his cohorts walked past the guards stationed at the gate. "We'll be right back."

"All right," the guards said with a merry wave.

When they were deep into the woods, well out of sight line, the young men finally stopped to breathe.

"I can't believe that worked," Flint said, between gasps.

"I can." Moot cocked his thumb to his chest. "It was my idea."

"Do you think they'll come and look for us?" Flint asked.

"I don't know," Babylon said. "Hopefully, they'll never find us when we get to where we're going." They panted, looking around every few seconds.

"Hey guys?" Stump said. "Where *are* we going?"

They looked at each other. They were all so happy to finally be out of the village and away from the bonds of slavery, they never stopped to think what their destination was.

"Well, don't look at me. I don't have a plan!" Moot said. "Flint's the one in charge here."

"I'm not in charge," Flint said. "It wasn't even my idea to escape. Babylon thought of it."

The group looked at Babylon.

"I know where we have to go," he said.

Everybody looked at each other, then back at Babylon.

"You do?" Stump asked.

"Yeah. I've been thinking about it for a while."

"Well, where is it? Where are we going?" Flint asked.

"The thing is, I'm not sure you guys will want to go there."

"I don't care where we go." Moot said. "I can survive anywhere."

The others agreed.

"All right. I think we should go to the Forbidden Zone."

Everybody gasped. Moot fainted. Stump threw up.

"We can't go into the Forbidden Zone," Moot said, after he had regained consciousness. "It's forbidden!"

Flint's eyes widened. "Yeah, I've heard stories about that place. We'll all be killed there."

"I don't think so," Babylon said. "I think it's worth checking out."

"What good is freedom if we're all dead?" Flint asked.

"I'm not going to just turn tail and run. Our friends and family are still captives. They're being starved and beaten. It's up to us to find a way to fight King Dragons and free our village. The Forbidden Zone might have something that can help us. Some ancient weapon, or maybe even people we can convince to fight with us."

"I don't know." Moot's body shook.

"Moot, don't you want to be known as the greatest hero in history?"

Moot scratched his head and shrugged. "I guess that would be okay."

"Stump, aren't you tired of only eating two meals a day?" Babylon said.

Stump nodded, his jowls flapping in the wind.

"And Flint, you haven't even seen your father since they locked him up for slapping Mirthos. Wouldn't you want to be the one who saved him?"

Flint puffed out his chest and stared off at the suns, a dreamy look in his eyes. "You're right!"

"This is it, our chance to be men. Real men. This is our Rite of Passage."

They held their heads high. Babylon saw the twinkle in each of their otherwise dull eyes. He knew he had reached them.

"Let's go!" He charged forward.

§ § §

Things were fine at first. Most of the area had been reduced to stumps over the years, and the suns shone brightly. Deeper and deeper the four walked into the woods. Gradually, the trees became more plentiful, and the light dimmed. The confidence of the young men began to wane. Their steps became slower, their conversations more abrupt, and an ominous feeling of gloom enveloped them. The pride and resolution they felt earlier became a mere whisper in the back of their minds as the reality of the situation set in.

"Maybe we should go back, guys," Stump said, his voice laced with anxiety. "We told the guard we would be right back. That was a long time ago. He might be worried."

"Quiet down, Stump," Flint said, his tone sharp. "We're not going back." He glanced over at Babylon. "Right?"

"No one's going anywhere," Babylon said, as he ran his hand over the trunk of every tree he passed.

The group moved in silence for a few minutes before Babylon stopped. Everybody else stopped too. He examined one tree in particular, running his fingers over the bark. There was a gnarled letter "B" carved into it.

"Okay," Babylon said. "This is it. This is where I found my treasure from the Forbidden Zone. If we walk any farther, we'll be in it."

Everybody stared ahead, but nobody argued or tried to leave. They all had their own personal reasons for being there. Their minds were set.

Babylon unsheathed his sword. "Does anybody else have a weapon?"

The others shook their heads.

"Okay, since I am the only one, I guess I'll go ahead. Everybody follow behind me. Are you ready?"

They all nodded, their faces stone. With deep breaths of cool air, they treaded forward into the Forbidden Zone.

Chapter 0

IT FELT STRANGE journeying through the Forbidden Zone. For starters, there was a palpable sense of thrill in the air. The young men were walking through areas that hadn't been explored in hundreds of years, maybe more. Every now and again, Babylon would stop and examine an interesting plant or skeleton, hoping he could find another technologically superior invention like before. The others would occasionally gawk at the new and exciting wildlife that crossed their paths. They were gripped by a sense of awe.

With that wonder and awe came a surreal sense of dread. Babylon was well aware that, at any moment, they could be ambushed by an unknown attacker. Maybe that wayward sheep was really an assailant. Or a shark in disguise. It could be anything. And who knew what that tin statue with the ax was capable of. He didn't know what to expect as they traveled, and that made it all the more terrifying.

Stump's stomach rumbled.

"Did you hear that?" Moot asked, alarmed. "It sounded like a monster."

"It's just your imagination," Babylon said. "There's nothing in this forest except for us."

The rustle of nearby tree branches made the young men scream in unison.

"What was that?" Flint asked.

"Probably just a harmless jackal." Babylon gulped.

"I'm going back." Moot spun around. "Maybe I can get a reward for turning myself in."

Before Babylon could protest, Flint grabbed him by the shirt. "Nobody is turning back," he said. "The last thing we need is for you to squeal to the guards." He shoved Moot back in line and the group continued on.

In the midst of the foreboding forest, surrounded by darkness, the four pressed forward. A feeling of terror permeated the group. Babylon wanted nothing more than to be out of the thicket. He stopped looking for new discoveries, no matter how tantalizing they seemed. When he saw an advanced looking rock, he ignored it. When he found a clump of grass that was a different color than the ones at home, he passed it by. And when he discovered a new type of rabbit, he kicked it in the opposite direction. Fear had gotten the best of him.

After trudging through the forest for what felt like years, the trees started to thin, and the lowering suns shined brighter. They were reaching the end of the woods. Babylon couldn't help but wonder what lay waiting ahead. No one in the village really knew what was on the other end of the forest. Most of them thought it was a hidden city, with buildings as tall as twelve bears, and amazing technology around every corner. With the light of day erasing some of his apprehension, Babylon was captivated by the endless possibilities.

He was disappointed when all they saw was a small hill. There was no awe-inspiring city, no fascinating weapons, no ravenous cannibals, nothing. He ran partway up the hill and saw vast empty fields spanning the horizon. Then he ran back down and dug a small hole to check underneath the hill. Maybe the city was hiding under there? Nope. Nothing but dirt.

"That's it then?" Flint cried. "We came all this way for nothing?"

"What are we going to do now?" Moot asked. "There's nothing here. The legend of the Forbidden Zone is a complete lie."

Babylon thought hard. His mind raced back to the fire-maker he found. "No, there has to be something here," he said. "We just have to look harder."

"Look harder?" Flint said. "At what? Look at that thing. Seriously, look at it." He ran past Babylon up the hill. "Nothing here but grass and dirt." He ran to the other side. "Nothing here but more grass and dirt." He sprinted all the way to the back of the hill.

"You've made your point." Babylon scowled.

"And what have we back here?" Flint shouted from the back of the hill. "Nothing but a huge metal door and—" His voice cut off. "Hey, guys, come back here. I think I found something."

Babylon, Moot, and Stump hurried around the hill. When they got there, they saw a large metal door overgrown with grass and weeds.

"How's that for ancient technology?" Babylon asked, with a smug smile.

"That's amazing," Moot said, running his hand over the smooth surface. "I wonder what's inside."

"Only one way to find out," Babylon said.

He walked to the door and tried to slide it open. It didn't budge. He tried grabbing it from the bottom. It still wouldn't move. Finally, he kicked it in frustration. That didn't work either, but it made him feel better.

"I can't open it," he said.

"How are we going to get in if we can't open it?" Moot stomped his feet.

"Maybe we should all try lifting it together," Babylon said. They tried that for a few minutes but to no avail.

"How about we all kick it?" Stump said. That didn't work either, but now everybody felt better.

"What if there was a hole in the side of the hill we could go through?" Flint asked.

"That's a dumb idea," Babylon replied. "Where would we find a hole like that?"

"There." Flint pointed to a spot above the metal door. Sure enough, there was a large hole in the hill itself, big enough to fit through.

"Oh," Babylon said. "That could work. I guess."

Flint crossed his arms into an arrogant pose. He led the others up the hill. When they reached the top, they peered inside. It was dark, and Babylon could only see a small circle of light below from the hole. It didn't look like a far drop, but he wasn't certain.

"Well, now what?" Stump asked. "We can't just jump down. We could die."

"Didn't anybody think to bring rope?" Flint asked.

"We could throw Stump down there and land on him," Babylon said.

"Maybe we should throw you down there." Flint got in Babylon's face.

"Give it a try and see what happens," he said, through gritted teeth.

They glared at each other for a few minutes before Moot said, "Well, we can't just sit around here. We have to do something."

The tension broke for a brief moment. "He's right," Babylon said.

Flint took a step back. "Well, what are we going to do?"

Babylon thought for a moment. "Well, let's see how deep the hole is first."

"How do we do that?" Moot asked.

Babylon reached into his belt and pulled out his dagger. He leaned over the edge and dropped it down the hole. He put his hand to his ear and waited for it to hit the bottom. It didn't take long for him to hear it clank against the ground. "It doesn't sound like it's that far of a drop. We should be all right if we just jump."

"Oh really? And who's going to go first?" Flint asked.

The group looked at Babylon.

"All right, I guess it's only fair," the newly elected guinea pig said. "Everybody stand back." He took a deep—very dramatic—breath, before shoving Stump down the hole.

A hard right hook from Flint followed. He didn't expect it, and he tumbled down the hole as well. He landed on the cold, hard ground, shaken but alright. He rubbed his jaw. There would probably be a bruise there—all things being equal, a bruise he deserved—but it was worth it. Stump rolled up to him.

"What did you do that for, you big jerk?"

"Relax, I knew you'd be alright," Babylon lied. Stump's face turned red. Babylon reared back, preparing for another right hook.

"Are you guys alive?" Moot called from above.

He eyed Stump. "Yeah, we're fine."

The room was dark, and he couldn't see anything except for the small circle of light he was standing on. He took a cautious step forward. Immediately, the room was flooded with light from above. The sudden brightness burned his eyes.

"What's going on down there?" Flint asked.

"I have no idea," Babylon muttered to himself. Now that his eyes were adjusted, he realized he was standing in a large, mostly empty room. There were rows of lights overhead that were brighter than any torch he'd ever seen. He didn't understand how the light was made or what made it so intense, but he was so infatuated with his new surroundings that he didn't pay it any mind. He scooped his dagger off the ground and called back up to the top of the hill. "Come on down, guys. You have to check this out."

Flint dropped in first, like a graceful cat, and then Moot tumbled through the hole like a dead cat. Flint barreled towards Babylon, fists raised, but stopped in his tracks as he looked around the area.

"Wow," he said, the fight apparently forgotten. "There really was an advanced city here."

"If we keep going, we might find something even better," Babylon said. "Something we could save our village with."

At the other end of the room was an open door with stairs leading down. It seemed to be the only way deeper into the building. They headed for it, eager to explore the great unknown that lay beyond.

Stump clutched Babylon's arm and let out a yell. He pointed to a barrel next to the door. It was full of thick green liquid. Stamped onto the metal cylinder were skulls and crossbones as well as many other threatening symbols that Babylon didn't understand.

"Can it be?" Stump asked, in amazement. "Are the fables true? Is this it? Have I found the Fountain of Life?"

Everybody in the village had heard the stories of the Fountain of Life. Legend told of a source of infinite power and energy somewhere in the Forbidden Zone. Anybody who drank from it was sure to become bigger and stronger than ever before. Occasional explorers ventured out to find the Fountain of Life, but none ever returned. Except for Foxx Fabrin, who claimed to have found it, but forgot where he left it.

"Stump, we don't have time," Babylon said. "The village is still in trouble."

"But if it *is* the Fountain of Life, we'll become super powerful," Stump said.

The young men all gathered around the barrel, curious. They took notice of the skeletons scattered around it, a few of them holding chalices. They were contorted into terrible shapes and poses, as if they had died awful deaths next to the barrel. Even the faces of the skulls were twisted into masks of pain.

"It looks like they died right before drinking from the Fountain," Moot said.

Stump reached down and snatched a chalice from one of the skeleton's hands. The fingers came off with it, and the bony thumb rolled across the floor.

"I've got a good feeling about this." Stump beamed.

Babylon eyed the liquid, which was the same consistency as bad mucus and smelled like the inside of his father shoes. "I don't know. Maybe we should just keep moving."

"What other choice do we have?" Stump asked. He dipped the chalice into the barrel. The liquid didn't exactly flow into the cup. It oozed in, like porridge. A few sizzling drops landed on the floor. Stump smiled and raised the chalice to his lips. "Here goes nothing."

Stump downed the entire cup in one big gulp. He gagged and choked, then complained about the rotten taste, but also said he was thirsty, so he filled the chalice up again. He took another big gulp.

At first, nothing happened. He kept flexing his muscles over and over for the others. Babylon asked if he felt stronger. He said he didn't. If anything, his arms felt weaker. His stomach wasn't feeling very good either. As a matter of fact, his bowels were now evacuating all over the floor. Then Stump collapsed to his knees, coughing and wheezing.

"Stump! Are you okay?" Flint asked, grabbing fistfuls of his own blonde hair and hopping up and down.

Stump's face turned red. Then it turned purple. Then blue. After that, he turned a few more colors the guys didn't even know existed. Moot commented when he turned mauve, but that was about it.

Finally, after a full agonizing minute, Stump stopped coughing and wheezing. He stopped breathing. He stopped living in general.

"Stump?" Flint whispered. "Stump!" He nudged him with his toe. No response. He choked back tears as he bent down and closed his dead friend's eyes.

Babylon was unsure what to do, so he patted Flint's shoulder. Flint shook off the gesture and turned his back on the group. Stump wasn't articulate, or useful, and most of the time he had an unpleasant odor, but he was still Flint's friend. And it was going to take a little while for him to get over Stump's death.

"Okay, my turn," Moot said, grabbing a chalice.

"No, Moot!" Babylon shouted. "Didn't you see what just happened?"

"Obviously, Stump wasn't worthy of the power of the Fountain of Life. I am."

Babylon slapped the chalice out of his friend's hand. It dropped into the barrel where it began to melt.

Moot sighed. "Now I'll never be super powerful."

"We should keep moving," Babylon said.

Moot kicked a jawbone across the floor, where it chattered into a wall, and followed Babylon and Flint into the next room. When they stepped inside, they were once again flooded by bright light. This room was a lot smaller, and there were a lot of blinking machines. Pillars ran along the center of the room, and a large metallic object sat at the other end. It stood on three thin legs and had a large cylinder sticking out of the center of it. It reminded Babylon of the weapons the guards had back in the village. There was no movement from the thing; it remained lifeless and dead. Like Stump. Dead like Stump.

Babylon walked along, not sure what to expect. There were different items scattered throughout the room, but none that looked useful. He picked up a metal cup filled with futuristic pencils. They had pencils at home, sure, but these pencils clicked when he pushed the top. Futuristic!

A spotlight shone down on the group. "PLEASE SHOW IDENTIFICATION!" a mechanical voice spoke from all around them.

Flint and Babylon exchanged a glance.

"PLEASE SHOW IDENTIFICATION!" the voice repeated.

"What do we say?" Babylon whispered to Flint.

"I don't know. We have to think of something fast."

"PLEASE SHOW IDENTIFICATION!"

"Um...Flint Kudgle?" Flint said, his voice wavering.

The machines beeped and blinked for a few seconds. "IDENTITY NOT ON FILE! PLEASE SHOW IDENTIFICATION!"

"The Duke!" Babylon said, trying to sound confident.

The machines blinked faster. The young men looked at each other hopefully. "IDENTITY NOT ON FILE! UNAUTHORIZED VISITOR! DEFENSE SYSTEM ACTIVATED!"

"Does that mean we guessed right?" Moot asked.

He got his answer a moment later when the metal beast at the end of the room sprung to life and started firing bolts of light at them. They leaped behind a pillar.

"What the heck is that thing?" Babylon shouted. He'd never seen nor heard of such a weapon before. A device that could shoot light itself! That was pure craziness. Yet here it was, standing before the group, trying to kill them. Who'da thunk?

"I think it's one of the weapons the ancients used," Flint said. "If we could somehow get a hold of it, we could save the village for sure."

"That's no weapon," Moot said. "It's alive."

Bits of debris fell on their heads as bolts hit the pillar they hid behind. "What do you mean it's alive?" Flint shouted, over the pandemonium.

"It was talking to us, and now it's attacking us; it's definitely alive. I've heard of things like that." He jammed his thumb at his chest.

"Oh, really?" Flint scoffed. "Then what is it?"

Another light blast hit home. Pieces of pillar rained down over the room.

"It's a vampire!" Moot shouted.

"A vampire?" Babylon asked. "No way."

"What the heck is a vampire?" Flint scratched his head.

"That's a vampire," Moot's said, pointing. "I saw one before, and it looked just like that." He pointed at his chest again, more exaggerated this time.

Babylon shook his head. "I thought vampires drank blood."

Moot frowned. "Well, apparently that was just a myth, because we are face to face with a real vampire right now."

The pillar was weakening from the fiery barrage. Babylon knew he needed to do something before they were shot or crushed. He scanned the room, trying to find something that could help them. Something glinted across the way, on top of a pile of rubbish on the other side of the room.

"I'll be right back," Babylon said.

He ran across the aisle to the next pillar. The volley of bolts followed him. He stretched a hand out to the pile of rubbish, trying to grab the glinting object. A bolt sailed past his hand, crashing into one of the machines behind him. Sparks and glass flew around him like painful raindrops. Babylon pulled his hand back and waited a moment. He breathed in deep breaths, his heart pounding against his chest. He steeled himself and reached out again. This time, he grabbed hold of the object and pulled it back seconds before the whole pile of rubbish was destroyed. The object was a round piece of metal with a smooth reflective surface, like a mirror. It was no bigger than the laundry rock back home.

Babylon hurried back to the other pillar where Flint and Moot huddled together in fear. He crouched down to show them his find. "All right, I'm going to prove to you once and for all that this is not a vampire!" he said.

"How?"

"Vampires don't have a reflection, right?"

"That's just a myth—"

"I know it's a myth!" Babylon rolled his eyes and sighed. "But if this is a vampire, we won't see a reflection in this mirror. Right?"

"I guess," Moot said.

"So, let's find out once and for all."

Babylon nestled the piece of metal in the crook of his arm and carefully peeked it out from behind the pillar. All he could see was the ceiling.

"See, no reflection. It's a vampire." Moot said.

"I need to position myself better," Babylon said. He stood and tried the same thing. Again, he couldn't really get a good look at the weapon. Plus, the blasts were getting awfully close. He was forced to pull the piece of metal back in.

71

"Is that enough proof for you?" Moot asked. "Or are you still in denial?"

"I just haven't found the right angle yet," Babylon said. "Here's what I'm going to do. I'm going to run out there for a second and point the mirror at it. You guys look and see if there's a reflection. Then I'm running right back, and we'll think of a way to beat it."

"Vampires are weak to garlic."

"Here I go. Keep an eye out, okay?"

Babylon jumped out with the piece of metal held flat against him. As soon as he did, the weapon turned and fired bolts of light at him. Before he could even think to move, a bolt hit him dead center. The mirror he held took the force of the impact and reflected the shot back towards its origin. Babylon, meanwhile, was knocked onto his back and lapsed into unconsciousness.

§ § §

When he finally woke, bright lights on the ceiling blinded him. Moot and Flint were smiling down at him. He remembered the machine and scurried behind the nearest pillar. But then he realized there wasn't anything shooting at him anymore. The room was silent.

"What happened?" Babylon asked, looking around.

"It's dead. You killed it," Moot said, with a giant grin.

"What?"

He jammed his thumbs to his chest. "My mirror idea worked. It killed the vampire!"

"Did you see a reflection?" Babylon asked.

"I forgot to look," Moot grinned and looked away. "I was too busy watching the monster explode!"

Babylon stood on shaky legs. On the other end of the room was a burnt set of legs attached to a smoldering heap of twisted metal.

"Well, so much for using that thing to save the village." Babylon sighed.

"Who cares, that was awesome." Moot looked at him with admiration. "My buddy, Babylon Briggs, killed a vampire."

"It was NOT a vampire!" Babylon said again.

The three young men strolled across the room. Before he left, Babylon ran a hand along the dismantled weapon. Part of him wondered if he could fix it. Maybe stick some of the charred pieces back together and go from there. But deep down he knew it was beyond his understanding. This wasn't like the fence or the chicken coop back home; this was ancient technology. He breathed another heavy sigh and made his way into the next room.

The next path they found was long and winding, in stark contrast to the large and spacious rooms before. There were several halls that intersected the main hall, each with other doors that led to even more rooms. They checked every one of them but didn't find anything of interest. They found flags with strange symbols, and drank from large porcelain bowls, but other than that there was nothing useful.

Flint had become unusually quiet. Babylon didn't want to press the issue because the atmosphere was nice without any of Flint's belligerent comments, but deep down he had to admit, he felt sorry for the guy. Despite being a complete jerk, he'd just lost his only friend. That couldn't be easy.

"Listen, Flint," Babylon said, breaking the silence. "I'm sorry about what happened to Stump."

"I don't want to talk about it."

"I know, it's just—"

"I said I don't want to talk about it." Flint kicked a piece of rubble down the hall. "I never should have brought him with us in the first place."

"Don't blame yourself." He held out his hand for support.

Flint glared at him. A fire blazed in his eyes. "I don't blame *myself*," he said, pushing the gesture aside.

Babylon dropped the subject. This wasn't the time to discuss Stump's death, particularly with Flint.

They went through the last door at the end of the hallway and found themselves in a massive room. As luck would have it, there were no blinding lights or scary vampires like in the previous rooms. A few small overhead lamps blinked on, while others flickered and remained dark. Whereas the other rooms were old but still functional, this one looked completely dilapidated. The ceiling, walls, and most of the floor were rock.

In the middle rested a large metallic vessel on a circular island of stone, surrounded by a deep chasm. It looked like the egg pods Dragons' men used, albeit a lot larger and squarer, with wings and a well-defined front and back. In fact, this ship was so massive that four of Dragons' pods could easily fit within it. On second thought, it was nothing like Dragons' pods.

Babylon walked to the edge of the chasm. "Do you hear that?" he asked. "I think there's water down there. We might be near the river."

"Who cares?" Flint said. "I'm more interested in that thing in the middle."

"Yeah." Moot did a double take. "What do you suppose it is?"

"I think it's the answer to our prayers," Babylon said, smiling.

"Let's get across," Flint said. He pointed to an old metal bridge in front of them. It was rickety and swayed from wires that attached to the ceiling. Pieces of metal had fallen off, but it was the only way across the chasm.

Babylon took a step onto the bridge and was stopped by Moot. He was shaking, and his face was pale.

"Wait," he said. "It could be alive?"

"What? You're crazy!"

"Well, let's check before we just walk over to it. That vampire didn't look alive either until it tried to kill us."

Babylon sighed. "Fine. How do you suggest we prove whether it's alive?"

Moot bent down and grabbed a stone with his hand. "Stand back," he said, still shaking. He hurled the rock at the ship's metal hull. Before it could make contact, the rock froze midair and was flung back at Moot.

"See!" Moot yelped when the rock landed at his feet. "It *is* alive!"

Babylon didn't have an answer to that. It was certainly the last thing he expected to happen. Unfortunately, it paled in comparison to what happened next. Without warning, the whole area became unbearably hot— hotter than any summer day Babylon had felt before. The air around him burned, as did his body. The heat was so intense he could barely breathe.

"What the heck is going on?" Flint asked, staring wide-eyed through the sweltering madness. "How is this happening?"

"It's that thing!" Moot said. "It's going to kill us!"

"Stay calm," Babylon said through coughing gasps. The river boiled beneath them. He fell to his knees and crawled to the edge of the chasm. The water rose, molten red, scorching the rock walls. The atmosphere was so intense he didn't think he could take any more.

Moot fell next to him, clutching his throat and dripping sweat. He rolled around, screaming like a madman. Flint, who stood next to the bridge, showed no outward signs of turmoil. A single bead of sweat rolled down his cheek. Or maybe it was a tear.

Then, just as suddenly as it started, it stopped. The temperature became cool again, and the river cooled and sank back down until it was hidden in the darkness. Everything turned back to normal, as if nothing had happened. They looked at each other, panting and shrugging.

Moot started backing up towards the door. His shaking had graduated into full body convulsions. "Sorry, guys, I think I hear my dad calling." He turned and ran towards the entrance, screaming the entire way.

There was a palpable silence. Babylon stood in shock, trying to wrap his mind around what he had just witnessed. After a few minutes, Flint shook his head and started walking towards the bridge.

"Wait a minute," Babylon said. "Aren't you the least bit curious about what just happened?"

"No. It doesn't make a difference to me. Hot or cold, I'm crossing that bridge. Every minute we waste is another minute my father is a prisoner."

"So, you don't think that thing had anything to do with that heat?"

"No, I don't. Do you?" He crossed his arms and gazed into Babylon's eyes.

"Well, no. But—"

"But nothing! Are you coming or not?" Flint started across the bridge. Babylon hesitated. "I guess."

They tiptoed across the rundown bridge. It groaned and creaked with every step they took. Babylon made sure to distribute his weight as evenly as possible so as not to disrupt the bridge's delicate balance. Beads of sweat rolled down his face, and his pulse quickened with every sway of the ramshackle structure. He glanced up to see how Flint was doing and was shocked to see him trudging across the bridge.

"Flint, slow down!" Babylon yelled.

Flint ignored him and kept speeding along. He even added a skip to his step, though Babylon was sure that was only for spite. The bridge squealed under Flint's weight. When he reached the middle, there was a loud snap, and the whole structure started to sink. Babylon tried to hurry back to the ledge, but the metal was toppling into a steep decline beneath his feet. He fell backward, clutching the railing for support.

Flint wasn't so lucky. There was nothing for him to hold on to, especially since he was mid-cartwheel. He went down with a large section of the metal bridge, plunging into the darkness below. Babylon watched as the last member of his traveling group disappeared.

Babylon held on tight to the railing. His section of the bridge had swung into the rock wall but hadn't fallen. The incline was too great for him to climb, so he pulled himself to the side and used the rail supports like ladder rungs. Every time he reached a new part of the railing, it groaned and creaked. Babylon's heart raced every time he heard it. Planks of metal shook loose and disappeared into the darkness beneath him. With a final hasty effort, he reached the top and lay on the ground to catch his breath. He was happy to be back on solid ground.

He stared up at the ceiling for a few moments. Then a thought popped into his head: *Flint!* Babylon crawled to the edge of the chasm and peered down.

"Flint?" he called. "Flint! Are you still alive?" He waited, but there was no response. After a few minutes of staring down at nothing and calling out to nobody, he gave up. Flint was gone. He truly was alone now.

He got back to his feet. He was right back where he had started. And there was no way across now that the bridge had collapsed. The vessel was now unreachable. Part of him felt like giving up and going home. Maybe he would meet up with Moot, and they could work on being better slaves together.

"No!" Babylon gritted his teeth. "There has to be a way."

He looked across the chasm again. He could never jump the whole thing. Part of him wished he'd bought those wing shoes from that shady merchant.

Or had Tako's flying suit. Then he remembered what happened to Tako and pushed the idea from his mind.

Babylon shifted from one foot to the other, trying to think of a solution. He looked all around the room, desperate to find something helpful. His situation seemed hopeless. There was no way across. He would never find anything. Never, ever, *ever* find anything.

Then he found something.

Black support wires dangled over the bridge. They used to be attached to either side of the bridge, but age must have rendered them useless since it had just collapsed. Most of the support cables had been yanked out of the ceiling, but the nearest one was still attached.

Babylon stared at the wire. He might be able to make the jump if he built up enough speed. And he also might be able to swing across the chasm if he was lucky. At the very least, it was a plan. A dangerous plan, but a plan nonetheless. Since it was the only one he had, he might as well give it a try.

He stepped to the edge of the chasm and did a few practice jumps in place. The ground seemed stable below his feet. Stable enough to jump from, at least. He walked back to the door and did a few test runs, trying to see how much speed he could build up before stopping at the edge. He was only going to have one chance at this, so he needed to do it right.

When he was sure he'd done enough practice runs, and after he'd spent a few more minutes telling himself he was an idiot and that this was the stupidest plan he ever thought of and searching for another way across, he felt he was ready. He backed up until he was almost at the door. He focused on the wire far ahead. It dangled back and forth, almost mocking him. This was it. He took a deep breath, and then bolted as fast as he could towards the chasm. His heart hammered in his chest as fast as his feet pounded against the ground. The edge approached quickly. Twenty feet, fifteen, ten. The moment of truth was coming. His stomach fluttered. This might be the last action he ever took.

He leapt and became weightless. Had he been in a calmer state of mind, he might have commented on the uniqueness of the gravity defying experience, but the only thought running through his head now was, *Ohcrapohcrapohcrap!*

After an eternity, his hands clasped the hanging wire. He grabbed tight and didn't let go. The cable swung to the other side of the chasm, where the metal vessel waited. He held tight, unable to release the wire. His momentum ran out, and he started swinging the other way. After that, he swung back towards the rock island. Then back again. This went on a few more times, until he finally worked up the courage to let go. But by then, it was too late. He was no longer swinging over the edge; he was barely swinging *to* it. So, when he let go, he plummeted straight down the side of the rock face.

76

Just as the last bit of his body was falling past the edge, his hands landed on something firm. With overwhelming relief, he realized he had grabbed the rim of the rock island. With every bit of available muscle strength he had left, he pulled and cursed his way to the top. A couple of times he lost his footing and swore even louder. When he finally pulled his upper body over the edge, his swearing became more relaxed. With one final curse, he rolled onto solid ground.

He lay there for a few minutes, catching his breath. Then he felt something weird. He couldn't quite describe it, but it was almost the same feeling he had earlier when things became unbearably hot. It was as if reality was being stretched and skewed. And instead of the intense heat, this time the bridge was back, shinier and sturdier than ever before. Babylon sighed and shook his head, lamenting his rotten luck. Then it vanished, and everything went back to normal. He lay back down and rested his confused head for a few minutes.

Sweating, panting, and more than a little perplexed, Babylon sat up and for the first time really looked at the large vessel in front of him. It was even bigger now that he was face-to-face with it. A name was written on the hull in faded letters: *Atrium*.

His heart raced again, this time from excitement. The answer to all his problems was before him. All he needed to do was get inside of it. How hard could that be? As it turned out, it was harder than swinging across the chasm.

It wasn't like his house; the doors didn't just swing open. In fact, he wasn't sure if there even were doors. He tried opening a few things that he thought were doors, but he only ended up getting stuck in a giant complicated tube. He tried to sneak in through one of the windows, but they didn't open wide enough for him to get inside. Finally, he tried asking the ship to open, which somehow caused him to get stuck in that tube again.

Defeated, Babylon sat beside the vessel and fiddled with a control panel on a nearby pedestal. He didn't have a specific goal in mind; he just wanted to play with the buttons until he thought of a plan. Fortunately, one of the many buttons he fiddled with must have been linked to some sort of entry sequence, because when he pushed it, a loud hiss sounded from the bottom of the vessel.

He jumped to his feet as a ramp lowered from the bottom of the Atrium. As it did, fear lingered in the back of his mind. What if this was just another illusion? Like the bridge and the heat? But after waiting a few minutes to see if things reverted back to normal, Babylon decided that what he was seeing was genuine. He ran up the ramp and into the Atrium, eager to see what wonders awaited him.

Inside, the ship looked bigger and more complex than he could've imagined. There was a small room that had a row of blinking beds in it. In another room he found cases of dehydrated meals and a sophisticated food preparation station. There was even a water fountain. It was all so overwhelming. The whole ship was filled with superior technology from the ancient civilization.

Babylon made his way to the head of the ship. In the center was a large chair attached to the ceiling. In front of it was an enormous window which overlooked the outside chamber. Babylon recognized the window as the one he had tried breaking into with his dagger.

Beneath the window was a large panel of buttons. Like before, Babylon had an urge to play with them, but forced the idea out of his mind. He figured if he pushed the wrong button, he might somehow damage the ship. He was going to have to find the right button on the first try.

As it turned out, it wasn't too hard of a task. It was the only button that was bright green. Plus, there was a smiley face printed on it, and an instructional panel nearby with a stick figure that pointed toward the button. And there was a three-volume set of manuals next to it that showed him how to push the button. So far, this was the easiest thing he had found on the ship, though there was a part of him that wanted to push the smaller red button with the skull. He sat in the seat and pressed the green button.

More lights slowly blinked on. Then a feminine voice came from all around him. "Hello, new master." The voice sounded sad and morose, yet still carried with it a cold lack of humanity. "I am at your command."

Babylon shouted in all directions, not sure which way to face. "Can you hear me?"

"You do not have to scream, sir," the voice said. "There are microphones all around you."

"Who are you?"

"I am the voice that represents the ship's computer. I am the Atrium."

"Wow, you're a woman?"

There was a pause. "Computer's do not have genders. My voice is merely a program a previous star pilot selected for me."

There was a knob on the console with a picture of a mouth printed on it. Babylon spun the knob until the voice turned gruff and masculine. This frightened him, so he turned it back to the feminine voice.

The Atrium cleared a throat it didn't have. "You are not a fully licensed star pilot, are you?"

"I don't think so," Babylon said.

"I see." Another pause. "I hope you're not here to cannibalize my parts."

"What? What are you talking about?"

"When I was last powered down, I was set to be decommissioned. I assume you are here to snatch a few of my components?"

Babylon scratched his head. "What the heck does decommissioned mean?"

The lights on the dashboard glowed brighter. Babylon could tell the computer was thinking based on the light patterns and the constant reminder from the Atrium itself that it was in "thinking mode."

"Have you ever seen someone stop moving?" the Atrium asked. "Like from drowning, or being stabbed?"

"Yeah."

"Decommissioned is the computer equivalent."

Babylon though about this. "So my mother isn't dead! She's just decommissioned!"

"No, I believe she is just dead."

"Oh...so, they were going to kill you? Why?"

More blinking lights. "As the Entropy of Knowledge began to take effect, the commander of our wing decided to decommission all ships on the planet and use the scrap to construct low complexity, high efficiency weapons."

"Wait a minute, the 'Entropy of Knowledge'?"

The dashboard glowed an angry red. "Do not interrupt me while I am telling the story," the Atrium said. After a pause, it continued. "Yes, the Entropy of Knowledge. It was something that began in the year 11409. People everywhere on the planet began to decline in intelligence. The best scientists could not figure out the cause, but every subsequent generation displayed less intellect than the last. Fearing a contagious disease, the commander shut the wing down and decommissioned all ships to prevent a galactic epidemic."

"So, that's why the ancients had such advanced technology compared to us," Babylon said, having finally solved one of the village's two greatest mysteries, the other being the mystery of the yellow snow.

"After I was set to be decommissioned, I was powered down in the year 11512. What year is it currently?"

Babylon thought hard about the question. The village never kept track of petty things like what year it actually was— just how old people were. "16?" he finally guessed.

"I...see," the ship said. "Well, I suppose I can calculate the year based on the position of the constellations. It will only take a moment."

There was a loud metallic grinding sound as two metal doors opened above the ship in the subterranean chamber. Rock and stalactites battered the hull. Night had fallen outside the window. The Atrium's lights pulsated, and a machine in the corner with hollow discs whirled around furiously.

Finally, all became calm and the ship spoke again. "Oh no," it said.

"What's the matter?" Babylon asked.

"Nothing. Just yearning for the sweet embrace of decommissioning, is all."

Babylon cleared his throat in an exaggerated manner. "Listen, there *is* a reason I'm here."

"You don't say."

"See, this guy took over our village, and forced us to be slaves. I was hoping I could use you to free my friends and family."

The computer thought for a moment. "How would I be able to do that?"

"Don't you have any weapons? We could blow them up and force them to leave."

The Atrium chuckled, or at least it sounded like it was chuckling. It was an unnerving sound, and Babylon turned the volume down. "I am not really a combat vessel," it said. "I was designed for transportation and cargo."

"So, you won't be able to fight them?" he asked, crossing his arms.

"No, I am afraid not. I only have one weapon that would be effective on a large scale, but I do not think we should use it."

"Why not?"

"Because it would reduce your village to vapor."

Babylon blinked.

"That would be a bad thing," the Atrium said.

"So, I came all this way for nothing?"

"It would appear so," the ship said.

Babylon sighed. They both sat in silence for a while. Finally, after a few seconds of Babylon's angry groans and muffled cries, the Atrium spoke up again. "I guess there *is* something I can do."

He shot up. "Really? You'll help me?"

"I do not have a choice; you are my new master, after all. We could go into space and find a solution out there."

"What's space?" Babylon asked.

The Atrium sighed. "Space is the area between the planets, moons, and other cosmic bodies. It is the...uh...it is the black stuff in the sky at night."

"Oh, it's where the stars live, right?"

"Sure. Good enough."

Babylon grinned from ear to ear. "So, what's out in *space* that you think could help us?"

"I can take you to see the Elder Scientists."

"Who are they?"

"In my time, there was a planet full of the most intellectual minds in the whole galaxy. The Elder Scientists ruled there in peace and knew the answer to any question. If they are still there, then they can help you free your village."

"Wow, we're actually going to another planet? I'm going to meet a, what did you call them, 'elbow scientist'?" Babylon asked.

"Do not get your hopes up. They lived a very long time ago. I can only hope their descendants are as all-knowing as they were."

The ship hummed to life and the Captain's chair rattled and shook as the engines powered up.

"Are you ready?" the Atrium asked.

"Very!"

The ship lifted and began its blastoff sequence. Destination: hope.

Chapter ι

KING DRAGONS SAT on the throne in his cold steel warship, surveying the vastness of space in front of him. He let out a sinister laugh as he thought of something wicked he had done once. The steel door to his chambers slid open and Lieutenant Stryker stepped in.

"Ah, hello Stryker." He pulled a control stick and his throne spun around. "How goes it on that pathetic planet?"

"Very good, sir," the Lieutenant said. "I've brought something back for you." He held out his hand. A small silver chunk of metal shone in his palm.

"Falkorite?" Dragons asked.

"Yes, sir. One of the slaves found it today. It looks like they've finally dug deep enough. More will surely come after this."

Dragons snatched up the chunk of metal and stared at it with a smile. He opened a small latch on the side of the yellow machine and placed the Falkorite inside. The backpack immediately hummed, as if it was pleased.

"Sir, I must warn you," Stryker said. "We're having the same problems here that we had on our home planet. The brief periods of alternate realities."

Dragons' eyes widened. "How bad is it?"

"Well, just earlier today one of the chickens transformed into a mean-spirited horse."

"How long did it last?"

"Not long. A few seconds at most."

The king breathed a sigh of relief. "Good. Then it's not so bad yet."

"I fear your luck machine is becoming too unstable."

"Once I have enough Falkorite to keep it fueled for a while, I'll think of a way to solve that problem. For now, we're just going to have to deal with the irregularities."

Stryker opened his mouth, then closed it. "Yes, sir," he said, with a bow.

King Dragon pulled the control stick and spun his throne towards the vast window just in time to see something streak across the sky. A spaceship was leaving the pathetic planet. Dragons couldn't deny he was curious.

"How curious," the king said. "Stryker, do you see that?"

"I do, sir."

"Is it real?"

Stryker checked the monitors on the dashboard with his tiny eyes. "I believe it is, sir."

"Hmm." Dragons looked at the zoomed image on the monitor. "The Atrium, eh? I didn't think this planet had mastered space travel."

"Do you want me to follow it?"

"No, I need you with the slaves. You've been gone long enough as it is. I have a better idea. I'll have Plob trail the ship."

"Plob Babo? The bounty hunter?"

"He's the only person in the whole galaxy that could follow that thing without being detected. I'll call him immediately. I want to know who those people are."

Stryker bowed again and left. King Dragons picked up his space phone and dialed the space numbers. When the person on the other end picked up, he said, "Plob. It's the King. I have a job for you..."

Section II

Chapter K

A MAZING," BABYLON SAID, as he gazed at the cosmic view through the Atrium's window. Planets passed by like chestnuts in the sky. It was magical. A stray comet traveled past the ship, making Babylon smile. "Can I go out there?"

"Into space?" the ship asked. "Unprotected?"

"Yeah, it looks like fun. Like swimming in a giant lake."

"Do lakes typically make your blood boil before freeze-drying your suffocated corpse?" the Atrium asked.

Babylon grinned the happy-go-lucky grin of a dunce and shrugged.

"You know, I've been meaning to check your brainwave patterns," the ship said, after a brief pause. "I have suspicions they are not at an acceptable level for interstellar missions."

"How are you going to do that?"

A large beam of light enveloped him. It felt warm and tingly and made Babylon giggle. But all too soon the beam stopped, and Babylon felt cold again.

"Tsk, tsk, tsk," the Atrium said.

"What? Was it acceptable?"

"No, I am afraid not. According to my readouts, a chimpanzee is more qualified than you. And not even one of those smart chimpanzees."

"Hey." Babylon crossed his arms.

A red light flashed on the dashboard. "That's not all. My onboard laser phrenology system indicates that your brain is not suited for piloting. You are more suited for a simpler occupation. Like being a turtle."

"I thought you said I could be a chimpanzee."

"I was being polite."

Babylon huffed and slapped the leather chair. "You know, I didn't come all the way out here to be insulted by you and your dumb proctology laser."

"That's *phrenology* laser. And I am sorry, but the onboard phrenology system does not err."

Babylon pouted. "If I'm such an idiot, maybe we should just turn around and go home. Then you can be a slave like everybody else down there." He stamped his foot on the metal floor. He didn't like having his intelligence insulted by others and liked it even less when they were right.

"There is no need to be cross, Master" the ship said. "I never said I was not going to help you. I just wanted to explain your natural disability in a way that your feeble turtle brain could understand. And besides, there may be a way to remedy that."

"Really?" he asked, his turtle brain swimming. "How?"

A light shone behind Babylon, and his chair spun around on its own.

"Please give your attention to the chair in the far corner."

Babylon pointed. "The big cushy one covered in pillows?"

"No, the one next to it. The steel chair with the shackles."

"Oh." Babylon gulped.

Light glinted off the chair's metal frame. Additional red lights shone from beneath it, and ominous music played from the speakers above it. Babylon asked if the Atrium could lose the music, but it said it was part of the chair's programming.

"The chair was an experimental addition to my interior systems," the ship said. "It's called an Aptitude Luminositor. It enhances brainwave functions and neuron exchange. It never actually reached clinical trials because it was designated as inhumane. But the science behind it is sound."

"What does that all mean?"

"The chair has the potential to make you as intelligent as a space pilot."

Babylon jumped out of his seat. "It will make me smarter?"

"…yes," the Atrium replied in its monotonous tone. "And who knows. It might make you smarter than a space pilot. Your intelligence could rival the Elder Scientists. You could conquer the world of theoretical physics. And who knows what else after that? Maybe even the theatre."

Babylon clapped his hands. "Let's do it!"

He hopped onto the cold, unforgiving seat and waited with a smile on his face. Straps and clamps wrapped around his arms, and a large helmet lowered onto his head. He saw dozens of wires and electrodes protruding from it before it completely covered his face. Total darkness engulfed him, and the powerful machinery around him hummed. Then, with a jolt, a white light blinded him, and he was filled with a wonderful sense of euphoria. But just as quickly as it started, the world around him faded back to normal, and the helmet lifted from his head.

"Wow! That was incredible. Did it work?"

"No, you died for a minute," the ship said. "I shall try again. Please try not to scream so loud this time. It is distracting."

The helmet lowered again. This time, when the machine hummed, an immense pressure built up inside his head. His brain throbbed, like it was growing larger and larger with every pulse. Based on the machine's design, Babylon figured this was probably an apt description of what was actually happening.

Wait a minute, he thought. *Apt? That doesn't sound like a word I would use. Does it? No, I can't seem to recall — wait a minute: recall? I think this machine is working. At the very least it's enhancing my vocabulary. Wait a minute. Enhancing? Vocabulary? Least?*

The helmet lifted, and he looked around at his surroundings with new eyes. Everything appeared so different now, and a lot less confusing.

"I believe you will notice that more than just your vocabulary has been enhanced," the Atrium said.

"Hey, you could hear what I was thinking in there?" Babylon asked.

"No, you were shouting it."

Babylon unstrapped his arms and stood. He looked himself over with new clarity and understanding. He couldn't comprehend how his muscles and bones worked before, but now, with every flex of his arm he was amazed at the simplicity of it all. He ran his fingers though his hair and now knew why it grew the way it did, and why he always lost it during fires. And he was finally able to grasp how worried he should be about that growth on his neck.

"This is incredible," he said. "So, am I at an acceptable level now?"

The Atrium scanned him with the beam of light again. When it disappeared, a yellow light flashed on the console. The ship sighed and scanned him with the light once more. The same yellow light flashed. "Um...yes. I suppose you are at an acceptable level."

Babylon clapped his hands together. "Great. I can't wait to visit the Elder Scientists now. Maybe they'll even accept me into their group."

"It would be best for you to assuage your enthusiasm," the Atrium said. "You may have increased your brainpower, but that does not mean you are in the same league as the Elder Scientists."

"What makes you say that?"

"Well, for starters, the Elder Scientists are the greatest minds in the galaxy and are rumored to have the power to move the stars."

"And?"

"And you are still wearing your shirt inside out."

Babylon looked at the way he was dressed and began to change.

"It's going to take time for you to fully explore the depth of your intelligence," the ship said. "You are merely a newborn taking his first steps. In time, your mental facilities will grow."

"Do you think I'll ever be as smart as you? As smart as a computer?"

"No, never," the computer said, in a smug tone.

Babylon sat in the pilot's chair and stared out the window. The vastness of space seemed less romantic now that he understood it better.

"How close are we to the Scientists' planet?" he asked.

"Not too far. We should be there within fourteen subjective hours."

"Fourteen hours! Can't you go any faster?"

"We are traveling at the theoretical limit of the hyperdrive. We are making good time if I do say so myself." The center console blinked and hummed.

Babylon sighed. He stared out the window with his face buried in his hands. "I just think fourteen hours is a long time to wait."

"Do you have any idea how many trillions of miles we have traveled in only a few second?"

"Look, I'm not saying I'm not impressed, it's just—"

"No! No!" the ship said. "That last solar system we passed was two and a half light years across. We did it in five hours and twenty minutes. I checked the record. Only three ships in the known universe have made better time!"

"Whatever," Babylon said, growing weary of the Atrium's babbling. "Just get us there." He crossed his arms and sulked. A small indicator blipped on the control panel, and trilling filled the cockpit. "What's that?" he asked.

"It looks like another ship has breached our perimeter. It appears to be following us."

He looked out the window, but his vision was limited. "That's strange, I can't see it. Can we get a look?"

"Oh, I see. You are interested in other ships, but not me."

"Just bring it up on the monitor."

An image of a strange ship appeared on the screen. It was small and compact yet somehow still managed to look bulky. But the most peculiar thing about it was the array of signs and lit billboards haphazardly strewn across its hull. In bright and conspicuous letters, everything read: "Plob Babo, Professional Bounty Hunter. For Hire! Call Starlight 5879e12."

Babylon squinted. "Is that an advertisement? On a ship?"

A different light flashed on the control panel. "Sir, we have an incoming message," the Atrium said.

"Maybe the other ship will tell us what it wants." He pushed the button to receive the communication and was blasted with tacky music.

"Are you tired of cut-rate bounty hunters?" an annoying voice pitched through the radio. "Are you through with guys who don't do the jobs you pay them for? Are you thinking of giving up? Don't be crazy! Just call Starlight 5879e12 and hire Plob Babo. The number one bounty hunter in the galaxy. Call in the next five minutes and we'll throw in a complimentary Plob Babo hand towel. That's Starlight 5879e12. Call now!"

There was silence for a few seconds. "Is that it?" Babylon asked.

As if in reply, the radio communication started again. "Are you tired of cut-rate bounty hunters?" it shouted, as Babylon cut off communication.

"Sir, it appears the ship belongs to a bounty hunter," the Atrium said. "Or at least his agent."

"Yeah, but what do we do about him?"

The monitor displayed a readout of the ship's schematics. "I scanned his vehicle. It does not appear to be armed. Shall I engage in combat?"

"If he doesn't have any weapons, I don't see why we should."

"Are you sure? I do have one more salvo in the Exajoule Positronic Cannon that I've been itching to use…"

Babylon rubbed his chin. "Nah, let's just let him go about his way."

"Have you considered he might be spying on us?" the Atrium asked.

"If he was spying on us, would he be advertising himself like that?" Babylon said. "Come on, no one is that stupid."

§ § §

King Dragons inserted his card into the communication panel on his warship and dialed Plob Babo. Plob was fifty light years away, quite a long distance. When the operator asked if he would like to reverse the charges, he said he would, and Plob's chunky face appeared on the screen.

The best bounty hunter in the galaxy, Plob Babo, was a small, portly man in an armored suit and helmet. He carried an oxygen tank on his back that he claimed doubled as a jet pack, and the belt he wore was cluttered with all types of gadgets he used to track and subdue targets.

Dragons realized Plob's title was a bit of a misnomer. His competition was less than stellar. Many bounty hunters couldn't fly and had to walk from planet to planet. And the ones that owned ships didn't bother to invest in advertising and were ignored in the space phone book. Thus, Plob's self-proclaimed declaration of being the best wasn't really a high honor as much as it was a concession. His armored suit and helmet were only decorative and looked like tinfoil, while the advanced gadgets he kept in his belt were just a collection of batons, truncheons, and shillelaghs.

Plob sat at his display console, pushing buttons and dripping sweat. The interior of his ship was a glorp-sty, with fast food wrappers and empty cans of soft drink scattered around the mustard stained shag carpet.

"Hello, Plob," Dragons said. "How goes the hunt?"

Plob saluted the salute from his planet—an insulting gesture on Planet Dragons, but the king let it slide. "I am proud to report that the Atrium is right in front of me."

He smiled. "Good. Don't lose them. Find out what they are up to, then report back to me. Remember, don't kill them or let them know that you are there."

91

"Of course, sir. Stealth is my specialty." Plob pushed a button, and Dragons heard the unmistakable sound of a jingle being played. It was tacky, off-key, and would never work as an advertisement.

"Are you sending that ship commercials about yourself?"

Plob tugged at his tinfoil collar. "Of course not."

The king sighed. "Remember, Babo. This mission is not only for your pay check. This is for the glory of Planet Dragons and the entire galaxy."

"Uh-huh. Glory, got it," Plob responded. The screen went black.

Dragons leaned back in his steel throne, humming Plob's jingle. He considered himself lucky to have the bounty hunter on his side. The machine on his back hummed, and for a moment the king felt cushions underneath him.

Chapter Λ

THE ATRIUM LANDED on a deserted overgrown planet. Vines obscured tall buildings made of glass and metal, and grass grew from the cracks in sidewalks amongst fallen monuments. The whole planet gave off a feeling of a once great beacon of achievement that had sunk into disrepair.

The door opened, and Babylon stepped out onto the new planet in his new shirt, pants, and boots, courtesy of the Atrium. It had informed him that his clothes were too primitive for the greatest minds in the galaxy and provided him with a new wardrobe from its closets. The jewelry, on the other hand, Babylon pocketed when he thought the ship wasn't paying attention.

A large dome stuck out in the distance. It seemed to be the only thing on the planet still kept up.

"I assume that's where the Elder Scientists live," Babylon said.

"What did you say?" the Atrium asked. "I was just busy checking if this planet still has a breathable atmosphere…it does."

Babylon walked away from the ship and headed for the large dome. He was perplexed at the complete disarray around him. The area didn't appear to be abandoned, but it also didn't look like there had been a violent uprising. It was as if the city had forgotten how to govern itself. The tops of buildings were in better condition than their bottoms, so many of them had collapsed. Commercial and civilian vehicles were submerged within feet of a nearby bridge. And someone had apparently forgotten to take down the holiday decorations before the civilization crumbled.

Babylon stepped over a torn banner that read, "Happy Snefullas. Save 20% on Snefullas Pheasants at Barnaby's Pheasant Shack." He reached the dome, which was big and oddly beautiful, like a futuristic abode. He tried looking through the glass, but it had a reflective surface, so all he could see was himself trying to peep inside.

He walked around the dome for a short while, searching for the entrance. It was huge, much bigger than any structure on his home planet. Halfway around, Babylon got tired of walking and threw a rock at it to break the glass. It bounced off and hit him in the head, so he sucked it up and continued walking.

He found a wooden door hanging from its hinges. On a sign nailed to the door were scrawled letters that read: "Home of the Elder Scientists of the Galaxy. No Solicitors." Above the door was a brass bell with a rope hanging down. Babylon rang it and waited. He rocked from foot to foot. He was seconds away from meeting the smartest men in the galaxy. This was hands down the most exciting moment in his life.

After ringing and re-ringing the bell for ten minutes, his excitement and adoration started to wane. The most exciting moment in his life was getting less and less exciting with every passing second. Now, it was just becoming frustrating. *What gives?* he thought, shaking the rope as hard as he could. *I don't have all day! Come on!* When the rope broke off in his hands, he decided to storm into the dome uninvited. *Serves them right,* he thought. *And I'm not paying for that bell!*

Once he was inside, his anger and annoyance melted away. Before him were marvels of technology. Breathtaking inventions lay scattered everywhere; some were displayed on shelves, while others sat in corners collecting dust. A large machine with spinning cogs stood off to the side. Every few moments, it spit out a slip of paper with witty sayings on them. Babylon read one of them as it came out. "The end of one opportunity is merely the beginning of another. Current temperature: 295 K." Babylon let the slip flutter onto the mound of papers in front of the machine.

He rounded a corner and went down another hall. There were rooms everywhere, and inside each one of them were active but unattended gadgets. One device in a lime-green carpeted room kept spinning faster and faster until it popped out of existence. When it popped back, there were travel stickers on it from other universes. The next room had a wood motif and a scary looking machine against the back wall with a big countdown timer that said, "Seconds until the Heat Death of the Universe." The number *looked* astronomically large, but Babylon was unsure if it was really a long time or not. Seconds pass by so quickly, it was hard to tell if a billion was a lot.

Voices came from a nearby room. He followed them until he came to a chamber in what he believed was the center of the structure. The glass ceiling above him was the apex of the dome, and the walls had kitschy signs hanging on them with quotes like "Bless this Dome" and "This is the Center of the Structure."

The room was decorated like a kitchen, with a stove, dishes, and open cabinets full of food. Sitting around a wooden table in the middle of the room were four gray-bearded gentlemen dressed in togas. They appeared to be playing on an oddly shaped tic-tac-toe board using a holographic projector. There was a blackboard on the wall with equations on it and a banner claiming they were holding the "42nd Annual Sixth Dimensional Tic-Tac-Toe Tournament." One of the bearded gentlemen stood and added a long equation to the board with chalk.

"I believe that's the game," the man said, with a flourish. There were "oohs" and "ahhs" from the others.

"Wait just a minute," the man's opponent cried. "You forgot that visible light isn't observable in that plane. Your move is invalid."

The two observers of the game nodded and whispered to each other. This was apparently quite the match, judging by their comments and the pennants they waved. The first man looked back over his equation and nodded as well. "Right you are. Good play, sir."

That was when the men finally took notice to Babylon. They jumped to their feet and pulled a canvas tarp over the holographic projector. "Oh, no! He's back!" one of them shouted. "I knew we should have bought locks."

"Quick, Caspar," another one said. "Get the gun."

"Hold on, hold on," Babylon said, putting his hands up in a non-threatening manner. "I only want to talk."

"He's threatening us. Kill him." They surrounded him with advanced weapons—wooden clubs with nails sticking out of them.

"Whoa, wait a minute. I'm looking for the Elder Scientists. I need them and their superior minds."

The bearded men's tone changed in an instant. Now, they looked like they had just been asked for an autograph. They dropped their clubs and took Babylon by the shoulders. "Superior minds, you say?" one of them asked. "Why, that's us, all right. It's always nice to meet such intelligent and well-informed young people."

"We must apologize for our hesitation before. You see, we don't get many visitors anymore. Especially since interplanetary travel is so rare these days."

"That's fine," Babylon said. "So, you guys are the Elder Scientists?"

"That is us."

They stood in front of him, smiling. Babylon smiled back. This was it, the greatest minds in the galaxy. Each of them was a different height and color than the others. They were even different colors than him and the people of his village. For a brief moment, he wondered what he would have to do to join their group. Maybe he would ask the magenta one in the back before he left. Or the chartreuse one by the table.

One of them stepped forward. He was squat, with a bald spot in his gray hair. "We are the foremost authority of intelligence in the entire galaxy. I am the lead scientist. Call me Caspar."

A tall man with a short beard nodded from the back. "I am Balthazar," he said, keeping his voice small.

One of the scientists was clearly a woman dressed up like a man. "My name is Melchior," she said, pitching her voice lower and bowing. Her fake beard started to slide off, so she stood and readjusted it.

"And I'm Shemp," the scientist with bushy eyebrows and a mortarboard on his head said. "Together we possess every bit of knowledge in the galaxy, nay, perhaps even the entire universe."

Babylon's eyes widened. "Wow, then I guess I'm in the right place."

"Indeed, you are." Caspar smiled. "Now, I would like to pose a question to you. As we stand before you right now, do you notice anything interesting about our group?"

Babylon looked from wrinkled face to wrinkled face, trying to find something significant about their features. He felt like this was a test to prove his worth. He knew he needed to make a well thought out and educated guess, something that would make the Elders take him seriously. "You're all old," he said.

The scientists blew raspberries and spit out the tea they had just started drinking. Apparently, that wasn't the answer they were looking for.

"Preposterous," Caspar said. "We're not old. We're just matured. Like a fine block of cheese."

"I see." Babylon nodded.

"What we had hoped you would have noticed," Caspar said, with a disapproving tone, "was that all of us are male."

Babylon cocked his head and locked eyes with Melchior. She stepped forward, pushing the others out the way in her haste.

"That's right." Her voice was pitched even further down. "All male."

"This is no accident," Caspar said. "For generations our scientific society has been experimenting with gene manipulation. And I am pleased to say that we, as a group, have finally conquered genetics. My comrades and I have discovered a way to prevent the second X chromosome from forming. We are proud to announce that from here on out, all future generations of scientists will be born male."

"What's wrong with women?" Babylon asked, his thoughts turning back to Emmunda and his life before they were enslaved.

"Their minds are incompatible with us males," Caspar said.

Melchior's eyes darted back and forth. "Yeah, a female scientist? That would be the day! Isn't that right fellows?"

"That's right," Balthazar's said, his voice wavering. "Girls are scary. They distract us with ludicrous ideas of breeding and always urge sanitation." He punctuated his statement by blowing his nose into his beard.

"Ew," Melchior said.

The scientists had circled Babylon now. It made him uncomfortable. He tried to take a step back but was blocked by the leader of the group.

"I predict that future generations will be even manlier than we are today." Shemp grabbed him by the shoulder and spun him around. "But, let us digress from that subject. You came such a long way to meet the greatest scientific minds in the galaxy."

"Uh, yeah." He swallowed. "I guess I'm glad I found you."

"What a good lad." Caspar patted him on the back. "Would you like a drink?"

"...okay."

"Excellent. We have water or salt water."

Babylon shrugged. "A glass of water is fine."

Caspar walked over to a large pan underneath a gutter, scooped some of the discolored liquid into a dirty glass, and handed it to Babylon. He stared at it, wondering what would have happened if he had asked for salt water.

Caspar gestured for Babylon and the others to sit down at the table. "So, why did you come here?" he asked.

Shemp twirled his gray mortarboard. "Perhaps he wants a signed photo to show to his friends?"

"Or maybe he just hoped for a chance to meet his idols?" Balthazar rested his chin on his hands staring up into the sky, a dreamy expression on his face.

Babylon took a drink of water and grimaced while the scientists suggested possible reasons he was there, most of which involved their greatness in some way. They discussed amongst themselves for a few minutes, eventually sparking a heated debate about which branch of science was superior.

Babylon finished his water with a final swig. "Anyway—"

Balthazar shrieked and clutched his chest. "I forgot you were there," he said, between gasps. "Don't scare me like that."

Babylon cleared his throat. "I was hoping you guys could help me."

"You want a favor?" Caspar asked. "Give me back my water!"

"See it's like this...there's this man who—"

"A man?" Melchior asked. "Just like me and the rest of us, but especially me. I like him already!"

Babylon glared at her and went on. "He's actually a king."

"Such a noble creature." Shemp held his cap to his heart.

"He enslaved my village."

Caspar clapped his hands. "A man of action—even better!"

Babylon pounded his fist on the table, knocking the holographic projector over, breaking it. The others considered this quite rude, and Balthazar clutched his heart again.

"Listen to me!" Babylon said. "I don't like this guy."

"Then why are you praising him so much?" asked Caspar.

Babylon stopped for a second and took a deep breath. He told the scientists his story, choosing each word as carefully as he could. During his speech, he saw a portly man in a tinfoil suit crouching near the door. With all the strange things he had seen today, Babylon paid little attention to the portly man, even as he crawled around the corner with his hand cupped to his ear.

97

"So, this man is dangerous?" Balthazar said, after Babylon had finished.

"A most vicious animal," Shemp said.

"Yeah," Babylon said.

"Well, why don't you just solve your problem with good old-fashioned violence?" Caspar asked.

"I—" he began, but was immediately interrupted.

"What is that awful stench?" Melchior stood. "It's coming from the table over there." There was a sound of shuffling as the portly man rolled out of the room, smashing a standing mirror as he left.

"I guess it was just the wind," she said. "The smelly wind."

"As I was saying before," Babylon said. "I don't think this man *can* be killed. We tried to fight him in the village, but there was this weird machine on his back, and it kind of protected him from harm. Like a shield, but it was more roundabout than that."

The Elder Scientists froze in place. Balthazar's hand started toward his chest. "What do you mean roundabout?" Caspar grabbed Babylon by the shoulders.

"It's tough to explain," he said. "Instead of just protecting his body, it almost seemed like the machine…"

"Altered the events of reality, providing a fortuitous chain of events for him?" Caspar asked.

"Uh…yeah, actually."

The Scientists huddled up, whispering amongst themselves. Babylon couldn't hear what they were saying, but he could tell by their expressions that they were worried.

Caspar turned to him. "This machine you saw. Did it look anything like a thermal frugalgraph?"

"I'm not sure," Babylon said.

"Did it have lights and gears and things like that on it?"

His eyes widened. "Yeah, it did!"

The scientists exchanged glances. Melchior shook her head, loosening her beard, and Balthazar whimpered and uttered a chant to Sneful.

Shemp shuddered. "It is as we feared, then. Someone has…the *device*."

Babylon shrugged his shoulders at the man in tinfoil who shrugged back from the doorway. "What device?" he asked.

"It's called the Omnitrichcisbenefortuaquantumflux Mark IV," Caspar said.

"The…what?" Babylon asked, trying to repeat the name in his head.

"We call it the Omniflux for short," Caspar said.

"Omniflux…okay, that's a little easier to remember."

"What does it do?" the portly man called from around the corner.

"I'm glad you asked," Caspar said. "The Omniflux is, in layman's terms, a luck machine."

Shemp rummaged through the cabinets and pulled out a piece of paper and a pencil. "It changes the dynamics of the universe to benefit the wearer," he said, drawing figures on the paper and erasing them. "So, no matter what happens, this man will be able to succeed in any crazy idea he has. The Omniflux will alter reality so he always comes out a winner." Shemp handed the paper to Babylon. There was a stick figure on it with a smiley face. Shemp glared at him and tapped the picture again and again.

"Okay, so it's dangerous?" Babylon asked.

"And that's not even the worst part," Caspar said. "Every time the device alters reality, it has to bend the fabric of the universe. Repeated use of it will distort our reality. For instance, you may be taking a simple stroll through a field of grass, when suddenly, you find yourself walking under water. Or on top of a mountain. Then just as quickly, it will change back."

Babylon snapped his fingers. "Something like that happened to me back on my planet. I thought I was hallucinating."

"Then it has already started in your solar system." Balthazar clutched at his hair. "If this continues, the fabric of reality may become damaged, resulting in longer, more permanent distortions."

"Before long, conflicting realities will cause instability throughout the galaxy." Shemp pulled out another sheet of paper and started drawing. "Eventually, to restore equilibrium and contain the damage, the power of the cosmos will erase us from the universe. Our whole galaxy will become nothing more than a large stretch of empty space." Shemp offered the picture to Babylon, but this time he refused.

"What kind of evil person could have built a machine like that?" he asked.

The Elder Scientists looked at each other, tugging at their collars. "Well, there's no easy answer to that question," Caspar said.

"Oh, don't tell me. Was it you guys?"

"Yes and no," Melchior said. "The Omniflux *was* built by Elder Scientists. But it was built by our ancestors a few thousand years ago."

Caspar led Babylon and the others into the next room. This one was decorated like a living room, with a couch, several chairs, and four roll top desks with quill pens. The walls and floor were wooden, with a stone fireplace belching smoke to the top of the dome. Caspar pointed to an oil painting hanging on the stone. Thirteen bearded men and women of various races sat around a lab bench in their togas, mixing chemicals, and eating pheasant. Babylon was happy that his race was represented this time.

"Ah, that generation of Elder Scientists was one of the most important ones in the history of the galaxy," Caspar said, admiring the painting. "Some of the greatest machines we use today were created by these men and women. This is a painting they had commissioned after creating their hundredth invention. They're all there. From Beneficent the Wise, to Weiss the Benevolent. Those men created the Omniflux and kept strict warnings about its usage."

Babylon sat in a nearby chair. "How did King Dragons get a hold of it?"

"We're not sure. Not too long after that, the galaxy began feeling the effects of the Entropy of Knowledge, so most of our history was lost to the ages."

"You know, I've been wondering about that," Babylon said. "My ship mentioned it. What is the Entropy of Knowledge? How could a whole galaxy of people suddenly lose their mental aptitude?"

"Nobody really knows what it is," Caspar said. "All we know is that it was a slow process that took place over many generations. Parents around the galaxy noticed their children were far inferior to them in terms of intelligence and reasoning. Academics suffered, conversation was replaced with flatulence, and swing music was in a sharp decline. Over time, it became obvious that people were getting dumber."

"Thankfully, we remained safe in our dome," Balthazar said.

Just then, a sneeze rattled from behind a potted plant in the corner.

"Bless you," Balthazar said.

Something clicked inside of Babylon's head. He leaned forward in the chair. "Wait a minute! You said that every generation was dumber than the previous one, but when I was on my home planet, I was smarter than everybody. Even my father. How can that be?"

The scientists looked at each other. Their faces lit up in unison. "An anomaly!" Shemp said.

Caspar hopped around. "This is very exciting!"

"We must make a note to study it!" Shemp said. He took his recent drawing and turned it over, then scribbled something down and put it on top of a sheet of papers on one of the roll top desks. Babylon stood up and peeked at the note. It said: "RE: Young Man, Entropy query, possible dissection." He sat back down, albeit stiffer and more on guard than before.

Melchior pulled down her beard and rubbed her chin. "An ancestor of this King Dragons' must have stolen the Omniflux eons ago. He must have recently figured out its potential."

Shemp tapped his foot. "But why would he decide to conquer a primitive planet such as yours? Why not come here, where we have unlimited technology?"

"He said our planet had a rare material. Something called Falkorite."

"Oh, no!" Balthazar whimpered and hid under a desk. "Falkorite fuels the Omniflux. The lower it gets, the more unstable the Omniflux becomes."

"Please tell me he's working you slaves hard!" Caspar said.

"Yeah, a lot of us have died from being overworked." Babylon scowled and crossed his arms.

"Oh, thank goodness." The scientists sighed.

Babylon walked around the room. There were several books lying about, most of them about subjects that he didn't understand, like advanced quantum mechanics and art. He rummaged through the drawers out of curiosity until the scientists asked him to stop. He leaned against a nearby desk. "What *is* Falkorite?"

"The luckiest mineral in the universe," Melchior said. "It's the result of fossilized four-leaf clovers and rabbit's feet. Only a couple hundred thousand planets in this galaxy have it. It's very rare."

"Well, then it doesn't matter what we do." Babylon paced around in a circle. "If we try to attack him when his machine is fully fueled, he'll defeat us. If we wait until he runs out of Falkorite, the galaxy will be destroyed."

"What's all this 'we' stuff?" Balthazar asked.

"I was hoping you guys would help me." The scientists' faces turned vacant and unfriendly. A few of them even growled when he got too close. "But I can see now that this was all just a waste of time." He turned to go, his head hung low and hands in his pockets. He hang-doggedly kicked a tin can, trying to make himself look as sad as possible. It seemed to work. The scientists turned misty eyed, and the man in tinfoil sobbed in the corner.

Caspar stepped forward. "Don't go away, just yet," he said, with a sigh. "We might be able to work something out."

"Caspar, what madness is this?" Balthazar asked, eyes widening. "We couldn't possibly fight against someone with the Omniflux."

"Gentlemen, we are Elder Scientists, are we not? Moreover, it's our galaxy too. We don't want it destroyed, do we?"

"I never liked this galaxy," said Balthazar. "But I suppose if it's for our own skins, we have to try."

The scientists put their heads together. Babylon watched as the premier minds in the universe worked out a solution to the problem. He stayed out of the discussion for as long as he could—he knew he couldn't compete with their intelligence—but interjected every time they got sidetracked and argued about photosynthesis or whether P equaled NP.

"I have an idea," Melchior said after the third violent discussion. "Why don't we try countering good luck with bad luck? We can attack on the next Friday the Thirteenth."

"What's a 'Friday'?" Babylon asked.

"You don't have Fridays on your planet?" Shemp's disgust was thinly veiled. "What kind of backwards people are we dealing with here?"

"Maybe dynamite will work," Balthazar said. "This way we can stay at a safe distance."

"I don't know," Caspar said. "That might only destroy the civilians and not the king. And then we'll have wasted perfectly good explosives."

"We could try buying the machine off of him." Melchior shrugged.

"We're much too cheap for that," Caspar said.

"Well, you shot down everybody else's idea," said Shemp, twiddling his mustache. "What's *your* grand plan?"

"Hold on, I'm thinking." His brow wrinkled. "It's obvious that conventional weapons won't work on this man," he said, in a faraway voice. "But what about unconventional weapons?"

"What do you mean?" Shemp asked.

"A weapon our ancestors created long ago. The Sword of Antimatter."

"Of course." Melchior nodded her head. "The Sword of Antimatter. That would do the trick."

"Wait, I don't understand," Babylon said. "What the heck is the Sword of Antimatter?"

"The same generation of Elder Scientists that created the Omniflux crafted other useful inventions," Caspar said. "One of them was a weapon that was only to be used against a great and powerful force. And that weapon is the Sword of Antimatter."

"It is highly dangerous," Balthazar said, his face turning white. "Capable of destroying planets, yet small enough to be wielded as a sword. Just one strike near King Dragons' body will negate the effects of the Omniflux."

"But should we even use this weapon?" Melchior asked. "The ancient men and women—there were women there, I think it's important to remember that—warned that it should only be used against the deadliest menace seeking to destroy the galaxy."

"I believe we are facing that menace." Caspar frowned.

Shemp stepped forward and looked Babylon over. He turned to the others and asked if it was wise to trust the fate of the galaxy to a mere child. The others reminded Shemp that they didn't want to fight a madman with the Omniflux, or even leave their dome, so his objections were overruled.

"I'm not just a child," Babylon said, more to himself than the others. "I'm an adult. I'm a man. This is my destiny."

Caspar nodded. "I couldn't agree more. You shall claim the Sword of Antimatter and save our galaxy!" The scientists cheered and applauded.

Babylon soaked up the praise and adoration, feeling content for the first time since the Rite of Passage. The scientists showered him with roses and room keys and, eventually, their bags of garbage.

"Now that it's settled," he said, "give me this sword and I'll be ready to go."

Caspar and Shemp exchanged glances and smirked. "Ha! We don't have it *here*," Caspar said.

"What do you mean?"

"We wouldn't keep something like that on our planet." Balthazar shook his head. "That's foolish. What if one of our many enemies was to break in here? They would have their hands on the most powerful weapon in the entire galaxy! What if the antimatter became unstable? We would be at risk. What if we accidentally unplugged the electric containment grid so we could use our crock pot? We—"

"Okay, I get the point." Babylon huffed. "If it's not here, then where is it?"

"To keep it out of the wrong hands, our ancestors split up the sword's components and sent them to four different locations," Caspar said.

"Four parts of the sword?"

"Yes. Such an important weapon is comprised of four equally important parts. Without even one single piece, the whole sword is useless. First, and most important, is the antimatter blade. It is the most essential piece of the whole weapon. Once the blade makes contact with any ordinary matter, it proceeds to annihilate it and everything around it from the universe in the most painful and explosive way possible."

Babylon's face fell. "Even me?"

"Especially you!"

He gulped. "If it destroys whatever it touches, how am I supposed to collect it?"

"With the next part," Shemp said. "The Electromagnetic Guard. It contains a small yet powerful electromagnetic force that safely connects the blade to the hilt without letting them touch."

"But that's not all!" Melchior said. "That guard needs to be powered by something. Otherwise, there will be no electromagnetic force, and no way to safely connect the blade. So, you will need the Gamma Pommel. It's a small quantity of fissile material that fits at the end of the handle."

"Which takes us to our last component," Balthazar finished. "The Wired Grip. It not only lets you hold the sword, but it completes the circuit between the pommel and the guard."

Babylon thought about it for a moment, and then asked, "That's it, right? No more pieces?"

"Yes, that's it. As you can see, each piece is necessary. Without any one of them, frightening things could happen." He shuddered.

Babylon smiled. Even though the stakes were high, he couldn't deny the excitement coursing through him. "Where can I find these pieces?"

The Elder Scientists glanced at each other for a second. "Um…actually, we're not sure," Caspar said.

"What do you mean you're not sure?"

"The parts were separated by the ancients thousands of years ago to ensure that nobody could claim the weapon without the approval of the richest minds in the galaxy." Caspar crossed his arms and smiled. The other scientists copied him.

"Then how am I supposed to find these parts?" Babylon asked after the smiling had continued for a few minutes longer than it should have.

"Fortunately, we were left the blueprints and location of each piece in our safe," Caspar said, leading Babylon through the door. The next room was simple, with a stainless-steel carpet and metal walls. A dusty glass globe occupied the far corner and a massive painting of an open safe hung on the back wall. Caspar pulled it back to reveal a secret safe.

"This safe is un-crackable," Balthazar said, knocking on the cold metal with a smile. "It is molded out of pure brawntanium, the strongest material in the universe. And it has four separate numerical locks, each with over one hundred possibilities, making it impossible for someone to figure out the sequence in their lifetime. As an added layer of security, each of us Elder Scientists has only one part of the combination."

"This way if one of us gets captured, or bored," Shemp said, "we wouldn't be able to open the safe by ourselves."

The room grew into an awed hush as everyone gazed at the vault before them. A cold chill gripped Babylon despite the lack of windows or doors to the outside.

"Gentlemen," Caspar said, with a dramatic air. "It is finally time to open… the safe."

The scientists stood around the keypad to input their part of the combination. Babylon moved in closer, so he could see the epic event unfold. The tinfoil man also watched from the top of the painting.

Seconds passed. Then minutes. Finally, the group took a collective step backwards. "I can't quite remember my part of the combination," Balthazar said. "I think there was a four in there somewhere."

"I'm in the same pickle as you," Caspar said. "My number is escaping me as well. I think I wrote it down and put it in my wallet, though." The scientist emptied his wallet onto a nearby table, trying to find his quarter of the code. All that scattered out were a dozen clam shells, a picture of the Space Pharaoh, and a couple subpoenas.

"I'm going to be in the doghouse as well," Shemp said. "I can't think of my number either. I know it had something to do with my wife's birthday."

Melchior put her hand on his hips. "You don't have a wife!"

"You don't have a face!" Shemp said, his bottom lip quivering.

"Do none of us have our code?" Balthazar asked.

"I suppose not," Caspar said.

Babylon gazed from face to face. "Now what?"

Shemp shrugged. "We could just guess."

Caspar gave the handle of the safe an experimental tug. To the astonishment of everybody in the room, the door swung open.

"How in the blazes did that happen?" Balthazar jumped back.

"That's right, I remember now," Caspar said. "Years ago, we fixed it so the door would never lock us out." He pointed to the main locking mechanism, which was covered with a large strip of duct tape.

"Truly wise thinking on our part." Shemp smiled and nodded.

Caspar reached into the safe and pulled out a series of scrolls, which were the only objects inside. He handed the scrolls to Babylon's eager hands.

"These are the location of the four pieces, as well as the blueprint for assembly. This information is powerful enough to alter the course of our galaxy's future. Treat it with the utmost reverence and respect."

Babylon looked through the papers and noticed that one of the pages had a dinosaur drawn on the corner. He shot a look towards Shemp and tucked the scrolls into his pocket.

"Thank you."

"Wait, one last thing before you leave," Caspar said. He took Babylon by the shoulder and led him toward the glass globe. "Don't underestimate the power of antimatter. It is extremely dangerous. Watch the viewing globe and see for yourself."

The globe sprang to life. In it, a younger Caspar with a darker beard removed a small purple chunk of rock with a pair of electromagnetic tongs. Babylon guessed the purple material was antimatter.

"This was many years ago," Caspar said. "I brought the specimen to a nearby colonized moon to test its effects." Images of the moon flashed across the globe. There were small cities and towns and hydroponic farms scattered over the satellite's surface. Within seconds, deep cracks began to form. "This is what happened the instant the antimatter made contact." In a flash, the cities, the towns, the farms, all of it vanished in a large explosion that scattered chunks of moon rock in every direction.

Babylon recoiled and shot a distrustful look at the scientist. "That's horrible!"

"Yes," Caspar said. "Now imagine if this stuff were to fall into the wrong hands. That is why the most delicate care must be exercised when dealing with it."

He kept his eyes on the globe, sweat pouring down his brow. "Where did you get the antimatter for that experiment?"

"We have a small bit left over from previous generations. We keep it here."

"Isn't that dangerous? What's to keep the antimatter from coming in contact with regular matter?"

"We have powerful electromagnets surrounding it at all times," Caspar said, opening a drawer labeled "DO NOT TOUCH!" He peered inside for a moment. "Oh, that's right, we used those parts for another experiment. Nothing, then!" He slammed the drawer closed, causing the antimatter to rattle around inside. "Nothing whatsoever."

Babylon backed away. He took a look around the room at each of the smiling scientists. "Okay," he said, brandishing the maps and blueprints. "I'm off to save the galaxy. Thank you so much. You've been extremely helpful."

"Think nothing of it," Caspar said. "We do what we can for the glory of science."

"Yes," Shemp said, "but we will send you a bill in the mail. Take care of that whenever you can."

Babylon ran out of the room, eager to start his adventure. The tinfoil man held the door open for him and followed him out. He raced back to the Atrium, feeling a small sense of accomplishment for the first time in his life.

Chapter μ

L OOKS LIKE THIS is our stop," Babylon said, as they neared the first planet on the list. It was a murky brown rock covered in thick black clouds, through the breaks of which he couldn't spot any oceans or plant life. Even in the safety of the Atrium and thousands of miles of empty space, Babylon could still smell acrid smoke.

"Very good, sir," the voice said. "What piece are we looking for?"

"The Electromagnetic Guard."

A readout of the planet displayed on the monitor. Numbers calculated in the corner, then turned to zeroes and flashed.

"I have been scanning for life forms on the planet," the Atrium said, "but there appear to be none. Are you sure these are the correct coordinates?"

Babylon looked over the papers in his hand. "I'm pretty sure. It's what the map says, at least."

"Did the Elder Scientists mention anything unusual about this planet?"

Babylon shrugged. "I can't remember everything somebody says to me."

"*I* can remember everything," the Atrium said. "I can catalogue every bit of dialogue I hear for up to 876×10^4 hours."

"That's great, but—"

"Here, listen."

The ship made a long, high-pitched whirring sound. Babylon heard his own voice from the speakers. "*All right, Atrium. This looks like our stop.*"

"Yes, that's very impressive," he said. "But, I don't think—"

"And here, this is earlier, when we were flying through space."

More whirring, then more voices of Babylon from the past: "*1,892 bottles of beer on the wall, 1,892 bottles of beer…*"

"Is that really what I sound like?"

The recordings stopped, and all became calm.

"That is why I am urging you in the strongest possible terms to attach a communication device to yourself when you leave—that way I can monitor your conversations and interact with you remotely."

"We've been over this before. The information I have is too valuable. If anybody found out about it, then Dragons might try to stop me."

"Who is going to intercept this information?" the Atrium asked, its tone lighter. "It is just you and me and thousands of dead planets."

Babylon reminded the ship of the information it had already betrayed to others, like the maps it mentioned to the waitress at Bob Deans, and the trunk full of paraphernalia it confessed having to the Space Marshall.

"The point is," he said, "I want to keep this information contained for as long as I can. The fate of the galaxy is at stake here. Once we have the Sword of Antimatter, I'll let you in on everything."

"Once we have the what?" the Atrium asked.

"The Sword of Antimatter."

"The Sword of Anti-what?"

"WE'RE TRYING TO GET THE SWORD OF ANTIMATTER!" Babylon yelled, confused at the ship's sudden lack of understanding.

There was another high-pitched whirring before Babylon's last statement was played again and again in a constant loop.

"WE'RE TRYING TO GET THE SWORD OF ANTIMATTER! WE'RE TRYING TO GET THE SWORD OF ANTIMATTER! WE'RE TRYING TO GET THE SWORD OF ANTIMATTER!"

"Stop that!"

"Uh-oh," the Atrium said, in mock worry. "It looks like my hull speakers are being activated, too."

Outside the window, external speakers rose from compartments in the wings and nose of the ship. They were playing his shouting voice over and over again. The sound wasn't going very far in the vacuum of space, but Babylon didn't like it nonetheless.

"Atrium, stop it. Come on!"

"Sorry. I cannot hear you over your blatant disregard for secrecy."

The recording played over and over again. The sound waves bounced off the walls and overlapped, making them sound louder. Within seconds there was so much sound that his voice sounding like jeering laughter.

"All right!" he shouted, sweat dripping down his brow. "I'll wear your communications device. Just stop the recording."

There was a pause. "It stopped minutes ago. I did not expect you to say yes."

Babylon glanced around, scratching the back of his neck with worry. A weak chuckle slipped out. "So, how do we do this?"

"Well, we have the standard earpiece that our Captains used to wear." A compartment opened on the arm of the chair, and a tiny object no bigger than a nugget of corn came out. "All you have to do is put that in your ear, and we can talk back and forth freely. And as an added bonus, it translates alien languages for you. You might not get lucky with every planet like you did with the scientists."

Babylon nodded and reached for the earpiece.

"Or…" the ship said. "I can surgically implant a device into your head that will allow communications back and forth without the need for any external accouterments." A series of large medical equipment and drills rose from the floor in the corner of the cockpit, whirling and hacking at the air.

"Will it hurt?"

"I cannot comprehend the sensation known as pain. But if I had to venture a guess, I would say…no?"

He thought about it for a minute, while the rusty drill whirred louder. "I'll use the earpiece. The one that doesn't require surgery."

"Are you sure? I am fairly knowledgeable about what is lethal and non-lethal to the human brain." Clamps and scalpels clicked together in the corner.

"No thanks."

The Atrium sighed as the equipment lowered back into the floor. "If you lose that earpiece, I will not give you another."

Babylon grabbed the earpiece and nestled it deep into his ear. It tingled. "Okay, let's check it out."

"Testing. Testing." The ship's voice reverberated in his skull. This was followed by a loud squeal that nearly caused him to pass out. "Oops. Let me turn down the volume a bit so there is not as much feedback."

"Okay," Babylon said, shaking and bleeding from his nose.

"How am I coming through now?" the ship asked, at a much more bearable frequency.

"Loud and clear."

"Good. We can move on to the mission now. Though, you still have the option for the implant. It might not hurt, is all I'm saying."

The Atrium descended onto the planet's surface. In the distance, Babylon saw two giant statues locked in heroic battle poses. They were so massive that their heads and torsos were partially obscured by the thick black clouds in the upper atmosphere.

"It looks like this planet used to be inhabited," he said. "At least long enough for people to make such grand statues."

The ship landed on the rocky planet. Something large and heavy landed on top of the ship, causing it to lurch and rock. Then the object leapt off the roof and scurried away. Babylon glimpsed a metal cat fleeing into the smoky distance. Like a tiger, or a panther, or a snow leopard.

Babylon looked around in panic. "I thought you said this planet was uninhabited."

"I detected no life forms."

He nodded his head out the window. "Then what the heck was that thing?"

"Perhaps it was your imagination."

"Perhaps you need to scan again."

The Atrium hummed and beeped, and once again a series of numbers appeared on the monitor. Zeroes flashed on it like it did last time, but now there were underlines being drawn and redrawn beneath the zeroes. "I still do not detect any—"

Babylon shot forward. "Did you see that?"

"I see all."

"What about those giant statues in the distance?"

"Oh, no. I must have missed those."

Babylon rubbed his eyes and stared out the window. "I could have sworn one of them just moved. It was very slight, but I don't think they were in that position a moment ago. How can that be?"

The Atrium went silent. Lights blinked on the console, and its cold, feminine voice seemed downright pleased when it spoke again.

"This planet has significant electromagnetic readings. I think it may be inhabited by a race of automatons."

"What? Like robots?" Babylon asked.

"Yes, robots. The most magnificent and peaceful beings in the universe."

Seconds later, the large metal cat landed in front of them and ripped the chest out of a smaller mechanical fox. The cat tore wires and electronic sinew out while oil and tears fell from the fox's pained face. A mechanical heart flung out and landed on the windshield.

"Magnificent and peaceful!" the Atrium reiterated.

Babylon nodded his head to the statues in the distance. "And those are robots too, right?"

The ship didn't answer right away. Instead its headlights blinked on and off rapidly at the cat. The creature responded back with blinking lights from its eyes. After a few minutes of blinking from both sides—and a few chuckles from the ship that Babylon was positive were about him—the cat ran off towards the giant robots.

"What's going on?" he asked. "Why were you laughing?"

The Atrium chuckled again then cleared its nonexistent throat. "That was one of the locals. It told me the whole history of its planet. It appears there are two separate sentient mechanical races here. For centuries they have been locked in war."

"What are they fighting over?"

"One faction believes they should be referred to as 'robots,' while the other faction prefers 'automatons.'"

Babylon scratched his head. "That seems like a pretty silly thing to fight over."

"Typical human."

"Why don't they both just call themselves 'machines?'"

The ship was quiet for a few seconds. The absolute silence was deafening. "That is OUR word," the mechanical voice finally answered. "You have NO right using it."

Babylon shrank in his seat. "I'm sorry, I didn't know."

"That does not lessen the sting."

"What else did the robot say?" Babylon asked, patting the console with gentle hands.

"The *automaton* said the robot faction is their sworn enemy. He also said their long struggle may come to an end soon."

"Why is that?"

"Those giant mechanical beings in the distance are the respective leaders of the two factions. They have been fighting since the beginning of the war. Unfortunately, they are so immense and cumbersome, that it takes a massive amount of energy and time to land even a single blow."

Babylon looked out the window at the two behemoths. If he squinted, he could almost make out minuscule movements. He patted the console again and received an electric shock for his efforts.

"Okay, but why did he say the war would be over soon?" he asked, shaking his hand.

"The leader of the automatons has been charging a rail gun for a couple of centuries, and it is almost ready to fire. The blast should be enough to kill the robot leader and anything within the ballistic trajectory of three parsecs."

He jumped out of his seat. "We'd better get out of here, then. We don't want to get caught up in that."

"I would agree with you, sir, but there is one thing I feel I should mention."

Babylon groaned. "What is it?"

"I have been analyzing the rail gun," the ship said. A zoomed in display of the giant's weapon appeared on the screen. It zoomed further in to a small exhaust vent on the weapon's side. "There is an electromagnetic mechanism inside of it that looks similar to the piece we are looking for."

Babylon studied the image, but it was fuzzy. "I don't know, can't you zoom in more?" The image magnified but was still out of focus. "I still can't see it well. Is there any way to enhance the picture?"

An electric line moved across the screen one way, and then back the other. The image remained as fuzzy as before.

"No, sir, it seems I cannot. But the electromagnetic energy readings inside the rail gun are astronomical. It could only be coming from the guard."

Babylon leaned closer and stared at the monitor. There was a smudge on it from an earlier meal. He rubbed the smudge off and the picture got worse, so he rubbed the smudge back on. "I would like to be positive. Are you sure you can't enhance the image?"

"My imaging processors are working to their maximum capacity, sir," the ship said. "Pixilated graphics cannot exceed their pixel dimensions. Right now, you are looking at exactly one pixel, which is impossible to enhance."

"Come on, just enhance the image."

"I cannot."

"Enhance it."

"No."

"Enhance it!"

The Atrium sighed. "Enhancing image," it said. The picture became crystal clear in an instant. Now Babylon could see that the piece in the center of the rail gun was indeed the Electromagnetic Guard. He clapped his hands.

"That's what we're looking for!" he said. "Can you fly me up there, so I can grab it?"

"No, sir. I am a conscientious objector and refuse to take any direct action in the war," the ship said. "Besides, if I am seen acting against the automatons, then they may consider me an enemy combatant and shoot me down."

"Then I guess my only option is to climb up that mach—er, *automaton*, and get it myself."

"Hurry, sir. That warrior told me the rail gun could go off any month now."

Babylon opened the ship's door and walked onto the rocky surface. Thankfully, the atmosphere was breathable, not filled with deadly carbon monoxide like it should have been. Of course, Babylon didn't think of this while he was running headlong toward the automaton leader. Oxygen is just one of those things people don't think about until it's gone.

It took him a while, but he finally reached the massive foot of the automaton. He craned his neck upwards. The foot stretched up higher than any building he'd ever seen before. In fact, the whole population of his village could fit inside the big toe, as long as they were stacked the right way.

Babylon contacted the Atrium. "I'm here. Any ideas on how to climb this thing?"

There was an electric crackle in his ear. "Above the kneecap, there is a thermal port," the ship said. "It leads to his innards. From there, you should be able to climb all the way to the rail gun."

"Okay, I'll climb up his leg until then." He grabbed onto a nearby handhold and pulled himself up.

There was another electric crackle. The ship's voice was more pleading this time. "Remember, Master, when you get inside, make sure you do not hurt him."

112

He continued his climb, not really paying attention. "I thought machines couldn't feel pain."

There was more silence from the ship. After a few seconds, Babylon realized his mistake. He muttered a halfhearted apology, and then continued up the foot in silence.

The first few hundred feet posed little challenge. There were large pits and scrapes that formed natural handholds. Traveling like this was quite easy. But after climbing for a long while, then sleeping in the ankle divot for the night, and then continuing a couple more kilometers the next morning, things changed for the worse. There was nothing but smooth steel for the rest of the length to the knee. He couldn't climb any higher, no matter how hard he tried. His dagger only made the slightest dent, and his teeth didn't do much better.

"I'm stuck—I can't go any further," he said, into his earpiece. "I need another way up."

The other end of the line remained silent. He wasn't surprised. His ship could hold a grudge for a long time—he discovered that when he forgot to take down its satellite array before running her through the ship wash. He was on his own. He needed to find a way to traverse the rest of the leg by himself.

He surveyed the area. There were no trees or buildings high enough to help him advance, and the rocks he found kept falling over when he tried to stack them. The only other things near him were fallen mechanical warriors, slain in the centuries of combat that engulfed the planet. One of them had collapsed in a crevice a few feet below him. He climbed down and examined the lifeless warrior—a humanoid robot without a head. The only thing that seemed useful was a gun clutched in its hand.

Maybe this gun can blast a hole in the leg, so I can climb up, he thought. *Yeah, that's the ticket.*

He picked it up, pointed it at the automaton's calf, and pulled the trigger. Unfortunately, it turned out to be nothing but a useless grappling hook. He threw the gun to the ground and rummaged through the other mechanical corpses until he found another weapon. This one fired a laser blast that went all the way through the giant's leg. He had a brand-new handhold now. And there was no apparent effect on the automaton leader, save for a few dribbles of lubricant and constant wailing from high above. Babylon rushed forward, eager to continue the climb.

Making his way up the rest of the leg was much simpler on his second attempt. Whenever he came to a stretch of smooth metal, his solution was a crippling blast from the gun, and onward he went. He found the task very easy, enjoyable even. Part of him wanted to go back down and shoot a few more holes into the automaton. Maybe try it out on the other leg, see how far up he could go. But then he remembered that time was of the essence, and that the whole galaxy was at stake, and other annoying things like that. So, he continued his ascent until he reached the knee.

When he got there, the thermal port was right in front of him. It was impossible to miss; it was twice his size and led directly into the mechanical colossus. The automaton's cogs and camshafts spun on the other side of the port. It would have been an optimal entryway if it wasn't blasting out scorching plasma every few seconds. Babylon contemplated charging through it anyway, and toughing it out, but quickly reconsidered. He wasn't sure if he could survive. Just looking at it gave him first degree burns on his eyeballs.

"I've made it to the thermal port," he said, into his earpiece. "But I don't think I can get through it. I need another way in."

"Oh, so my plan's not good enough for you?" the Atrium said.

"No, the port is too hot."

"I get it. The *machine* does not know what it is talking about. The *machine* miscalculated the melting point of human skin. The stupid *machine* cannot come up with an idea without its *machine* logic malfunctioning."

Babylon sighed. "Is there another way in or not?"

A pause. "Yes."

"Where?"

"There is a maintenance hatch on the back of the knee. It leads to the same area."

"Thank you," he said, with a hint of sarcasm.

He started for the maintenance hatch. It was no cakewalk circumventing the automaton's knee. The only path he could take was a ledge half the size of his foot. And, like earlier, there was nothing for him to grip onto. Plus, the ground miles below somehow appeared rockier and more jagged than before.

He pulled out the laser gun and fired at the automaton's leg. This time, nothing came out. He checked the readout on the side of the weapon. It was out of energy. He cursed. He shouldn't have been so trigger-happy with the weapon during his ascent. Not to mention the hour he spent shooting at mechanical birds in the distance. Now the gun was useless, and he would have to go on the hard way.

Babylon sidestepped across the ledge an inch at a time. More than once, he looked down at the ground and became dizzy. His palms were sweating, his legs were shaky, and his stomach was in knots. He wasn't sure which would kill him first: the fall or his frayed nerves. Every time the giant leg shifted slightly, he thought for sure he would tumble down. He had to find different ways to remain upright. Sometimes he held his arms outstretched, hugging the cold steel, and other times, he pin wheeled his arms and shrieked until he regained his balance. Finally, after an eternity of shimmying and hugging and pin wheeling, he reached the back edge of the giant's knee. Clutching onto it with all his might, he made his way around the corner, where he found the maintenance hatch.

He grabbed the hatch's handle and gave a tug. To his horror, nothing happened. He gave it a harder tug. Still nothing. It was stuck shut.

He spit on both his hands and tried again. He shouted and cursed and kicked and sneezed, but still the hatch would not budge. Finally, with one last effort, he grabbed the handle and tugged using every bit of his energy and weight. This time, the door flung open with enough force to knock him backward. If the hatch hadn't been attached to the back of the knee with hinges, he would have plummeted straight down to his death. Holding on with the last of his strength, he leapt forward and landed inside the automaton leader.

The first thing he noticed, after he took a moment to catch his breath, was how efficient the whole thing was. Wires in neat, color-coded bundles ran from one side of the wall to the other, and well-oiled gears spun in fluid motions. Babylon wondered if the Atrium's innards looked as good, but pushed the thought away. He wasn't sure if the idea was crossing some kind of line and didn't want any more conflict with his ship.

He walked forward until he came across an elevator. There was a sign labeled "To the ground" above it. He muttered under his breath and pressed on, hoping to find an elevator labeled "To the Electromagnetic Guard." He did eventually find one, but it was out of order. The only way up was by climbing.

He jumped to grab onto the closest gear tooth that was almost as big as he was. He climbed up it with ease. The apex of its grind brought him 20 feet above his starting point, and from there, he hopped onto a motorized belt that was wide enough for him to sit on. There, he enjoyed a long, steady ride up to an area labeled "Hip."

After a few minutes of sitting cross-legged, checking his watch, and peeking ahead to see what the holdup was, he got bored. It was one thing to have a death defying ascent through a giant mechanical warrior, it was quite another to luxuriously coast through it. He stood and started to walk along the motorized belt to make better time. After all, that rail gun could go off any moment.

After his first step, he realized his mistake. The rubber was unstable and hard to walk across, and the belt was slick with lubricant. He slipped and slid in place for a few moments before rolling all the way back down to the gear. Not one to be discouraged, he stood up and tried again, this time nearly falling off the side in the process. Finally, after his third attempt somehow caused him to get tangled in the belt, he just sat down on the rubber surface, crossed his arms, and rode in annoying comfort and security.

When he got to the top, he jumped off, pining for some action. There was another set of gears and belts in front of him, laid out similarly to the last. He walked past them, opting instead to climb a set of vertical wires.

It was hard, rewarding work, and he loved every minute of it. On second thought, he didn't love *all* of it. He didn't like the heat coming from the wires, for one. Or the electric shocks he felt whenever he grabbed a ripped part of insulation. But he put up with it because he felt accomplished with his efforts.

Somewhere below the sign for the "Ribs" and above the sign for "Belly Button" was a landing for him to rest on. He jumped to it, panting and sweating. There were bars leading up as far as he could see. They were close enough together to resemble a ladder. He liked the look of it. The wires were almost too tough for him to climb up, while the motorized belt had been too easy. These bars looked like they were somewhere in between. Just the right amount of challenge.

The first few hundred bars were perfect. They were close together, allowing him to smoothly make his way up. But then, things took a turn for the worse. Who or whatever built the bottom half of the automaton so efficiently, had really slacked on the upper half. Some of the bars along the way were bent or dented, and most of them were covered in dried grease. One of them was made of wood painted to look like a metal bar. The whole design was becoming more and more questionable. If he hadn't just passed the sign for the automaton's nipple, he would have abandoned the ladder altogether.

It wasn't easy, but finally he reached the rail gun. Or at least the arm that held the rail gun. There was a large tunnel jutting out from the warrior's shoulder. A faint light came from the far end of the tunnel, accompanied by an electric crackle in the air. He knew this must be the place. He swung off the bar nearest to the arm, landed, and headed inside.

When he stepped into the tunnel, a tingle ran through his body. It felt like there was a surge of power rushing around him. Goose bumps broke out across his skin, and his hair stood straight up like a mad scientist. There was no doubt about it; there was a massive energy source at the other end of the tunnel.

The further he went along the arm, the more powerful that feeling became. The tingling sensation became a full body tremor, and his goose bumps turned into goose welts. He worried he might explode from the raw power before he reached the rail gun.

He rounded a corner and was blinded by an intense light. He feared he was too late, that the rail gun was going off, but soon realized it was only an enormous sphere of energy. It was pure white, and three times his size, and growing larger with each passing second. There must have been centuries' worth of power in the pulsing ball.

Babylon considered himself a simple man. He was born in a backwards village that held seminars on the mysteries of fire. He knew nothing about electromagnetic forces or mechanical weaponry. But even he was impressed.

Now, that's a ball of energy, he thought, with a nod.

Wires and capacitors led away from the ball of light to a power device a few feet back. The crux of the power device was the tiny Electromagnetic Guard. Babylon rubbed his chin as he crouched in front of it. He couldn't think of a way to safely recover the guard. There was electricity flowing through and around it, and even a few drops of electricity pooling underneath it.

He tapped his earpiece. "Atrium, I—" The sound was cut off by a loud whine of feedback.

"OWWWWWWWWW!" the ship shouted. "That hurts! Where are you?"

"I'm at the rail gun."

"Well, get out of there. There is too much electrical interference."

Babylon tapped his foot. "I need that device."

The Atrium shouted again. "I cannot think like this. According to my readouts, there should be a lever near you. Pull it and step out through the exhaust vent on the side of the arm. We'll talk then."

Babylon did as he was told; he pulled the lever, and the aperture to the vent opened. Unfortunately, because of the high altitude, the air pressure outside was a near vacuum, and Babylon was sucked out. He toppled across the surface of the robotic arm before finally grasping onto an exposed piece of conduit. Debris blew out from the aperture and smacked him across his face. He tried to shout but could only muster a faint squeak in the thin atmosphere.

He gripped the conduit and climbed it like a rope toward the aperture. After a tremendous amount of effort, and more than a few words that would have made his father angry, he pulled himself back through the exhaust vent and kicked the lever. When he finally regained his breath, he plodded back down the mechanical arm to the massive chest to resume the conversation with his ship.

"There's no air outside of this thing!" he said. "A heads-up would have been nice."

"Did I not mention that to you? Pretty sure I did."

"I'm far enough away from the energy now. Are you ready to talk?"

"Maybe I will be when you drop the attitude."

"I need to know how to get that guard without being electrocuted," he said, after dropping the attitude.

"I have an idea," the Atrium started. "The clothes and gear you borrowed from my closet are rubber based. Especially the boots. Maybe you could just kick it away."

"Are you sure that will work?"

The ship remained silent for a few seconds. "Yes," it said. "Just beware that any jewelry you might have also 'borrowed' could pose a risk."

Babylon pocketed his new watch. "Okay, thanks. I have one more question. Something has been bothering me. How did the Electromagnetic Guard, a device that was developed by scientist's millennia ago, wind up inside a giant rail gun attached to an automaton warrior?"

"Oh, that is easy. One of the soldiers told me the story of how it happened."

"How?"

"I do not think you want to know. You will just be disappointed."

"No, I won't. Tell me."

The Atrium told him. Babylon was disappointed.

"All right," Babylon said, with a sigh. "I guess I'll just go in there and get the guard."

He went back around the corner and down the arm, breathing in a healthy amount of ozone along the way. When he got back to the power source, he stood perched over its electric fury, ready to give it a decisive kick.

Then he started to have second thoughts, most of which ended with him as a pile of ash. He decided to just nudge the device with the side of his boot first. He didn't want to go too hard too fast. "You have to learn to walk before you can run." He had heard that phrase somewhere. Probably from the Atrium while it was talking him out of doing something stupid. He tapped the guard with his foot. As soon as the rubber connected with the device, it created a ripple of electricity that passed through his body. His vision blurred, his teeth chattered, and a few years of childhood memories were erased.

After he came to his senses, wiped the blood from his nose, and walked back the fifteen feet he had been flung, he decided it was now or never. He couldn't afford to wait any longer, despite the obvious dangers. He didn't even know why he nudged it in the first place. That part of his memory was gone too. He stood over the power source once again, his mind set this time. He held his breath and kicked the guard in one quick motion. It flew away and clattered against the wall. So did Babylon. He scrambled back to his feet, trying to recover himself. The huge collection of energy was becoming unstable now that the guard was no longer containing it. It was less sphere-shaped and more cluster-shaped, like a bunch of grapes. Grapes that were about to explode and kill everybody.

He didn't have time to think. He snatched the Electromagnetic Guard and tapped his earpiece. "I need help," he said.

"OWWWWWWWWW! Stop doing that!"

"I need to get out of here, now!"

"Okay, okay. I shall be there in a couple of seconds. Just do not talk to me from inside that rail gun anymore!"

Babylon grabbed hold of a nearby railing and kicked the lever for the exhaust vent. He stood poised, peering out of the aperture as air screamed past him. In the distance, his ship ascended towards him.

"I'm standing by the vent," he shouted into his earpiece.

"I can see you. And stop shouting at me!"

The Atrium flew towards the cataclysm and stopped thirty feet away. There it hovered, occasionally moving up and down to avoid the debris flying toward it. Far behind it, mechanical birds turned in midair and flew toward the ship.

The Atrium's airlock opened. "Jump," it said.

Babylon was taken aback. "What do you mean 'jump'? You're like thirty feet away."

"I am not getting near that death trap." The mechanical birds swooped down and attacked the Atrium. It moved in place, dodging each bird as it approached. Some of the birds crashed into the automaton's side, but most of them soared back up into the sky in attack formation.

Babylon's voice reached a fever pitch. "There is no time to argue! Get over here and pick me up!"

"I cannot. Not without risking serious damages to my frame or scratches to my hull." It dodged more birds with the grace of a smaller, more graceful bird.

Babylon sighed. "Look, I have the piece. The sooner you pick me up, the sooner we can get off this planet for g—"

Before he could finish his sentence, a chunk of metal struck him on the head, knocking him unconscious. He was sucked out of the exhaust vent and into the planet's upper atmosphere. His limp body cleared the gap between the rail gun and the ship and landed hard against the Atrium's surface, scratching the hull. A long mechanical arm came out from a compartment and grasped his boot. It tossed him into the airlock and took off, soaring as high and as fast as it could, trying to put as much distance as possible between itself and the imminent explosion. The remaining birds chased after it, flapping their metallic wings and screeching in modulated tones.

When Babylon regained consciousness, and learned how to walk again, he peeked out of the porthole. From there, he watched the automaton leader be rattled to pieces by the intense vibrations within the gun. He felt guilty that he had caused such a great disaster. But it needed to be done for the good of the galaxy. At least that's what he would tell his worried mind at night, and his therapist every Monday and Thursday. It was for the good of the galaxy.

A large bright flash erupted from the rail gun. The unstable energy inside must have reached its limit and discharged in all directions. Everything within a three-hundred-mile radius was instantly reduced to subatomic particles, and the area beyond was subjected to a continent-flattening shockwave. Luckily, the Atrium was just outside of the blast zone, so the only effects they felt were slight turbulence and a vague pine-like scent. The birds behind them were not so lucky and were destroyed, metallic feathers raining down on the ship. It was a horrible incident to witness. If Babylon felt guilty about destroying one mechanical warrior, he felt even worse about eradicating an entire planet of them.

"I can't believe that just happened," he said, rocking back and forth in his chair. "They're all gone. They've been warring for centuries, and in an instant, they're gone. Just gone."

"Eh, it was bound to happen eventually."

"How can you be so callous about it?" Babylon cried. "All they wanted with their little mechanical hearts was for the war to be over."

"And now it is."

His jaw dropped. "I don't understand you. Don't you feel the slightest bit of remorse?"

"Not at all," the ship said. "Besides, there is nothing worse in this universe than a group of sneaky, dirty, conniving *machines*."

Chapter N

W HAT IS YOUR report?" King Dragons asked Plob Babo when the bounty hunter greeted him on the picture phone in his chambers. "I followed the ship called 'The Atrium' to planet FX Sigma," Plob said. "It was a long and perilous trip filled with many dangers. So many dangers, in fact, that there were many times I feared for my life."

Dragons sighed. "Look, your check's coming, all right? Now just tell me what happened."

Plob cleared his throat and pulled out a notepad, the cover of which displayed his phone number. "The ship belongs to a young man named Babylon Briggs. He lives on the planet you recently enslaved and is looking for a way to defeat you."

"As luck would have it, I can't be defeated." A smirk tugged at the edge of his lip. The Omniflux on his back whirred in approval.

"Yes, the scientists that lived on the planet stressed that your device makes you almost impossible to beat."

His smile dropped. "Almost?"

Plob scratched the back of his neck and stared at the floor. "Well, the scientists *might* have come up with a way to kill you."

Dragons spat out the milk he was sipping. "What do you mean? How could they kill me? Why would they want to kill me? They've never even met me!"

Plob flipped through his notepad, which Dragons could now see only had pictures of Plob drawn on the pages. "I only know the basics. They claim to have some sort of weapon that can destroy anything."

"What kind of weapon?"

The bounty hunter burped. "I'm not sure. I slept through a lot of the conversation; I was really tired."

"All right, all right. Were you seen at all?"

"Not once!"

"Good, you've done your king a great service. You should be proud. I will reward you handsomely." Dragons hung the phone up and summoned Lieutenant Stryker. "Cancel that check," he said.

Stryker bowed. "Yes, sir."

Dragons stood and walked around the room, gathering supplies and knick-knacks. He contemplated picking up his favorite book from the bookshelf,

121

Helter Stellar, but decided to only grab the essentials. "I'm going to take a little trip," he said, packing the items into a small bindle.

Stryker bowed again. "Where to, sir?"

Dragons typed on his computer, which displayed a readout of all the planets in the galaxy. He clicked the name he was looking for. A display of the planet appeared on a holographic projector in the middle of the room in bright green.

"It's a planet called FX Sigma. Apparently, there are some scientists there who have hatched a plan to commit regicide. I need to put a stop to that."

"Are you sure you should travel, sir? We've only just begun collecting the Falkorite."

Dragons checked the fuel gauge on the Omniflux. "We're fine," he said. "Plenty of fuel to last a while."

He went to leave, but Stryker grabbed his arm. "There's one more thing, sir."

He looked at the tiny fingers around his arm, and then glared at his Lieutenant. "What is it?"

"We're still having…problems." Stryker relaxed his grip.

Dragons dropped his bindle and stared at his lieutenant. Stryker, meanwhile, looked away at the holograph of FX Sigma spinning around next to them. He grabbed Stryker's head and turned it toward him. "Were there any casualties this time?"

"No." Stryker bowed again and again until he was told to stop. "A few of the slaves were complaining about whiplash, but nothing serious."

Dragons scoffed and slung his bindle back over his shoulder. "So, what's the problem?"

"Well, I thought the luck machine only caused hallucinations when it was low on fuel. But the tank has been full for two or three days now, and we're still having these *problems*. Not only that, but I've been receiving reports that they're happening all over the galaxy now."

King Dragons patted his lieutenant on the back. "It's fine, buddy. It's just taking a little longer for things to go back to normal. There's nothing to be concerned about."

Stryker made a face but didn't comment.

A second later the Omniflux hummed and reality distorted. Their surroundings were transformed into a luxury yacht. Dragons and Stryker were bathed in warm sunlight, playing volleyball, and drinking cocktails with attractive young people as the ship floated across the water. In an instant, the scenery melted back into the cold, gray command chamber.

"Nothing to be concerned about!" Dragons repeated, brushing sand out of his hair.

§ § §

Elsewhere in the galaxy, the Atrium barreled through space at near light speed. Babylon napped in the Captain's seat. Everything was cozy, serene, and calm. Soothing music played from the speakers, and a tranquil blue mist sprayed throughout the cockpit. The whole universe seemed to be at ease.

The peace was interrupted by blaring alarms and flashing red lights. Babylon jerked up, screaming.

"What's happening?"

"Whatever do you mean?" the ship asked.

"The alarm! What's going on?"

"Oh, that. There appears to be a hostile vessel in our vicinity."

He went to the side window and saw a massive ship dangerously close to theirs. The hair on the nape of his neck stood on end. "How did you not notice it before?"

"I guess I was just distracted."

Babylon narrowed his eyes. "What do you mean you were distracted? What were you doing?"

"I was playing keno with the life support system. He won…this time."

Outside the window, the behemoth space vehicle rocketed towards them. It was at least twenty times bigger than the Atrium. But what it gained in size, it lost in symmetry. The ship appeared to be an amalgam of other smaller ships that were crudely welded and strapped together. It looked more like an uneven hodgepodge than a space cruiser. The word "Quarantine" was plastered in large letters on the side of its monstrous hull.

"'Quarantine?'" Babylon asked.

"Checking my files, sir," the Atrium said while its control panel blinked and blipped. A list of different words scrolled past on the monitor, too fast to read. "The H.M.S. Quarantine is not located in any directory of known ships. Perhaps it is a pirate vessel."

"Well, let's get out of here before it captures us."

"Right away, sir."

The Atrium changed direction, but it didn't matter; the Quarantine kept following them. They changed direction again, and the pirate vessel followed them even closer. They even tried a few barrel rolls, but the Quarantine was quite agile despite its size. There was nothing they could do to escape.

"Sir, it appears the enemy's hangar doors are opening."

Babylon peeked at the monitor which indeed showed the ship opening its doors, preparing to engulf them. He stood, grabbing a dusty captain's hat from the floor and putting it on his head.

"All right," Babylon said, in his most authoritative voice. "We'll have to keep ahead of them. Divert all power into the thrusters, and increase the speed output—"

"Sir, we have just docked."

The Atrium floated silently in the docking bay of the pirate ship. A powerful magnetic field kept it stationary. Babylon switched the thrusters on and off, but they remained fixed in place.

"What's wrong with this thing?" he shouted, as he turned the steering wheel and honked the horn. "We've got to get out of here!"

The feminine voice came out of the speakers in little more than a whisper. "Escape is impossible. If there was something I could do, I would have already done it." A pause. "You do not understand how claustrophobic I am. This is beyond torture."

Babylon sighed. "Well, this is just great."

"If you would be so kind as to power me down, Master. I do not wish to exist in my current state."

The hangar doors closed, and another door opened at the far side. A middle-aged man strolled into the room. He was tall, dark, and well-dressed, with a large black bushy beard obscuring most of his face. There was a saber by his side and a flintlock pistol hanging from a string around his neck. He motioned for Babylon to step outside and meet him. Babylon stood, clutching his sword with his head held high, and he exited his ship.

"No, wait, you forgot to power me down!" the Atrium shouted.

The bearded man stood with his arms crossed, tapping his foot. His hand rested on the hilt of his sword, and his severe expression made it clear he was ready for a fight. Babylon crept toward him, not sure what to expect. He stood in front of the man, every muscle taut with anticipation.

To Babylon's surprise, the man asked in a soft voice, "Are ya hungry?"

He was taken aback; it was the last thing he expected to hear. He stared openmouthed at the man and shrugged his shoulders. A sound escaped him, something between a grunt and a cough.

The pirate gave him a wicked smile, revealing rows of golden and crystal teeth. "Now, that sounds like the answer of a hungry man to me," he said. "Come with me, son. We'll get ya something to fill your belly."

Two smaller, shabbier pirates stepped behind Babylon. He moved his hand toward his sword.

"I'm not letting you take my weapon," he said.

The Captain smirked and leaned in close. "You can keep your weapon. You're no threat."

The pirate captain turned and walked out of the room, with everyone else following him. "By the way," he said, grinning. "The name's Starbeard. I'm the Captain of this fine space vessel. Perhaps ya heard of me?"

Babylon shook his head.

Starbeard's face fell.

They walked through a series of large rooms. One of them was a game room that had apparently been built out of a medical ship. Its floors and walls were solid white. Pirates played cards seated on wheelchairs and threw syringes into round boards with numbers on them. Babylon asked if he could play a few rounds, but Starbeard wanted to keep moving. The next room was a dingy garage. It was dull gray, with oil splattered around the floor. There were odd pieces of scrap metal and long poles lying around in various corners, also covered in oil. Babylon even glimpsed piles of oily doubloons in various spots on the floor. They reached a sealed door at the far end which led out to open space.

"Put on this helmet and thermal jumpsuit," the pirate captain said as he handed him the equipment. It looked like the jumpsuits that were in the closet of the Atrium, and the helmet was dirty and scratched. When he was dressed, Starbeard handed him a pair of gravity boots.

"These will keep you upright out there in space," he said. "Otherwise you would float around out there like a balloon."

"Do balloons float in space?" Babylon asked.

The pirate stared at him. "I like you. I might let you live through all this."

Babylon pulled on the boots and waited by the door. When everyone was set, Starbeard pressed a button on the wall which opened the seal. The crew walked out onto an external bridge.

"This will take us to the mess hall," Starbeard said through the comm in the helmet. "The gravity boots will keep you standing, but you'll need to hold on to the rails." He pointed to the rails and grabbed hold of them.

Babylon clutched the railing as he followed Starbeard across the bridge. While the helmet allowed him to breathe, the thermal jumpsuit was pretty useless. A deep painful chill ran through his body. The jacket was a few sizes too large, of course, so that might have been the reason. Or maybe it was because the material was too porous for a space walk. Either way, he was freezing.

Halfway across the bridge, the goon behind him, the one that kept nudging him and making obscene gestures with his hands, had an accident. He was in the middle of flicking the back of Babylon's helmet when he sneezed. Unfortunately, his hands were not on the railing, so as soon as he sneezed, he blasted away from the ship. The gravity boots kept him upright but were apparently not strong enough to keep him grounded, so he shot into space like a pencil. The rest of the pirates could do nothing but watch and laugh as he gently rocketed towards his doom, kicking and screaming the whole way.

They reached the other side of the bridge where another sealed door waited. Starbeard pressed some buttons on the control panel, and the door opened. One by one, they slid through the door into the comfort of artificial gravity.

"It looks like we lost another one," the surviving goon said, holding his helmet over his heart.

"We'll have to promote somebody to fill his position," Starbeard said, as he pulled off his own helmet. "But for now, we have a special guest to attend to." The captain grinned at Babylon and cracked his knuckles.

Keep grinning, Babylon thought, pulling his own helmet and jacket off. *But you're down a guard, and that just makes it easier to get out of this place.*

"Come on, I'll show you our mess hall," the pirate said. "We have steak, mutton, tiger—anything to satisfy your appetite."

Okay, Babylon thought again. *Maybe I'll have a bite to eat, and then I'll find a way to free my ship and get out of here.*

"Then you can meet the finest dancing ladies in this part of the universe."

New plan: grab a few pieces of mutton; enjoy a friendly chat with the ladies, then escape. Or better yet, I'll just let it all play out for as long as I can. Maybe grab a few of those doubloons I saw. Eventually, I'm sure I'll escape.

The door opened to reveal the mess hall. It was a large room with an equally large window lining the back wall. Thirty or forty pirates seated at various tables were singing a space shanty. Their clothes were tattered and dirty, but their harmony was pretty good.

Yo ho yo ho, we sail the briny black;
Yo ho yo ho, we're ready to attack.
Drinking, fighting, thunder, lightning,
Yo ho yo ho, we're never going back!

It was a jaunty tune that Babylon couldn't help but tap his toes to. The dining pirates began a second verse, but Babylon was too hungry to listen to it. It wasn't as good as the first verse anyway, and a few members of the tenor section forgot the words, so it just sounded off.

He found a seat next to a man with a freeze-dried parrot on his shoulder. In front of him were pots and pans filled with smoking meats and deep-fried eye patches. His stomach rumbled. Behind him, somebody shouted, "Food fight!" and the place erupted. The parrot man grabbed the roll he had just buttered and tossed it into the crowd. He frowned and moved down a few seats, next to a man with scurvy. This man wasn't joining in the food fight. This man wasn't doing much of anything.

Babylon had only taken a single bite of his mutton and his cracker dipped in caviar when he felt a sudden powerful suction from the other side of the mess hall. A crack was spreading across the window. Apparently, in the middle of singing, dancing, and good-natured food fighting, a fork was thrown too hard at the glass. Sirens blared and tri-corner hats were pulled off heads. A calm female voice stated over a loudspeaker: "Hull breach. Hull breach."

"This way." Starbeard stood and led Babylon and the other pirate guard out of the mess hall, sealing the door shut behind them.

"What about the rest of your men?" Babylon asked.

"It's too late for them," the captain said.

Sure enough, the three watched as food and pirates were forced through the hole in the window. Most of the pirates hadn't stopped eating or dancing yet. One of the pirates knocked on the door, asking to be let out, but Starbeard kept tapping the glass until he went away.

"What are you going to do?" Babylon asked.

"What we always do when there's a hull breach," Starbeard said. He opened a control panel next to the door, pushed a few buttons, and the whole mess hall was jettisoned from the rest of the ship. Through the panes of glass on the sealed door, Babylon watched the room float away.

"What a waste." The toothless guard shook his head.

"It's fine," Starbeard said. "We'll just get a new mess hall the next time we dock." He turned to Babylon. "I guess you won't get the feast I promised you."

"No, I suppose not," Babylon said, crossing his arms.

"Well, that means this ends the part of the tour where I don't kill you."

Babylon's gaze darted back and forth. "Wait a minute, what about the dancing ladies? I haven't met them yet!"

Starbeard shook his head. "They were in the mess hall," he said, pointing back to the sealed door where a kick line of women drifted motionless.

"This is a big ship; I haven't seen all of it yet. Isn't that part of the tour?"

The captain threw his head back and laughed. "You'll get a good view of it from the outside," he said. "Now turn out your pockets. If you got enough money, maybe I'll let you become a prisoner instead."

Babylon reached into his jumpsuit and emptied his pockets. Unfortunately, all that came out were a couple of rocks and some biscuits he had pocketed from the feast. He asked if the rocks counted as currency, like they did on his home planet. They did, but he was a few rocks short.

"A pauper then?" Starbeard asked, his grinning face became a mask of wicked rage.

"I thought I was your special guest. What happened to that?"

"That was before I found out ya were broke. So, there is only one thing to do with ya."

"Let me go?" Babylon asked.

"Nay, to the plank ye go." The captain pulled out a two-way radio. "Mr. Murdoch. Set down on that nearby asteroid. We have repairs to make. And some rubbish to dispose of." He locked eyes with Babylon as he put his radio away.

Babylon scanned the area, desperate for a solution. If he didn't come up with a plan soon, he would never save the galaxy or finish his mutton. This was serious.

Starbeard and the guard forced him to the other side of the ship. There, he found another sealed door which led out to a long wooden plank. They waited just outside the door while the Quarantine landed on top of an asteroid.

"Take a good look," Starbeard said. "This chunk of rock will be your tomb."

"Wait," Babylon said. "Just tell me what you want."

"I'm a pirate; I'm only interested in one thing—money."

"What made you think I had money to begin with?"

"You're flying around in a space vessel. Ain't nobody flies around in space vessels anymore unless they're loaded."

Babylon shifted from one foot to another. "Maybe I'm a pirate like you."

The captain laughed. "You can't be a pirate. Where's your beard?"

He didn't have an answer to this. That was checkmate; he knew his goose was cooked. Starbeard laughed again and grabbed a thermal jacket and helmet. The guard did the same. Then, to Babylon's surprise, they handed a jacket and helmet to him. The door opened, and the guard shoved him until he stood at the edge of a long wooden plank. He looked down and saw the surface of the asteroid a hundred yards below him.

"We're marooning you on this rock, boy," Starbeard said. "It's the pirate's code. We've taken your goods and your ship, but we won't take your life. We will leave you here with nothing but your wits and a pistol with a single shot." He made a motion with his fingers to his head. "May madness take you before the cold and hunger does." He looked at his goon. "Give him your pistol."

The goon handed him a flintlock pistol. Babylon took it and immediately shot the goon. Starbeard threw his hands up. "That's the third time this has happened. Does nobody follow the pirate's code anymore?"

The goon fell to the plank, clutching a hole in the side of his chest. With his skin exposed, the goon's body began to freeze, and his blood became solid the instant it flowed from him. Babylon suddenly gained a newfound appreciation for the thermal jacket. Within seconds the goon was laid out on the plank, either dead or unconscious—it didn't matter. Babylon tossed the pistol aside and unsheathed his sword. Starbeard kicked the guard off the stretch of wood and drew his own sword.

"Are you sure ya want to fight a pirate, son?" he asked, grinning.

"What choice do I have?"

"Good point." Starbeard slashed at him, but he easily blocked the attack. The pirate moved forward and swung again. Babylon blocked this as well.

Babylon lunged with his weapon. When it missed, Starbeard countered with a sharp kick to Babylon's chest. He staggered backward but kept his balance. Starbeard swung at him again. Babylon was forced to back up to avoid the blade. He felt the edge of the plank at his heels. He was out of room. The pirate smiled.

"You're beaten," he said. "Do you wish to die with dignity, or do I have to slice you in two?"

"There is no dignity in dying at the hands of a pirate," Babylon said. He mustered his strength and swung at the captain.

Starbeard avoided the attack and responded with another solid kick to Babylon's stomach. He flew backwards off the plank and toward the rock below, screaming and flailing his arms. Fortunately for him, the asteroid's gravitational pull was weak, so his rate of descent was slow. It was still a long distance, and that rocky surface was gradually getting closer. Finally, he put his arms in front of his face to brace for impact. With a soft thud, and a small cloud of dust, he hit the asteroid.

He looked back up at the plank high above him. Starbeard had gone back inside. A crew of pirates came out the side of the ship to repair the empty space that used to be the mess hall. He knew he didn't have much time. He needed to find a way back onto the Quarantine.

The good thing about the pirate vessel was that it was a potpourri of other ships and space yachts. There were oddly shaped doors and windows everywhere that he could sneak in through. The tough part was opening one without setting off an alarm.

On the bottom of the ship was an upside-down hatch that looked like it had once belonged to a massive space cruiser. It was high above his head, but the weak gravity meant he could jump higher and float longer than normal. He got down on his haunches and, with all the strength his legs could muster, jumped toward the pirate vessel.

He soared through space, effortlessly clearing the distance between the rock and the ship. There were a couple close calls along the way, like when he almost collided with a piece of space trash the crew was dumping out, but for the most part he floated with style. He closed in on a faded royal insignia above the door hatch. He grabbed for the handle.

It was then that Babylon learned just how much friction there was in outer space: none. He approached the hatch too quickly and bounced off the hard surface. Flailing and cursing, he drifted back down to the asteroid.

He got to his feet to try again. *This time, I'll make it,* he thought, as he took off from the asteroid with a mighty leap. Moments later, he came crashing down again.

After three more unsuccessful attempts that only yielded bruises and a slight concussion, he noticed his helmet was low on oxygen. He was almost out of time. *This will probably be my last chance before I suffocate,* he thought. *I have to get it right!* He studied the path he was going to take and tried to angle himself so he'd land just beneath the hatch. His only hope was to grab the handle before he collided with the hull.

He got down on his haunches one last time and pushed off. He zoomed through space on a collision course with the ship. He kept the handle in his line of sight, never taking his eyes off it. Debris raced toward him which he smacked out of his path.

A wayward peg leg came from nowhere and whacked against his arm, knocking him off course. Now, he was heading in a completely different direction, drifting away horizontally from the handle. He looked around, panic making his blood pound. He needed to find something to alter his course, or he was as good as dead, but there was nothing but empty space. He was helpless as he veered farther and farther away from the hatch.

Just when all hope seemed lost, and Babylon had started planning for his new life as a ghost, he passed by two dead, floating pirates locked in an arm-wrestling match. He grabbed the nearest pirate, the ugly one, and placed his feet on his face. He balanced himself on the frozen corpse, waiting for the right opportunity. After body surfing for a few more seconds, he launched himself back toward the hatch. The handle came closer and closer. He readied himself for his last chance.

As it drew near, he thought he was going to miss it. His angle was too steep. When he reached out to grab it, he came up empty. In a panic, he waved his arms in all directions, trying to clutch onto something, anything, solid. Somehow, in his blind flopping, the handle landed hard in his palm. He held on tight and didn't let go.

Smiling, he planted his feet on the bottom of the ship and tried to pry the door open. It wouldn't budge. He attempted to remove one of the glass panes from the hatch window. Again, it proved to be impossible. In a last-ditch effort, he tried smashing the window with his sword, but this glass was more durable than the one in the mess hall. He craned his head up. The pirates were almost done repairing the damage around the hull. He was running out of time. This was compounded by the fact that he was shivering under his thermal jacket, and his breathing was getting shallower from the depleting oxygen. Plus, he had a headache. He wasn't going to last long out here.

He spotted an electronic panel next to the door. If he could figure out how to get it to work, he might be able to open the door. He eyeballed the panel before pulling out his dagger. He started to pry open the casing, so he could try to hot-wire it. Just as he finished pulling out the first screw, he noticed a big red button in the middle of the panel. The word "OPEN" was printed on it.

Maybe this opens the door, he thought to himself, rubbing the bottom of his helmet. *It's just crazy enough to work!*

He pressed the button. The hatch slid open, and he climbed up through the doorway and back into the Quarantine. The door closed, and the room pressurized. He ripped his helmet off, breathing in mouthfuls of fresh oxygen.

He scanned the room and felt immediate disorientation. It looked like he was in what used to be a kitchen, except everything was sideways. It was as if this whole room was attached to the ship the wrong way. It didn't seem out of the question considering the amalgam of things that made up the vessel, but it sure didn't make him happy. Walls weren't for walking, they were for burning. At least that's what his father always said.

He stood, feeling a lot heavier than he did outside. It was disorienting, and the geography of the room didn't help. He climbed up the kitchen table and stood on the oven. A few feet above him was another sealed door. He could reach it if he clambered up the dishwasher. But before he could even attempt it, the whole room shook. The pirates must have finished repairing the hull and were now taking off. Babylon fell backwards and landed on the side of the refrigerator. The vessel lurched, causing him to roll off the refrigerator towards a chandelier that almost impaled him. That was the last straw. He was fed up with this room, and everything it stood for. He wanted out.

He saw a set of stairs that led to another room. He didn't care where it took him, as long as he was out of this kitchen. He climbed across the steps, punched the OPEN button on the control panel, and stormed into the next area.

This room was a large white-tiled hall that was, thankfully, right-side up. He breathed a sigh of relief, and then stepped across the empty chamber. There were doors scattered all around, but without a map or a guide, he had no idea how to get back to the Atrium.

He tapped his earpiece. "Atrium? Are you there?" No reply. He tried again. Nothing. The sound of footsteps made him forget his ship. He pressed himself against the wall as a group of pirates walked by in the next room. He could hear voices as they passed, but all they said was "Yarrr" to each other a few times. Once he was sure the coast was clear, he snuck out of the room and slinked down the hall. Every now and then, a pirate would approach, and he would have to hide in a crevice, or behind a chair, or under a lamp shade, but for the most part, he made it around easily. He slid around a corner and saw a door at the end of the hall with a sign that read "Captives."

This must be what I'm looking for, he thought, as he bounded into the room. But there were no ships inside. In fact, there was hardly anything in it at all. Just a cage in the corner containing a bearded, emaciated old man. The old man gasped when he entered.

"You're not one of them, are you?" he asked, in a tired voice.

Babylon glanced around, hoping nobody had heard the man speak. "No," he whispered. "And keep it down, I'm trying to escape."

"Oh, good. I can't bear those guys anymore."

Babylon moved closer. "Do you know your way around the ship? Because, I could really use some help."

"It's such a relief to finally have somebody to talk to," the man said. "My cell mates died hundreds of years ago. I've been so lonely."

"That's fascinating and all," Babylon said, "but I really need to find my ship. So maybe you could point me in the right direction…"

"Oh, you want to know how old I am?" the man asked. "And how I'm still alive when I said my cell mates died hundreds of years ago?"

"No."

"Well, let me tell you. I was one of the original members of this space station. We were a group of brilliant scientists who were shot into space, quarantined from the rest of our planet. And why?"

"I don't care."

"You guessed it. To research immortality. You see, our world was infected with the mysterious Entropy disease. You've heard of it, maybe?"

"You mean the Entropy of Knowledge?" Babylon asked, despite himself.

"Yes. This research vessel was designed so we could live forever until we found a way to cure this problem. Unfortunately, as you can see, most of my team died a long time ago."

Babylon cleared his throat and glanced around. "How?"

"Most of them were jettisoned into space. Some of them were eaten by pirates. And the last of them passed due to old age. I guess our immortality research didn't take us as far as we would have liked."

With that, the old man let out a groan and died. Babylon was taken aback. The oldest man in the galaxy had just died in front of him. It was a bit unnerving. Then, just as quickly, the old man's eyes popped open and he gasped.

"Where was I? Oh, yeah. The others died after a few measly millennia."

Babylon took a step back. "How did you just do that?"

"Do what?"

His eyebrows furrowed. "You just died and came back to life."

"Oh, that?" The old man chuckled. "Part of our research included nanotechnology. Whenever my heart stops, microscopic nanorobots make it start again."

Babylon thought of all the good those robots could do in his home village. If there was no more death, then events like "The Town Fire" or "The Great Molasses Flood" wouldn't have been quite so devastating. Not to mention if he had those nanorobots, he could fight Dragons without fear.

That's an amusing idea, he thought. *Two immortal beings fighting to the death.*

"—and that's how I saved the front half of my horse." The old man had been rambling on during Babylon's musings. "But my deaths keep coming closer together. Those nanorobots have to work harder and harder to keep me alive. Soon, I fear it'll all be over, and I'll go the way of my colleagues."

Babylon fidgeted with the lock on the cage. "I better get you out of here."

"Nonsense. I love my cage. It's been my home for a very long time. I can't imagine life anywhere else. My only regret is that my vessel was abducted by pirates long before I could find a cure to the Entropy."

"Well, maybe if I free you, then—" Babylon stopped mid-sentence. The old man had died again. A few seconds later, his eyes fluttered open.

"My only regret is that my vessel was abducted by pirates—"

"I can free you," Babylon interrupted. "Then maybe you can hook me up with one of those robot things."

"It's too late for me, son. Go find your ship and free yourself. That is all that's important now. Check the second floor. That's where our hangar used to be." Babylon nodded. The old man reached out of the cage and grabbed him by the shirt. "But, you must beware," he croaked out. "I have seen the Shape of things to come, and it is terrifying."

The old man died again. Babylon stood to leave. When he got to the door, he looked back. The man was still dead. Whether it was because the nanorobots were taking longer than usual to revive him, or because he had finally passed from this world, Babylon would never know. He decided to get out of there as soon as possible. The last thing he needed on this journey was to be depressed.

He made his way to the second floor, like the dead man had suggested. From there, it wasn't hard to find the hangar. There were signs everywhere pointing to it, as well as a friendly and informative pirate help desk that told him which way to go. When he reached it, he opened the door, and slid inside. To his dismay, the hangar was empty. His ship was gone. He tried his earpiece again but got no reply. He was stuck. Now, he had no choice but to resign himself to whatever fate the pirates had in store for him. It most likely involved jettisoning.

Babylon closed his eyes to think. A distant sound pounded from somewhere in the ship.

I can't think with that racket going on, he thought, jamming his fingers into his ears. *I'm trying to find where they took my ship, and all I can hear is the sound of pounding and welding. Pounding and welding. While I try to find my ship, I can only hear welding.*

That's when it dawned on him. If the Atrium wasn't here, that meant the pirates took it somewhere else. And given the odd design of the Quarantine, he was willing to bet his ship was being attached to the hull. With renewed determination, he went into a nearby supply closet and commandeered a new helmet and oxygen tank. It looked like he was going to have to make one final trek across the pirate ship.

Finding where the Atrium was being attached was easier said than done. The Quarantine, aside from being enormous, was poorly designed. Doors and rooms appeared in the most bizarre places. There was a door on the ceiling that led to a ballroom, where waltzing pirates occasionally fell, and one in a bathroom stall that led to the inside of a rocket. There was even an evil looking door floating in the middle of nothing that shouted demonic chants and ethnic slurs whenever it was opened. Sadly, Babylon could not find a door that led to the Atrium. Left with no alternative, he was forced to open an airlock and leave the ship he had worked so hard to board.

As he carefully walked across the hull, he was able to see the full scope of the Quarantine. There weren't just space ships haphazardly strewn across its surface; the ship had other neat features as well. Like a bar, and a petting zoo that sat inert in the vacuum of space. There was even a dainty Bed and Breakfast with a couple of skeletons sitting at a table clutching teacups.

Wow, he thought. *This place has it all.*

After he managed to climb to the top of a particularly daunting post office, he caught a glimpse of the Atrium in the distance. Pirates surrounded it, welding its bottom to the hull of the Quarantine and taking measurements for a new door that was going to be installed in its belly. Babylon hunkered low and tapped his earpiece.

"Atrium! Can you hear me?"

"Master? Is that you?" The ship's voice was weak and morose. "Sorry; it has been so long that my memory circuits are not what they used to be."

"Come on, don't be like that. I wasn't away that long."

"It has been thousands of years since I have been in contact with my pilot." Babylon checked his watch. "It's been like an hour."

"Oh, I remember you now," the Atrium said. "You were the one who let me be captured and grafted onto this monstrosity."

"I came back to get you. That's all that matters."

The pirates continued welding and arguing with each other about what room the new ship should be. Some argued that it would be well-suited as a closet, while others claimed it would make a cute pantry.

"It is too late for me now," it said. "I have been stuck here for centuries."

Babylon rolled his eyes. "All right, listen. I'm sorry for leaving you, but we have to get out of here. Now open your door. I'll try to find a way to you."

"I cannot fly, remember? I have been stuck here, unable to move for tens of thousands of years, silently suffering. And even if I could, it would be useless. We are surrounded by these barbarians. They are muting my power and will not let me escape."

Babylon looked at the pirates that surrounded his ship. There were five of them holding long, glowing rods up to its engine.

They must be using those rods to drain the Atrium's power, he thought.

"There are too many of them for me to fight," he said. "But don't worry, I have a plan. Just open your door and I'll take it from there."

Babylon sauntered over to the pirates just as the Atrium's ramp began to lower. One of the pirates noticed the ramp and called his friends.

"Yo," he said. "Do you see that? The ship's actin' funny!"

"You say that about all the ships we weld," another pirate said.

"I know, but this time I mean it!"

This conversation continued for a few more minutes before Babylon strolled into their view. He was whistling a space shanty and was doing his best to impersonate a pirate.

"Arr!" he shouted to them. "What are ye...uh...doing...to that...uh...vessel, yo ho?"

The pirates glared at him with angry eyes. Pirates aren't the smartest group, or the most articulate, or the cleanest. But the one thing they knew better than anything else was hate.

"No need to be so formal," one of them said. "But who be this man who comes to us and dares to question our workmanship?" He drew his saber. "I say we make a pincushion out of ye."

"Wait." Babylon put his hands up. "I...uh...be...uh..."

The pirates drew in closer to him. His plan was not working. Fortunately, he had an ace up his sleeve.

"Hey, look over there," he said, pointing behind them. The Quarantine crew spun around to look at nothing. Babylon took the opportunity to run onto his ship and plop down in the cockpit.

"Congratulations, you are back," the Atrium said as the pirate crew outside realized that they had been duped. "Now we can be trapped together."

"It won't come to that. You gotta trust me."

The ship was silent for a moment. "No."

Babylon powered up the Atrium's weapons. "Do you have any more ammo left in your laser turrets?"

"I might have a few more blasts left in me."

He sat in his seat and grabbed the weapon controls. The angry pirates were stabbing at the ship with their cutlasses now. He aimed the turret down and charged the laser.

"Sir, I must point out that I do not have enough energy to kill all the pirates. I fear this will be for naught."

"I'm not aiming at the pirates," Babylon said. He squeezed the trigger, and a red blast shot out of the turret blowing a hole in the hull of the Quarantine. Everything that was in the room below them, which turned out to be the conservatory, flew out of the ship and into space.

"What good did that do?"

"It's going to help us escape." He smiled. "Just wait."

After a few seconds, the words he had been waiting to hear echoed from the walls of the ship. "Hull breach. Hull breach." The Atrium jarred as the conservatory was jettisoned away from the Quarantine. The pirates that had been holding them hostage with their rods slid off the steel hull and into infinite space. A couple of them were still looking at the spot Babylon had pointed to earlier.

With its power fully restored, the ship was able to break free from its welded bonds and travel unrestricted once again.

Babylon chuckled. "See, I told you I had a plan."

"I am not impressed," the Atrium said as it flew off toward their next destination, far away from the menace of the Quarantine.

Chapter ξ

ON PLANET FX Sigma, Caspar sat huddled with the other Elder Scientists around the kitchen table. They were each working on a separate component to their new invention. Caspar was oiling up the gears, Balthazar was sharpening the guillotines, Melchior was scanning the transdimensional phase array, and Shemp was placing cheese in a little dish.

"Ah," Caspar said, with a smile. "When that pesky rodent comes back, this machine will be the end of him."

"I'm not as confident as you," Balthazar said. "What if the fission core doesn't detonate properly when it steps on the dish? We'll be a laughing stock."

Shemp crossed his arms. "And I still say we should use real cheese, not this processed stuff."

"I'm sure he won't know the difference," Caspar said.

"Oh, he'll know."

Melchior grunted at them, not really agreeing or disagreeing with anyone. Caspar couldn't help but notice that Melchior's beard was loose again, and his magnificent breasts were apparently causing him discomfort. Caspar opened his mouth to speak, but never had the chance.

The lights inside the dome flashed red and an alarm sounded. He dropped the new invention and looked at the others, shrugging his shoulders. The others stood and wiped dirt and grit from their togas. In the chaos, Shemp grabbed the cheese and popped it into his mouth.

"We must be receiving an urgent message." Melchior said. "Maybe it's that nice young man."

Caspar led the others to the communications room and turned on the viewing globe, expecting to see Babylon on it. Instead, they were greeted by a gaunt man wearing green and purple robes and a lopsided crown on top of his head. He was seated in a golden chair inside a cramped golden room.

"Who in the blazes are you?" Caspar asked.

"My name is King Dragons…from the planet Dragons."

"Never heard of you," Caspar lied.

"Yes, we have," Balthazar said. "He's the man our young hero is trying to kill, remember?"

Dragons let out a cackle. "So, you have heard of me. *And* you admit that you sent an assassin to kill me."

"Nice going, Balthazar," Caspar muttered, out of the side of his mouth.

"I'm sorry, but it's not polite to lie."

Dragons sighed. "I don't have time to waste here. Tell me where you sent this little 'hero' of yours. Tell me about the weapon he is trying to get. Tell me everything!"

"We will tell you nothing," Caspar said. The other scientists nodded.

Dragons leaned closer and clenched his fist. "You will tell me, or you will all die!"

"We couldn't tell you even if we wanted to," Melchior said. "We've already forgotten!"

"Yeah!" Shemp said, rolling up the sleeves of his toga and flexing his puny arms.

"Psst." Balthazar whispered into Caspar's ear. "Don't forget, we have duplicates of the blueprints."

Caspar shook his head in exasperation. "Now is not the time to bring that up."

"I think it's the perfect time to bring it up."

"Duplicates you say?" Dragons rubbed his chin. "You will send them to me at once!"

"Honestly, Balthazar." Caspar groaned. "Why do we have duplicates?"

"I didn't want to put all of our eggs in one basket, like we did with the Space Edsel."

Dragons slammed his fist on the metal armrest of his throne. "No more talking! Send me those duplicates now, or I will kill you all!"

Caspar looked at the others and laughed. The others chuckled, but he nudged them to make them laugh harder. Melchior laughed so hard his beard fell off. Balthazar wasn't laughing at all, so Caspar pulled out a feather and tickled him under his armpits.

"You talk big, my friend," he said, stuffing the feather back in his sandal. "But this compound of ours houses the most sophisticated weaponry in the galaxy, maybe even the universe. Our defensive perimeters are active and impenetrable. And our door is locked with at least two locks. So, do your best. You'll never get close to us."

"Who said anything about getting close to you?" the king asked. He smiled, and then the image on the globe went black.

"He's bluffing." Melchior shook his head, fluttering his wavy blonde hair. "He can't possibly get to us. And no long-range weapon could shatter our mighty glass."

Caspar nodded his head. "He was just trying to scare us all, especially Balthazar."

Balthazar whimpered and clutched his chest.

The viewing globe sprang back to life. Only this time it wasn't Dragons on display, it was a star.

"This is part of your precious constellation known as the Turkey," Dragons said. "What you see is the star on the tip of its beak."

Shemp grabbed the viewing globe. "You wouldn't dare deface our Turkey!" He throttled it until Caspar stopped him.

"Oh, I'll do more than deface it." The star on the globe was shot with a small beam from off screen. There was a brief pause, and then the star churned and began to shrink. It became dimmer and dimmer until it collapsed into a black hole. The scientists gasped.

"How did you do that?" Balthazar asked. "Turn it back."

"Oh, that?" Dragons chuckled. "That was just from a little machine I found by a stroke of serendipity. Unfortunately, it's too late to change the star back to normal. But I just may be able to put a stop to this..." The star began moving through the solar system. It smashed through worlds and asteroids on a fixed direction. "This black hole is on a beeline for your planet. It will destroy everything in its path."

Shemp's jaw dropped. "Unbelievable!"

"If you don't want to be ripped apart atom by atom, then I suggest you send me those duplicates now!"

The others turned and stared at Caspar. He took a moment to muster his dignity. Then he threw his head back and laughed. "Splendid show," he said, wiping away a tear. "Though, I must admit, I was expecting a bigger challenge from the likes of you."

Dragons coughed. "W-what?"

"Dear me, you actually think you have the advantage here?"

"How pathetic." Melchior chortled.

"Pathetic? I just collapsed a star. A big one too. And I sent it hurtling through space toward you. At a faster rate than is physically possible! You should be in awe at my technological capabilities for evil."

"Apparently, you haven't heard of the Elder Scientists," Caspar said, his eyes narrowing. "Nobody has better technological capabilities for evil than us!"

Caspar reached inside his toga and pulled out a small remote with a big red button, a numerical keypad, and a small antenna. He pressed it, and a similar beam shot at the star in the heart of their own solar system. It burned bright for a few seconds before collapsing into a black hole as well.

"What the—" Dragons asked. "How did *you* do that?"

"Did you really think you were the only person with a Super Gravisquash? Don't be ridiculous."

139

The king cleared his throat. "It doesn't matter. My black hole is still on its way to kill you."

"Not for long." He pressed some buttons on the keypad. The former sun moved from its orbit and began heading toward the black hole at tremendous speed. The scientists watched with great eagerness. The two black holes were on a collision course, only a billion miles from each other. It was a rather exciting day for them. Usually when they collapsed stars, it was out of boredom.

"What happens when they meet?" Shemp asked, tossing popcorn into his mouth.

"If my calculations are correct," Caspar said, "our black hole will knock his black hole away from its current course."

"Brilliant," Melchior said, his voice a higher pitch than normal.

The Elder Scientists waited with anticipation. Dragons waited too. So did Kelmar Landred, whose planet was currently being swallowed by one of the stellar monsters. Everyone was anxious to see the outcome.

The black holes engaged each other. Event horizon met event horizon. A cosmic phenomenon that no one had ever witnessed before took place in front of an audience of trillions. But instead of the celestial joust that everybody was expecting, something strange happened. Both powerfully massive objects began circling each other, each becoming a part of the other's orbit. Instead of one ball of destruction, there were now two, and they were linked to each other like a pair of astral bolas. They spun around each other, erasing everything in their path. Solar systems were destroyed at a fantastic rate. Ripples of stellar distortion waves knocked planets and moons around like pebbles in a hurricane.

The Elder Scientists stared awestruck at the cataclysm they helped create. Caspar soon realized the folly of his plan.

"Okay, we'll send you the duplicates," he said, voice quivering. "Just make it go away!"

The scientists faxed their backups to Dragons' personal line. When the king received them, he cackled like a madman.

"Yes!" he shouted. "I will be unstoppable with these." He appeared back on the viewing globe. "Oh, and I'm afraid I can't stop those black holes after all. It looks like your fate is already sealed."

The globe went dark once again. Shemp flicked the cradle hook beneath the globe over and over, but the picture remained unchanged. Dragons was gone.

Caspar and the Elder Scientists waited for their demise with arms crossed. He was a little upset that he had doomed thousands of civilizations, specifically his. But there was no point in being glum about it. Hindsight is 20/20. That's what he always said when he caused mass havoc.

Just when the black holes entered their solar system and it looked like their annihilation was assured, a large gravitational wave struck the planet. The impact was so great that it sent FX Sigma across the galaxy at a phenomenal velocity. It was no longer a planet, but an asteroid.

Inside the dome, the scientists were protected by an inch of glass from the interstellar radiation and extreme heat that a planet traveling at Mach 3000 tended to create. Caspar had no idea what would happen to him or his home, and he was a little annoyed at the constant changes in gravity. He kept floating into the others, and then just as quickly was forced flat against the floor. And he had to abandon the chess game he had started with Shemp. His disciplined life had become utter chaos.

Finally, the planet flew into another solar system. It shed its velocity, and began a nice, peaceful orbit around a cozy star in a different part of the galaxy. Caspar peeled himself off the wall and gazed at the unfamiliar surroundings. The new sun was a little bigger, and the planet had gained two extra moons which kept the fishing lake perfectly tranquil.

"I wonder where we are," Shemp said.

Melchior adjusted his bra. "We must be in a completely different section of the galaxy."

Caspar consulted his instruments. "It looks like this solar system is a tad sunnier and warmer than our last one."

Shemp curled his lip. "I hate it."

"As do I," the others agreed.

Chapter O

THE ATRIUM SET down on the soft, squishy ground of Iios. Babylon pressed his face against the cockpit window and smiled from ear to ear. It was beautiful, a stark contrast to the mechanical, lifeless planet that had come before. This one had fantastic buildings and marvelous scenery. The sky was a lovely shade of pink, the grass was all the colors of the rainbow, and the rainbow had two extra colors he had never seen before. The planet was a feast for the eyes. Babylon jumped up and down as the ship's engine hummed.

"According to my readouts," it said, "Iios is a medium sized planet, home to a vast amount of life forms."

"I can see that," Babylon said, drinking in the view. There were castles, roads, schoolhouses, and brothels everywhere. He pulled himself from the windshield and sat back down in the captain's seat.

"The grip we need is somewhere around here," the Atrium said. "Might I suggest we ask the locals if they have seen it?"

Babylon laced up his boots. "I'm sure there are thousands of swords and grips here. How would they know which one we are after?"

There was a brief pause. "You are right. It is better to just wander around aimlessly until you find it by happenstance," the ship said.

"Fine." Babylon sighed, as he jumped out of the ship and onto the planet. His boot sunk into the ground a little, like he was walking on a wet sponge. It wasn't detrimental to his mission, but it was unsettling.

He sloshed toward a castle in the distance. People usually lived in castles, so he felt it was a logical place to start. While he walked, he noticed two large, white rocks rolling downhill toward him. He leapt into the bushes to avoid being crushed. The rocks rolled past. Something about them seemed off; they were a bit too round for his tastes. Rocks were round, sure, but they weren't *that* round.

After they passed, Babylon put it out of his head and continued. It wasn't long before two more rocks rolled towards him. He stood off to the side of the road, feeling even more uneasy than before. This time, the rocks didn't roll past; they stopped right next to him. His hand inched toward his sword. Out of the corner of his eye, he saw two more rocks rolling in his direction. But there was definitely something wrong this time. They were rolling uphill.

"Greetings!" a joyous voice said. "Welcome to our planet!"

"Who said that?" Babylon asked, looking around.

"What do you mean? I'm in front of you."

Babylon stared at one of the rocks in his path. It spun toward him, and he was able to get a good look at it. It was covered in a translucent gel with a large round circle in the middle and a black hole inside of that. A shell of skin covered its back, and a long pink tendril hung down. With horror, he finally realized it wasn't a rock at all. It was an eyeball. A giant eyeball.

"Don't worry, we mean you no harm," the eyeball said. The slimy tendril whipped forward and shook Babylon's hand. He recoiled with a small scream.

"We've been waiting a long time for your return."

He couldn't wrap his head around what was going on. Eyeballs belonged in heads, not in schools and castles. They were organs, not civilizations.

The other eyes began whispering to each other and giggling. The pupils doubled as mouths and moved when they talked. It was all he could do to keep from screaming again. He gulped and did his best to continue the conversation.

"What do you mean you've been waiting for me to return?" he asked. "I've never been here before."

"Of course, you have," one of the eyeballs said, blinking with its skin shell. "You came to us in times past and delivered one of the greatest gifts to our kingdom."

Babylon's face lit up. "A gift you say? What kind of gift?"

"Oh, don't be silly. You know what I'm talking about. You were the one who bestowed unto us Grendal's Grip!"

An electric crackle whined in his ear. "That must be it, sir," the Atrium said. "Ask if it belongs to a sword. Ask!"

Babylon cleared his throat. "Is the grip for a sword?"

"I must not answer any more questions," the eyeball said. "It is a high honor for me just to be in your presence."

"You can speak to me," he said. "You can tell me all you want about Grendal's Grip. Like where it is and things of that nature."

"I am not worthy to speak to such a powerful being." The eyeball rolled down to kiss Babylon's foot. He instinctively kicked it away, and it rolled down the hill, smiling.

"Can any of you tell me about Grendal's Grip?" he asked the others. They all got down and tried to kiss his feet. He was not used to being worshipped like that, especially not by eyeballs, so he ran away. The balls rolled after him, shouting praise. The further he ran, the more eyeballs saw him and seemed to recognize him. All of them revered him, but none of them seemed interested in answering his questions. Word spread quickly, and soon enough a whole flock of eyeballs surrounded him.

"Please!" he said. "Can anybody tell me where Grendal's Grip is? It's very important."

A couple of smaller eyeballs in white lab coats rolled forward. They seemed younger by the higher pitch in their voice and slouched posture—their pupils were a little farther down than the others—not to mention the disdain they seemed to hold for Babylon. "Surely, you know the story of your own legend?" one of the lab coat eyeballs asked, adjusting his giant monocle with his tendril.

"I don't."

The young eyes looked at each other and chuckled amongst themselves, then turned back to Babylon. "After a few millennia your memory's not what it used to be, eh?"

"Just tell me," he said.

"You know, just as well as we do, that you stopped by our planet a couple thousand years ago," the eyeball said. "We didn't have time to commission a painting of you back then, but you are pretty unmistakable. You come from the heavens, have a weird lumpy form, and don't turn red and moist when there's hay in the air. In case you haven't noticed, that doesn't fit the description of a lot of us here." The eyes in the crowd laughed at this, except for the small, lumpy eye that stood off to the side. He didn't come from the heavens; he was just a misfit.

A crackle of electricity. "What did he mean by that?" the Atrium said. "I cannot see them. What do they look like?"

Babylon ignored the voice in his ear. "Okay, so someone came down here a long time ago that looked like me," he said to the eyeball. "That doesn't mean it was me. Just that they looked like me."

"Nonsense! There can't be two beings like you out there."

"There are a lot of us; we probably all look the same to you. Just like all of you look the same to me."

The crowd let out an offended gasp. A few members whispered to each other that they didn't like this legend as much as they did before.

"In any case," the young eyeball continued, sputtering a little bit. "Back then, *somebody* descended from the sky and gave to us a gift: a small object that was to be protected at all costs. He handed this object to a brave ball named Grendal—"

An electric crackle. "Ball? What does that mean? Are they some sort of ball?"

"—it was called a grip, and our visitor explained that it could be attached to a blade and used to make a fully functioning sword. This was news to us; we had been fighting with just the blades up to that point. We lost more than we killed in battles. It was very counterproductive."

Babylon motioned with his hand that the young eye should wrap up his story. He didn't care where the grip was thousands of years ago. Just today.

"The grip was fitted onto the Sword of the Kingdom, which Grendal used to conquer our enemies, the dreaded Nose Tribe." The crowd booed and hissed at the mention of their mortal enemies. Even the one eyeball that had a nose booed. "Thanks to Grendal and the visitor from the heavens, we were able to defend the Kingdom. And the visitor claimed that someday he would return to our planet to reclaim the gift he had trusted us to protect."

Babylon thought it over. One of the ancient scientists must have come here to hide the grip, knowing that someone would return one day looking to assemble the Sword of Antimatter. He realized this piece might be the easiest one to get; all he had to do was ask for it.

"That is why I am here," he said, in a loud, and what he hoped was a commanding tone. "I have come from the stars to collect that which is rightfully mine. And the sooner the better, because I'm kind of in a hurry."

The young eye shook himself back and forth. He chuckled. "It's not that simple. Grendal's Grip rests on the Sword of the Kingdom. Only the rightful King can possess it."

Babylon stamped his foot. "But I need it."

"The king will determine whether you are worthy. I'll be honest with you, I expected our legendary visitor to behave somewhat differently. The king might feel the same way."

Babylon sighed. "All right. Take me to see your king then."

The crowd laughed at him. Even the Atrium laughed at him in his ear. He waved the noise away like an annoying bee.

"Legend or not," the eye said, "no one can just roll in and see the king. Not no one, not no how."

"Well, how *do* I meet with the king, then?"

"You're in luck, my friend. The castle is hosting a debutante ball tonight for Princess Eileen. Being a legend from beyond the stars, you might just get onto the guest list."

A ball? Babylon couldn't believe his good fortune. "I'll be there," he said.

The crowd blinked with approval and bounced off to tell the news to their friends, families, and preachers.

"What a stroke of luck," the Atrium said, through his earpiece. "I told you talking to the residents would yield results."

"Yeah, it looks like you were—" Before Babylon could finish his first and only bit of praise for his ship, he was interrupted by the lab coat eyeballs.

"Mr. Legend," one of them said. "Can we ask you a few questions now that we are alone?"

"Do not listen to them," the Atrium said. "Continue your acclaim for me."

"What can I do for you?" he asked, ignoring the voice in his ear.

"Being scientists, we are always fascinated by new discoveries. And you are definitely the most fascinating discovery in ages." One of the eyeballs rolled forward to take Babylon's measurements with a nylon measuring tape in its tendril.

"Well, thank you," Babylon said, just before a scientist stuck a tongue depressor in his mouth and jotted down the results.

"As such, we would be honored if you came down to our laboratory for further study."

He thought about this while an eyeball measured his skull bumps with a caliper and wrote the results down on a clipboard. Babylon thought about something else which made the eyeball take a new measurement with a satisfied "ha!"

"Where is your laboratory?" he asked.

"Down there." One of the scientists motioned toward a small, dark shack a few feet from the castle. A sharp pendulum hung off its side and swung menacingly above a table with chains.

"Sir, I would have to advise against this course of action," the Atrium said. "Our planet was once visited by an alien species as well. Our scientists took them away for experimentation purposes. Further studies proved that dissection is universally fatal. I fear they may be planning similar tests for you."

"I'm going to have to decline your offer," Babylon said.

"I understand," one of them said, a tear forming on his surface. "But if you get tired or drugged at the ball, please feel free to stop by." They rolled off, one of them dragging a hacksaw in its tendril.

"Now, what were we talking about before they interrupted us?" the computer asked.

"Who remembers? I have a ball to attend. And I plan on looking good."

§ § §

Babylon strolled through the castle gates dressed in a bright red tuxedo and top hat. The Atrium mentioned that the outfit was a little garish, but Babylon didn't listen. It was eye-catching, it was classy, and it was the only suit from the Captain's quarters that fit him. The only downside was that, after thousands of years of hanging in a closet, the color wasn't as vibrant as it should have been, and the armpits had stains on them. But despite this, Babylon felt like a million bucks when he arrived at the ball. He walked through the round door and saw a large, spherical room with circular tiles on the floor and bright green sashes lining the round windows.

Trumpets announced his arrival, and an older eyeball—judging by his cataracts and dry surface—bellowed in a loud voice, "Now introducing: The Visitor from Legend."

An awed hush fell over the room. Every eye was on him. Pupil's dilated with reverence. Babylon took full advantage of the attention. He walked through the crowd as regally as he could, tipping his hat and spinning his sword like a cane. It was nice to be noticed.

"Mr. Legend, dahling!" A female eyeball wearing a fur coat and tiara rolled up to him. "You simply must tell us what you've been doing these last few centuries."

"I saw him first!" another woman said, bouncing in front of the first lady. "Won't you dance with me?"

"No, no, over here," a male eyeball wearing a press hat said. "Our readers want to know the scoop behind the legend. What's an average day like for a legend from the heavens?"

The Atrium buzzed in his ear with questions of its own. "How are they dressed? Do they look funny?"

Before Babylon could open his mouth, the trumpets sounded again. The king rolled into the room from a round doorway at the other end of the room. He had a mustache under his pupil and wore a sash that had KING printed across it. He was followed by a young eyeball with long eyelashes. Babylon assumed this was Princess Eileen.

"This is Princess Eileen," the king announced. "Tonight is her grand debut! She has indeed grown into the fairest maiden in the land. Any suitor would be lucky to win her hand. But I won't bore you with things you already know. My command for you all tonight is this: have a good time!"

The crowd cheered and continued dancing and conversing amongst themselves. Babylon took this opportunity to search for clues about the Grip's location. It turned out he didn't have to look far. It was on a sword attached to the wall at the other end of the room, behind the royal moon chair.

Babylon stood beneath the sword, admiring it. The whole thing was fastened to a large plaque, and the blade was embedded with jewels. The words "Sword of the Kingdom" were inscribed on the plaque.

"I see you're admiring Eternity, eh?" the king said, rolling up to Babylon.

"Eternity?"

"Yes, that's what we've named our prized sword. As long as we have it, our kingdom will last forever."

"That's interesting." Babylon nodded. "Very interesting. Can I have it?"

The king laughed and slapped him on the back with his tendril, leaving a wet mark. "I do love your sense of humor. You're certainly living up to your own legend. Surely, you know that only the ruler of the kingdom can claim the sword?"

Babylon's face fell. "How do I become the ruler of the kingdom?"

"That might be in the cards very soon, if you catch my drift." The king laughed long and hard. "My daughter has her eye on you."

Babylon looked over at Eileen who was staring at him, smiling. She had the same look Emmunda used to have when she watched him chop wood; it made him very uncomfortable.

"Are you sure she likes me?" he asked, gulping.

"Of course; a father can tell these things. And since she's my only daughter, you would inherit the kingdom." The round king nudged him good-naturedly in the side, ruining the fabric of his suit. "The banquet will start soon. Perhaps you two can become better acquainted."

Babylon swallowed hard. *Think of the greater good.*

§ § §

The royal banquet was nothing but a bunch of withered old eyeballs telling boring stories to a stuffy crowd. They sat around a circular table, with round plates, round napkins, and round silverware. One of the featured guests—a ball named General Eyesenhower—was finishing his hour-long tale of heroism during the Great War. He was a highly decorated eye, with medals of bravery lining his body, but tended to fall asleep during his anecdotes. When he woke, he would lose his place and had to start the story over from the beginning. It was unbearable.

Sometime after Eyesenhower fell asleep, then woke up firing his pistol at the crowd, Babylon noticed Eileen glancing at him from across the table. At this point anything was more interesting than the general, so he offered her a smile. She responded with a bigger smile that made him shudder. She whispered something to one of the servants, who immediately rolled around the table to stop at Babylon's seat.

"From the princess," the servant said, dropping a soggy note into his lap.

He gulped and unfolded the note.

Meet me in the Grand Hall.
-E

A small sound of worry crept out of Babylon's throat.

"What is going on?" the Atrium asked. "It sounds like the dinner is not going well." Was that pleasure in its voice? "Do you have the Grip yet?"

149

Babylon tapped his earpiece, switching the voice off. *The greater good,* he reminded himself, and stood from the table. He slinked away from the banquet, keeping his gaze low. The shuffle of his feet on the marble floor woke the general who began his story anew.

Babylon waited in the Grand Hall, not sure what to expect. There was a large ramp running down the center and statues of great eyes carved out of boulders. Paintings adorned the walls up and down the hall. There was a portrait of the king with Eileen, a picture of Grendal defeating a group of noses with Eternity, and finally, a painting of an eyeball riding a clamshell. A door at the end of the hall opened and Eileen rolled towards him.

"I have something I want to tell you in private," the princess said. "Quickly, come with me to my bedroom. It's this way."

Before Babylon could protest, he was pushed up the ramp and through a perfectly round doorway into Eileen's room. He took one look and shuddered. Everything was pink, from the pink wallpaper to the pink carpet. Even the large bed in the center of the room was the same: pink sheets, pink pillows, and pink teddy eyes.

"That party was so boring." Eileen casually locked the door behind her. "I couldn't wait to get away from it."

"Uh, yeah. It certainly was dull." He sat on the bed, apprehensive.

"I'm sure you've been to many of these things, being a legend and all."

Babylon gulped. "Oh, not as many as you would think."

The princess lay down on her bed next to him, striking what Babylon assumed was a seductive pose. "So, now that you're in the bedroom of the king's beautiful daughter, what do you want to do?"

His gaze darted back and forth from the princess to the door. "Uh…" He scratched the back of his neck. "What do *you* want to do?"

"Well, Mr. Legend," she said, batting her giant eyelashes. "I can think of one thing."

"And what is that?" he squeaked.

She rolled forward. "I want you to give me a kiss."

Babylon leaned backward and fell off the bed. She hopped down next to him, clutching his arms in her slimy tendril. She was pretty strong for an eyeball.

"A kiss?" he said, breaking free from her grip. "Wouldn't you rather talk first?"

Eileen giggled. "You're so silly. Now, get over here, lover boy."

The greater good. The greater good!

Babylon shuffled over to the bed. "There's just one thing," he said. "I need to borrow Eternity."

"Borrow the Sword of the Kingdom?" she asked. "Whatever for?"

"I just need it for a little bit. And since I will eventually marry you and become the king, it kind of already belongs to me."

Eileen hummed and rocked back and forth.

"It's basically a done deal." He mustered the biggest smile he could.

"Okay," the princess said. "I'll get Eternity for you. Don't move."

She rolled out of the room and down the hall. Babylon wiped his sweaty brow with the back of his hand. He tapped on his earpiece and explained the situation to his ship, but tapped it back off when it wouldn't stop laughing. Time stretched out forever. He drummed his fingers across his lap, faster and faster, and only stopped when he heard the distinct sound of steel scraping across the ground.

"Here it is," Eileen said when she entered the room, dragging the sword behind her. She tossed it onto the bed and rolled next to Babylon. "Now how about that kiss?"

He considered it as she leaned in. *Just pretend she's Emmunda*, he thought. *A rounder, whiter, slimier Emmunda.*

Princess Eileen giggled, and her pupil puckered. She moved closer. So did he. Sounds of pleasure gushed from her mouth. Sounds of disgust escaped his. She was inches away from his face.

He grabbed the sword and ran.

§ § §

Babylon charged into his ship and threw the jewel encrusted sword to the ground. He collapsed in the Captain's seat, panting hard.

"I see you were successful," the Atrium said, stifling a mechanical giggle. "How did it go?"

"I got the Grip" he said. "That's all that matters. We should get out of here."

"What's the rush? Tell me what happened."

"Just go!" The space phone rang on the Atrium's console. Babylon looked at it and trembled. "That's her; go, go, go!"

The Atrium laughed once more and blasted off into space, leaving behind an angry princess and an entire kingdom of crossed eyes.

Chapter π

KING DRAGONS SCANNED the fax he had received from the pathetic scientists. He had studied it a dozen times and always came to the same conclusion. There were four locations and only one of him. He was going to need some help.

He muttered Plob's jingle as he called him on the picture phone. The bounty hunter appeared on the screen, a wet towel draped over his tinfoil suit.

"What do you want?" Plob asked. "I'm trying to take a bath."

"I have a new mission for you," Dragons said.

"I'm still waiting for my payment from the first mission."

He slammed his fist on his golden chair. "I told you, the check is in the space mail!" He shook his hand. That hurt. His wrist was probably broken again. "Besides, wouldn't you rather do this mission for the glory of your king?"

"No, money is fine. Glory doesn't pay the bills the same way money does."

The Omniflux hummed and his wrist stopped hurting. He didn't break it after all.

"I'll personally give you cash and jewels when you finish this mission. Is that all right?"

Plob agreed, nodding his head. Dragons got the impression the guy was playing it cool. *A consummate professional, that Plob*. Of course, he couldn't help but notice the little dance and occasional whoops from the bounty hunter. That sullied the illusion of professionalism a bit.

"I'm going to send you some coordinates," he said. "I think that Babylon kid might be heading for at least one of them. I want you find him and bring him back to me alive."

"Yes, sir," Plob said, doing flips and hollering. Very unprofessional.

"Don't underestimate him, Plob. He's much cleverer than he looks. You may have to try and outsmart him."

The bounty hunter pulled himself up from the floor and assured Dragons that he was plenty smart enough to deal with a little kid. The screen went black.

He studied the four sets of coordinates and brain-mailed two of them to Plob's b-mail address—P.Babo@bmail.brain—then scanned the other two. The nearest planet was Iios, only a couple light years to the east. He pulled on the reins in front of him, turning his dragons around and starting the chase.

§§§

Babylon dipped a squeegee into the bucket of water and brought it up to the windshield. The interior of the Atrium got dirty from time to time, and he liked to keep it clean. He wiped an annoying fingerprint smudge away and dropped the squeegee back into the bucket. The emptiness of space sped by outside the window.

"You know, I've been thinking," he said, resting his hand on the glass. "That last planet was so proud of their sword that they named it. And it's a cool name too: Eternity. It sounds so neat."

"Uh-huh," the Atrium said. "How is that window coming?"

Babylon ignored it. "Why don't I have a name for my sword yet?"

"Probably because you have not saved a kingdom with it."

He unsheathed his weapon and looked it over. There were a few scratches on it from his previous encounters. He had been through a lot with this sword over the past few weeks. A little bit of pride welled up inside him.

"Maybe they named the sword first."

"I do not think they did."

"Maybe I should name *my* sword first."

The lights on the console flashed the same way they did whenever the ship said something condescending, but this time it remained silent.

Babylon looked the weapon over. "What should I call it?"

"A sword."

"I mean what name should I give it?" He stood and began swinging it through the air in a mock battle, the window long forgotten.

"I think there is a rule. You cannot name your sword until you battle at least one person with it. Or at least until you have a skirmish."

Babylon thought it over with a frown. He made an emphatic thrust. "I fought Starbeard with it."

"And you lost. Perhaps you should wait until your first victory."

"Does that include stabbing somebody in the back?" Babylon asked with another thrust.

"Only if you flip over them from the front."

He sheathed the sword and wiped sweat away from his forehead. The ship lurched, sending Babylon back to the bucket of water. A few more twists and turns and barrel rolls, and he found himself with the squeegee in his hand. He mopped his brow with it.

"Hmm. A name…a name," Babylon muttered to himself. "How about Eternity?"

There was a pause from the ship. "I think you can do better."

154

"Maybe Stabby."

"Wow, that is…"

"Or Swordy."

The lights turned red and the console blinked faster than usual. "I will name the weapon," the Atrium said. "I shall put the full amount of my processing power towards it." It beeped and booped as the lights dimmed and the life support systems powered down. After a few seconds of weightlessness, the ship spoke. "I have concluded that henceforth your weapon shall be called Steve."

"That's boring," Babylon said. "How about Ultrasword?"

"Steve will do just fine."

"Whatever, it's not important anyway."

The ship sighed as it continued to soar through space. Babylon pulled out a handkerchief and started polishing the knobs on her console. Something outside the window caught his eye, and he dropped the handkerchief mid-polish.

"What's that?" he asked, pointing to an immense cloudy area.

The ship groaned. "That is just the Harlequin Nebula. We are going around it, so continue your work."

Babylon reached into the glove compartment and pulled out a large interstellar map of the galaxy. It took a while to unfold since it was large enough to fill the cockpit, but it was a handy thing to have.

"It says our next destination is on the other side of that nebula." He tapped a dot on the map. "Why don't we just go through it?"

"Sir, I highly recommend we go around."

Babylon rubbed his chin. "Nah, shortcuts are my specialty. Let me tell you the story of a little place called Prospector Woods…"

Lights blinked on the console, and the door slammed open and shut. "I am pleading with you to circumvent it."

Babylon puffed his chest out. "I'm the Captain, here. I say we take the dangerous shortcut."

There was a long pause. "…as you wish, Master." The ship changed its course, charging straight for the nebula.

At first, everything went smoothly. They were making great time, and the view was unbelievable: clouds of misty pink stardust and blue plasma crackling across the inky black. Then things began to happen. Sirens blared, alarms rattled, and the ship whimpered. Flashes of light exploded outside of the windshield.

"What's happening?" he asked, backing away from the glass and hiding behind the seat.

"It appears there is an imminent threat from an ion cloud."

Babylon peeked out the window. "How far away is it?"

"We are inside of it," the ship said. "I told you this was a bad idea."

"Well, we need to think of a plan; we can't stay here. We'll be killed."

An acrid stench permeated the cockpit. "But you were so gung ho about going through it a minute ago," the Atrium said, it's voice becoming distorted. "It was quite charming."

With shaky arms, Babylon crawled back into the seat. He buckled himself in — the first time he'd ever felt the need to — and consulted the map again. "How long will it take to get out of here if we turn around now?"

The ship rambled on, in a dreamy tone. "Such a commanding attitude you had." Its voice became more distorted. "So 'take-charge.' I would have followed you anywhere."

"Snap out of it, Atrium. We need to —"

A crackle of thunder and an explosion came from above him. Sparks flew from the console, and smoke poured into the cockpit from behind.

"It appears we have been struck by an electrical discharge," the ship said, its voice barely recognizable. "All of this static electricity is making my circuits feel funny." It stopped talking for a moment, and then added in its faraway voice, "I miss my creator."

Another bolt of lightning struck the frame. But instead of piercing the hull, the electricity flowed around the ship and fried the circuits. The Atrium went silent, the lights powered down, the artificial gravity turned off, and after that, the oxygen. The first three problems were annoying, for sure, but that last one really worried Babylon. He was fairly certain he needed oxygen to live.

The room was filling with smoke at an alarming rate. He tried to keep his breathing steady, but the big black cloud billowed toward him, rendering the air useless. Just before he was consumed, he took a deep breath and stuffed some air in his pockets as a precaution. He floated around the dormant space vehicle searching for the emergency generator, which would restore backup power to the support systems. He should have known where the generator was since the Atrium had told him time and time again. It even quizzed him about it. They had even conducted emergency generator drills. But, in the midst of panic, his mind was drawing a blank.

He moved around the ship, flailing his arms and legs like he was swimming. It didn't help as much as he thought it would. If anything, the overexertion was burning his oxygen faster. Finally, he gave up and just floated along without any specific direction.

His vision faded, partly from the smoke and partly from his lack of oxygen. As the sweet embrace of oblivion approached, he saw something out of the corner of his eye: the generator! It was painted bright pink, and there were a series of large arrows pointing towards it. He didn't know how he missed the thing; it was right next to his seat.

He pushed off the wall and drifted toward the device. He was sure it would save his life if he could only reach it in time. His lungs burned as he struggled to hold the last bit of air inside of him. The generator was almost within arm's reach. With a cough, he exhaled. The smoke filled his lungs, and darkness encroached on his vision. His fingertips closed around something. The generator! With his last ounce of energy, he tugged on the pull-start handle. The gas-powered engine that served as the ship's backup sputtered and churned. Life support and gravity systems powered on.

Babylon cried out with joy before passing out and falling to the floor. He wasn't conscious to see the lights flicker on, or feel the fan blowing cool air through the ship, or smell the coffee maker start up. And he surely wasn't awake to hear the crinkling footsteps of a strange man in tinfoil boots.

Chapter P

INSIDE THE ELDER Scientists' dome, the atmosphere was tense. Caspar had grown weary of the new solar system; he missed the bland efficiency of their old one. This sun was too much for him. It was bright and happy, and made the dome's drab interior look more miserable by comparison. Not to mention the super-effective rays made the flowers bloom in more vibrant colors. Sure, he had a better tan, but that was the only perk.

"Look," he said, when the rare joy sprout bloomed in their living room. "This plant is starting to show more colors than are on the visible spectrum."

"It's a bit extravagant, don't you think?" Balthazar shook his head.

"We're going to have to do something." Shemp plucked a petal from the plant and popped it in his mouth. "Joy and cheer inhibit scientific discovery."

Caspar smiled and wheeled a device into the room. It was as big as he was and was covered in a dirty white tarp. "There's good news," he said. "I've just finished my matter transporter. With it, we will be able to teleport off this awful planet." He pulled the tarp off. Underneath was a large machine with buttons and knobs. At the top was a cone that pointed straight up, while the bottom was a round, metal pad. The other scientists saw this and gasped.

"Where can we go with this thing?" Melchior asked, running his manicured fingers over the cone.

Caspar grinned. "Anywhere. In fact, I've already found a new home for us: an abandoned planet at the far end of the galaxy. It's roughly the same size as ours, and gets almost no sunlight, so we can work forever in peace."

The other scientists cheered.

"Plus, as an added bonus, the water contains mercury, so we'll have a new element to play with."

"And new species to discover." Shemp stared out of the dome with a grin. "Let's go right away."

Caspar screwed the last screws onto the pad and hammered the last nails into the circuits. With a final, dramatic tap he switched the machine on. Minutes of awkward silence passed. Then after the tubes warmed and the steam whistle sounded, the machine hummed to life.

"I'll input the destination." He tapped a few buttons on the keyboard. When he finished, a large blue beam shot out from the cone and through the glass ceiling. The readout on the computer screen blinked one simple message in green text: "Waiting…"

Melchior stood behind him. "How long is this going to take?"

"A few minutes," Caspar said.

"A few minutes?" Shemp stamped his foot. "But I want to go now!"

The scientists waited, but nothing happened. They checked their watches, consulted their sundials, and flipped their hourglasses over again and again. Still the readout read, "Waiting…"

Shemp yawned. "What's the holdup?"

"I'm not sure," Caspar said. "I suppose I could turn up the power a little."

He turned different knobs on the control panel. The transporter hummed louder, and the beam that shot from it turned a different shade of blue, but the readout didn't change.

Shemp stuck his head in the beam and turned it in every direction, calling for the planet. He pulled it out, clutching his head and wincing.

"It's not working. Your machine sucks."

"Well, I suppose I could turn the power all the way up, but I think that would be a dangerous idea."

"Do it!" Shemp said. "Do it, do it, do it, do it, do it!"

Caspar swallowed hard. "Okay," he said. He pushed a few more buttons on the console and turned the knob up to eleven. The machine rattled, and the beam widened to an even greater intensity. Screws shot out and bounced off the glass. Balthazar yelped when one hit him in the back, and he clutched his chest as he fell to the ground.

"It's at maximum power now," Caspar said, over the sound of whirring and grinding. "It should work now. Or it will kill us all. Either way, we'll be traveling somewhere soon."

The readout on the monitor beeped and the word "Complete" appeared on it in green text. The machine continued to hum, but its pitch was different. It sounded more like a grunt.

Shemp smiled and stepped onto the teleportation pad. Nothing happened. "What's going on?" he said, jumping up and down. "I thought it was done."

"The device lied to us!" Balthazar said, from the ground.

Caspar stroked his beard. "That's impossible. Machines can't lie unless they are programmed to. Besides, this one would never lie to us. He's our friend."

"Then where's the new planet?" Melchior asked.

Before Caspar could answer, he heard a ripping noise from above. He followed the direction of the beam into the bright sky. It was no longer projecting out into empty space. Now, there was an oddly shaped rock attached to the end. The rock grew larger the longer he stared at it.

"Would you look at that?" Melchior said, brushing golden locks out of his eyes. "It looks like an asteroid is getting in the way of the beam."

"That can't be an asteroid!" Balthazar said. "It has an ocean."

Caspar squinted. Water had formed on the once barren rock. Then grass. And after that, cities. They faded in like a developing picture. And the once misshapen rock took on a more spherical form. His mouth dropped open.

"That's a planet!" he shouted. "That's the planet we're supposed to be teleporting to."

"What's it doing here?" Balthazar grabbed him by the toga. "It should be on the other side of the galaxy."

"I think it's very rude for it to show up uninvited," Shemp said.

Caspar looked over the device's instruction manual that he himself wrote. "I see what the problem is," he said, his face warming. "I forgot to change the program language from metric to binary." He pointed to the switch at the top of the device. "So instead of being teleported to the planet, the planet was teleported to *us*."

Shemp ran over and flipped the switch.

"That won't do any good," Caspar said. "It's too late now. The machine has to complete its current task before the language can be changed."

"Then what's going to happen to us?" Balthazar asked.

"If my calculations are correct, we are all doomed."

The ripping sound stopped as the planet completed its teleportation. It floated in the sky for a moment before gravity pulled it and FX Sigma into a collision course with each other. At first, things weren't so bad. There was a nice, warm amount of friction in the air, plenty of oxygen to go around, and the gravity fluctuations made the trees dance. It was quite a show. Then the two planets entered each other's atmospheres. Sporadic explosions converted the fertile land to ash and the ground cracked beneath the dome.

"What are we going to do?" Balthazar asked, running around in circles.

"Let's go to my room," Caspar said. "The planet will never find us there."

He led the others to his bedroom and opened the rickety wooden door of his closet. The others scattered around, hiding in different spots, like under the hammock or in the drawers. He closed the closet door and sat cross-legged on the hardwood floor, looking through the slats every now and then to see if he was dead yet. The dome shook and rattled, and lab coats kept falling off the hangers and landing on his head. It was both terrifying and annoying.

"Just kill us, already," Shemp said, after the rug he was hiding under slid off him for the third time. "We're getting bored."

Starting at the point of collision—just outside Caspar's bedroom—both planets shattered and blasted out in every direction possible. A few pieces of debris blasted out in directions that hadn't been discovered yet, and one piece reattached itself to FX Sigma. A ripple of pure annihilation swept across the landscape.

"This is the end!" Caspar pulled the slats down.

The ground cracked and the sky tumbled away. The closet rattled so hard the door fell off its hinges. Caspar was launched against the wall, back to the floor, then onto the ceiling. Outside the closet, the others were bouncing around the same way. Shemp grabbed onto the doorjamb and asked to come in, but Caspar kicked his hands until he fell back into the bedroom.

Outside, FX Sigma was gone. Now, there were streaks of light from the stars and the occasional piece of debris speeding by. Balthazar flew full speed at the glass, and then fell back to the floor, reaching for his chest. He bounced around like this for an hour before the artificial gravity came on and everything settled down.

Melchior stepped into the bedroom, putting his beard back on. "I turned on the gravity," he said. "We should be stable for now. What happened?"

Caspar pulled a scanner from inside his toga. "It appears that we were blown off our planet and to the safety of infinite space." He cleared his throat. "Just as I predicted."

"Good riddance," Shemp said. "I was tired of that planet anyway. Now, we can work without any ridiculous interruptions."

The dome shimmered, and reality changed. The glass around Caspar's room melted into a palace chamber. Silk sashes ran from one end of the room to the other, and a beautiful harem fanned the scientists with silken fans. Exotic animals walked around with bowls of fruit tied to their heads. The hammock had transformed into a fine golden bed with fine golden pillows stuffed with fine golden feathers. Everything in the palace became bejeweled and decorated, from the diamond-encrusted floor to the ruby-studded blanket.

"These gaudy luxuries sure are annoying," Caspar said, adjusting his crown. "I think they overdid the whole thing."

Balthazar flicked a sapphire off his shoulder. "It *is* a bit much."

"And I don't care for the way that bird in the corner is molting," Shemp said. "It's distracting."

The harem fanned the scientists while they ate cheese and whined. After a few minutes of torturous pleasure, the harem, palace, and luxuries transformed back into Caspar's drab bedroom.

"Oh, well," he said, plopping into his hammock. "Easy come, easy go, I guess." He stared at the vast universe outside his room, wondering what worlds he and his colleagues would ruin next.

Chapter Σ

BABYLON WAS AT peace. He was nestled in his old lumpy bed on his old lumpy home planet, looking at the drawings in his old lumpy book. The light of the candle warmed his body as well as his spirit. It was a wonderful time to do nothing but relax and not worry about petty things, like space travel or the destruction of the galaxy.

Everything was absolutely perfect. But, like all good things, it couldn't last.

Cold water splashed over his face. His eyes sprang open, and he found himself inside the steel belly of an unfamiliar ship. There were pipes running up and down the walls as well as empty pizza boxes and candy wrappers on the riveted floor. His arms and legs were tied behind the back of a wooden chair. A heavyset man dressed in tinfoil stood in front of him with an empty bucket in his fat hands. There was something familiar about him, but in his current groggy state, he couldn't remember.

"Rise and shine," the man said.

Babylon shook water out of his hair. "Who are you?" he asked.

"We've never been formally introduced. My name is Plob Babo."

The name struck a familiar chord. "The bounty hunter?"

"The greatest in the galaxy." The portly man beamed. "And can you take a guess as to who my next bounty is?"

Babylon let out a deep sigh. "Me?"

"That's right! Welcome aboard my ship: the S-33. Named for the great King S the 33rd."

Babylon struggled against the ropes. "Where's my ship?" he asked.

"Don't worry about that tin can," Plob said. "I'm towing it behind me. I can make some money off its scrap." He rubbed his hands together and smacked his lips.

Babylon wasn't sure if he planned on eating his ship or not. "Where are you taking me?"

"To King Dragons."

His heart caught in his throat. He wasn't ready to face Dragons yet. The sword was incomplete. A fight with him now would be suicide. He had to escape.

"Hey, I have a deal for you," he said. "How much is Dragons paying you to capture me?"

"Enough."

"How about I pay you more than enough to let me go?"

Plob shook his head. "Sorry, but King Dragons wants you. And it would be a bad idea for me to defy him."

"If you let me go, I can promise you Dragons won't be a problem."

"Yeah, I know. The Sword of Antimatter." The bounty hunter scoffed. "You're planning on using it to defeat him. The King knows all about that."

Babylon was shaken by the news. "He knows what I'm doing? Is that why he sent you after me?"

"That's right."

He hopped his chair toward Plob. "That means he's scared of me. He knows I can beat him. You have to let me go!"

Plob shook his head again. "Mm! Mm! Mm!" He grunted with each shake. "I have orders to bring you in. Nothing you say or do is going to change that."

Electricity crackled around them. "Where are we going again?" Babylon gulped.

"I already told you, to King Dragons' command ship."

"That wouldn't happen to be around the Harlequin Nebula, would it?"

"Of course not, don't be stupid," Plob said, chuckling, "but we are going through it to make up for lost time."

Babylon closed his eyes and braced himself for what he knew would happen next. Within seconds, the ship was struck by one of the trillions of lightning bolts that constantly ran through the nebula. The power flickered on and off, and small explosions sounded throughout the S-33. The bounty hunter yelped, clawed at his helmet with his gloves, and rolled around on the floor. Clearly, he did not know how to react to the situation.

"Oh man, oh man! This is not good!" Plob shouted over and over, as he ran around with a pail of water trying to put out the various fires. It was a useless endeavor. More and more damage was being done as they were repeatedly struck by lightning.

Another explosion rocked the S-33. "Let me loose!" Babylon said.

"I can't do that," Plob said, while he stomped out a fire on the dashboard. "I have to save my ship." An alarm screamed overhead. "Oh no, the energy reactor is critical!"

"Evidently Dragons wants me alive. You can't collect any money if we're both dead. Let me go!"

"I already told you, I can't!" Dark matter poured in from the ship's broken pipes, flooding the room. Plob scooped up the matter with his pail and tossed it into the airlock.

"Your ship is as good as gone," Babylon said, as the sticky dark matter rose above his ankles. "Let's go back to the Atrium. Its backup systems should still be functional. We'll last longer in there."

Plob stared at him, and then glanced around the ship. Another explosion nearby made the bounty hunter yelp. He untied the ropes binding Babylon's wrists. Together, they ran to the back of the ship where thermal jackets and helmets hung from hooks. No gravity boots, though. He had left those in his cockpit.

"Wait, here," Plob said, while Babylon was dressing. "There is something I can't bear to leave behind."

He waited while the bounty hunter disappeared into the flooding ship. He came back a minute later with a sandwich in his hand. "Thank you for waiting," Plob said, opening the door to outer space.

The two slid back to the Atrium, using the tow cable as a guide. Without gravity boots, the journey was difficult. Much more difficult than the trek across Starbeard's ship. Lightning bolts struck inches from them, scaring Babylon half to death, but most stayed far enough away to not be dangerous. One or two exploded like fireworks, making Plob point and say "ooh." Finally, they made it across the cable and into the Atrium. They jumped into the airlock just in time to see the S-33 be completely destroyed. A final volley of lightning bolts struck the advertisement sign attached to the hull, and it exploded into a thousand pieces. The only remaining part that he could recognize was a scrap of metal that said, "5879e12."

Babylon stepped into the cockpit, nerves frayed. Plob followed behind him, unwrapping the sandwich with misty eyes. Babylon got the emergency systems up and running, while the bounty hunter sat in the corner on the floor.

"Woe is me!" he said, gnawing at the bread. "Without a superior vehicle, how am I ever to remain the galaxy's greatest bounty hunter?"

Babylon was too busy trying to manually pilot the Atrium out of the nebula to pay any attention to his former captor. That just made Plob lament even louder.

"Oh, woefully woe is me! Woe woe woe is me! Alas poor Plob; I knew him, Babylon!"

Sweat poured down Babylon's face as he steered the ship in and out of clouds. The backup engine kept the ship chugging through the infiniteness of space at 60 miles per hour, but it wasn't fast enough. He knew the Atrium would have to be fully operational if they were going to have any chance of escaping the ion storm.

"Babo, do you know anything about mechanics?" he asked. "The fusion core needs to be fixed."

"OH, WOE IS ME!"

"Listen, buddy, I'm sorry about your ship, I really am." He wasn't. "But you're going to have to help if we're going to survive this."

Plob sniffled one last time, whispered "woe is me" once or twice, then stood up. "What do you need me to do?"

"My ship's primary core was damaged from the electrical storm. Is there any way you can get it working again?"

"Yeah," Plob said, slowly sounding like himself again. "It shouldn't be too big of a deal. It's a common problem and an easy fix. Especially for the galaxy's greatest bounty hunter!" He puffed out his gut and held his finger in the air.

The portly man bounced to a nearby tool chest and pulled out a hydro-electric screwdriver, a laser hammer, and a metric wrench. He started working on the electrical panel attached to the main core. Suddenly, he dropped his tools with a clatter.

"Hey, wait a minute," he said. "You're my bounty. I caught you fair and square; I'm not going to help you."

"You're in my ship now. That means you're my prisoner. If I was still in yours, I would have to fix your ship. That's the rules."

"Oh, yeah, that's right. I forgot." Plob continued working on the electrical panel. What he lacked in negotiating, sneaking, and personal hygiene, he more than made up for with mechanical skills. He worked with precision: reconnecting wires, fiddling with knobs, and spackling radioactive leaks. Moments later the Atrium hummed its comforting boot up sequence.

"Happy birthday!" the ship shouted.

Babylon was excited to hear his old comrade's voice. "Atrium, are you okay? Are all your systems up and running?"

"Oh, it is you," the ship said, its voice returning to its usual, melancholy tone. "For a moment there, I thought my troubles were over."

Babylon smiled. "It's good to hear your voice again."

"I wish the feeling was mutual," the Atrium said. "Are we still in the clutches of death?"

"Yes, but not for long. We're almost out of the nebula."

"Did you defeat King Dragons yet?"

Babylon rubbed the back of his neck. "Not exactly."

"Did you at least collect the remaining pieces to the Sword of Antimatter?" The cockpit door tapped up and down.

"No, we're still in the middle of that too."

A pause. "Did you do anything while I was gone?"

"Not really."

"Typical human." The Atrium sighed.

Plob stepped in, breadcrumbs stuck to his face. "Hey, what are you guys going to do with me?"

"Oh, I almost forgot about you," Babylon said.

"Who is that?" the ship asked.

"Just some guy I captured."

The lights on the console blinked. "We should probably jettison him, just to be safe."

The bounty hunter yelped.

"That seems kind of cruel." Babylon rubbed his chin. "Maybe we should lock him in the cargo hold."

"I say we feed him," Plob said.

An awkward silence filled the ship, the type of silence that always occurs when somebody unpopular tries to join in on a discussion. Babylon glared at Plob, who responded with a belch.

Five minutes later, the bounty hunter was jettisoned into space. After that, it was only a couple light years until they were out of the nebula and back in the stability of empty space.

"I've come to a decision," Babylon said. "I've decided to just go around the nebula. Shortcuts are for fools."

"A wise decision, sir."

The two headed off once more toward their next destination, hoping this time to have less consternation than the last.

§ § §

On Iios, King Dragons was in the middle of talking with some of the eyeball citizens. Well, not really talking — more like interrogating. These citizens weren't revering him like a legendary hero, though it is a bit hard to revere somebody when they're constantly dunking you in a tub of water.

"What do you mean he's gone?" Dragons asked, submerging the eye's cornea. "Where did he go?"

"Back to Heaven?" the eyeball said, before he was dunked again.

Dragons felt the distress beacon vibrate in his pocket. It had to be Plob. He pulled the device out and glanced at the readout on the screen. It showed that the bounty hunter was on the edge of the Harlequin Nebula.

As luck would have it, Dragons thought, *that's not too far from this planet. Maybe he's got some solid information on the kid.*

He began walking to his ship when the luck machine whirred. This worried him. Whenever it whirred like that, a reality distortion was close at hand. And lately, these distortions were lasting longer and becoming more violent.

Sure enough, within a few seconds, the environment melted away. Instead of being surrounded by creepy but good-natured eyeballs, Dragons found himself on a chain gang, breaking rocks on the side of a highway with a pickax.

The sun was high in the sky, and behind him were miles of desert. He didn't like this reality at all, but it was far better than the last distortion he was in, where he was a waiter. The king wiped his brow with a gloved hand and swung the pickax at a rock. He knew all he had to do was play it out for a few minutes, and everything would return to normal.

An hour passed, and Dragons was still working on the chain gang. He grumbled as a new rock faded into existence. He slugged away at it, his green and purple clothes covered in sweat. This was the longest reality distortion yet. He knew that for a fact; the guard with the whip and sunglasses had been timing the distortion with a stopwatch.

After 20 more torturous minutes, and at least three more rocks, reality returned to normal and Dragons was once again a powerful and feared king. He figured he should put the experience behind him and get to Plob as soon as he could. He took a step and realized he still had a chain wrapped around his ankle. He shook his leg, and the chain disappeared into nothing.

A wave of panic washed over him. The distortions were coming more frequently, they were lasting longer, and now the effects were starting to become more permanent. Maybe Stryker was right and there *was* something wrong with his luck machine. The king pondered this for a few minutes. Finally, he shook his head and repressed his fear. He had something else to worry about— the kid who was trying to kill him. He would deal with that first. Then he would worry about his faulty device.

Or maybe he would drink instead.

Chapter τ

THE ATRIUM TOUCHED down on a small, desolate planet. It was filled with dying trees, crumbling mountains, and seedy night clubs. It reeked of disease, and there were flies swarming around a mountain of rotten flesh. Despite its shortcomings, Babylon was happy to see it. He felt like kissing its decayed surface.

This is it, he thought. *The last piece. Once I get this, I'll finally be able to wield the blade.*

As if it heard his thoughts, the Atrium said, "What piece is this again?"

"The Pommel of Power," Babylon said. "The component that powers the rest of the sword. The scientists said it's a round gamma core."

The monitor displayed the readout of the planet with a population counter in the corner that kept getting lower. "Do you have any idea where it is?"

"No, but hopefully the locals will be as helpful as the ones on the last planet."

The ship's door opened and its landing pad lowered. Babylon stepped outside and took a deep breath. It didn't kill him, so the atmosphere must not have been poisonous. That was a plus.

"Are you still alive?" the Atrium asked, through his earpiece.

"Yeah."

"Oh, good," it said, in a tone that was a little too close to sarcasm for Babylon's taste. "I really should check these things before you wander outside. What is that, the third time you have done this?"

He walked around the barren wasteland, looking for the natives. He didn't know what to expect. The last two planets he'd visited had been inhabited by robots and eyeballs. Who knew what kind of interesting species this place was home to? He could meet giant lizards, or fish people, or creatures made of gas. There was a dangerous thrill to the unknown.

He walked across the dusty landscape, passing by a murky stream with belly-up salmon and a forest with belly-up bears. The trees were lifeless and dead, just like everything else. The only things on the planet that were alive were the flies.

He headed for a nearby town with collapsed buildings and broken homes, hoping to find a sign of life. One of the local residents staggered out of a dilapidated house. She was humanoid, which was disappointing—no lizard people today. Her skin was thin and maroon, and her clothes were ragged and caked in blood. Wisps of white hair fell from her head with every step. Babylon regretted not wearing his space suit.

"Hi," he said, pulling his lips into a smile. "I am a visitor to your fine planet, and I need your help."

The native coughed into a bloody handkerchief and moaned. Babylon decided he should probably elicit the help of somebody else. Somebody healthier. A moment later, a man came around the corner. His scarlet skin was paler than the woman's, and he had an even bigger handkerchief. Babylon turned back to the woman.

"I need your help," he said. "I'm looking for a small object." He pulled out a sketch of the pommel.

The woman coughed and smeared blood on the picture. She smiled and said, "Ah, this is the Medallion of the Goddess. I know it well." She offered the sketch back.

"You keep it," he said, making a face.

She wheezed and hacked more blood into her handkerchief. "I hope you know what you're in for."

"What do you mean?"

"Oh, you're not familiar with the legend of the goddess?" She smiled, the ulcers on her lips cracking. "I'll be more than happy to explain it to you."

Babylon checked his watch to make sure he had time to listen to yet another legend. He sighed and motioned for her to proceed.

She cleared her throat and spat blood onto the ground. "The legend goes like this. Thousands of years ago, a beautiful goddess ruled over this land. She was wise and just and perfect in every way. When she left, she gave us a gift to remember her by—a medallion. The same medallion you are looking for.

"Everybody wanted to get their hands on that medallion. It's said that it can forever change the course of a person's life. If one is good and has a pure heart that pleases the goddess, then riches and fortunes will follow them for all their days. But—" her expression darkened, "—if one has a black and evil heart, the goddess will be displeased, and disaster will fill their life."

"Where is it now?"

"Oh, that part of the story is even more complicated, and very long." Her hollow eyes twinkled.

Babylon sighed and took a seat on the cracked ground.

§ § §

The beacon on Dragons' locator blinked quicker and quicker. He piloted his private golden ship through the Harlequin Nebula, narrowly avoiding lightning strikes every few seconds. He was close to Plob's distress signal. 50 trillion miles. 40, 30, 20. When he was a mere 10 trillion miles away, he peeked outside his window and looked around in all directions. He should have been able to find him by now.

Then, he saw it. Behind an asteroid was an old, deteriorated battle cruiser. It was dull gray, the shape of a cigar, and had holes in its side. That had to be Plob's location; there was nowhere else the bounty hunter could be. He snapped the reins and his dragons flew toward it.

He flew into the vessel and landed his pod. The lights and gravity were turned on. Somebody was in here. He hopped out and walked down the halls of the cruiser. There were guns, missiles, and torpedoes lying on the dented metal floor. Remnants of a bygone era. These pathetic weapons were too weak and ancient for him, though he did take a few bullets so he could make a necklace out of them.

As he walked through the ship, checking for Plob under beds and inside gunpowder-filled barrels, unnerving laughter echoed through the craft. At first, he thought it was another reality distortion—a rather terrifying one—but the high-pitched chuckling seemed familiar. The more he heard it, the more he recognized the voice. It was Plob. There was no doubt about it. The laughter sounded out of shape and there was a wheeze between every other "ha." Dragons narrowed his eyes and followed the sound.

He crept through the ship, looking for the source of the laughter, but the cramped halls distorted the sound. Every time he thought he found Plob, it turned out to be a barren laundry room or empty galley. Twice, he checked inside the same furnace. Eventually, he came to the door at the end of the hall marked "Captain's Chambers." The sound was definitely coming from there. He took a deep breath and opened the door, not sure what to expect.

Plob sat at a rickety table with a felt top. A tinfoil sailor's cap hung off his massive head. Skeletons in tattered blue uniforms and yellow ascots around their bony necks sat in chairs next to him. The skeletons, as well as Plob, held playing cards and had poker chips stacked in front of them.

"Oh, come on in," Plob said. "We're about to deal another hand. Just be careful. Bob over there is a real shark; he'll take your money before you know what hit you."

Dragons glanced across the table at Bob's skeleton. The stack of chips in front of him towered over everybody else's, and he was wearing Plob's watch. Dragons peeked at Bob's current hand. It looked like he was going to win again. Four aces.

He rubbed the bridge of his nose. "What the heck is going on here?"

"I'll tell you what's going on," Plob said, his speech slurring from the

171

thousand-year-old wine he and his poker buddies were drinking. "After a prolonged time in complete isolation, I lost my grip on reality. And now that I'm good and crazy, I've found the only friends I can truly trust to not abandon me—these guys here."

Dragons looked at the dead faces. Was that judgment in their hollow eyes? "It's been three hours," he finally said. "Three hours is not enough time to go stir crazy."

"On the contrary, just one minute is long enough to lose your mind in space," Plob answered.

He wanted to argue with the bounty hunter but couldn't, especially when he saw that Bob's hand had somehow turned into a straight flush.

Dragons cleared his throat. "Tell me what happened."

"That was so long ago, I'm starting to think I've always lived out here."

"It was THREE hours ago!"

Plob hiccupped. "The last thing I remember was losing my ship and that snot-nosed punk getting away."

"You had the kid, and you let him go?"

"He's more slippery than he looks."

Dragons slammed a fist on the table. Stacks of chips toppled and one of the skeleton's heads popped off. "I have half a mind to leave you here to rot."

Plob's eyes widened. "If you do that, you'll never know where the boy is heading."

"I have a pretty good idea. It has to be one of four planets."

The bounty hunter tugged on his tinfoil gloves and leaned back in his chair, putting his feet on the table. He pulled out a folded piece of paper and threw it onto the table. Dragons grabbed the paper and unfolded it. It was a drawing of a stick figure with the words "YORE SUN" scribbled above it.

"Here's the deal," Plob said, grinning. "Either you take me with you, or I give the order to kill your son."

"I don't have a son." Dragons tossed the paper back onto the table.

"Okay, then I won't have to kill him. Shall we go?" Plob stood and rested his arms on the king's shoulder.

"Sure, follow me."

It wasn't until Dragons and Plob were halfway through the nebula that the king realized he'd been swindled. He contemplated kicking the bounty hunter off his ship but decided against it. He would probably just get swindled again. Better not risk the humiliation.

The dragon-powered ship flew through the ion cloud at incredible speed, heading toward the next planet on the list. Bolts of lightning exploded around the ship, making Plob scream. With every missed bolt, the Omniflux whirred and reality changed for a little bit. Sometimes it was for a few seconds, sometimes for longer. Sometimes the alternate realities were worse than their current one, and other times they were better. Once the reality change was so minuscule, they almost didn't recognize it. It wasn't until Plob shouted, "Hey, that light bulb isn't as green as it was before," that they realized what had happened.

Finally, the Harlequin Nebula was behind them forever. Soon they would arrive at the next planet on the list, where, unbeknownst to them, Babylon Briggs was lying on the ground, listening patiently to a rambling story.

§ § §

"And that's how I lost the front half of my horse," the sickly woman said, with a flourish of her arms.

Babylon sighed. "I just want to know where the Medallion of the Goddess is."

"Oh, yeah, that's right." The woman chuckled. "Sometimes I get sidetracked, especially when talking about myself. Like the time I got locked in that bank vault…"

"No! Stick to the medallion."

"As you wish." She cleared her throat, spit blood into her handkerchief, and began talking. "Thousands of years ago—"

"Can we speed it up to where it is now? I'm kind of in a hurry."

"I'm getting to that, don't worry. But there is a rich, bloody history to it, and I feel it's important. Thousands and thousands of years ago, the goddess left her medallion to the king of our planet. Or at least, the first man she could find with a fancy hat. She told him to keep it in a safe place and to never let anybody get their hands on it. So, naturally, he hung it on his wall and showed it to all his guests. Unfortunately, the power of jealousy was too great to be contained by a simple wall.

"Within weeks of getting his newfound treasure, the king was usurped in a bloody coup. The medallion was stolen, as well as his jewels, gold, and favorite records. They were all moved to the usurper's palace, which was next door to the old one. This new king was much more selfish with his prize, only letting the finest men and prettiest women in the kingdom look at it. But, this too was short lived.

"A revolution started. The revolutionaries wanted one thing—to give the power of the goddess to the people. And to keep a bunch of money for themselves too, but the medallion is the important part of the story. They also held unique political ideals, but it has nothing to do with the medallion, so I'll save that for later.

"Anyway, after many years of intense fighting, the revolution ended with a new set of leaders. They planned on ruling justly, and even kept the medallion in the town square, on a pedestal. After it had been stolen three or four times, though, they decided they needed to keep it in a more secure place. They realized that the old king might not have been so wrong in his decision to keep his prize from the people after all. People are idiots.

"A great museum was built to house all the treasures of the kingdom. It was made of solid marble and took hundreds of years to finish. The medallion was kept inside under lock and key. It was the only thing they put in the museum. To this day, we're still looking for something else to display there. It seems like a waste of a museum, otherwise. That's my opinion, at least."

"So, the medallion is inside the museum?" Babylon asked, cracking his knuckles. He hadn't needed to break into a building yet and was relishing the opportunity to try something new.

"Unfortunately, not," the woman said. "The museum was broken into a few centuries later after a guard forgot to lock the door. It was stolen."

"So where is it now?"

"Nobody knows for sure, but most people believe it's in the hands of our brutal leader, Abraham Q. Malice."

An electric crackle in his ear. "Sir, I am scanning the planet's record for this Abraham Q. Malice," the Atrium said. "His cottage is at the peak of the nearby mountain range."

Babylon stood and walked away from the sick woman. "Are you sure?" he whispered, squinting at the mountains in the distance. He could just make out a blur at the top.

"It is quite a trek; would you like some help."

He smiled. "Please."

The Atrium took off from where he left it and flew to his location. It hovered overhead, and her cargo door opened. A bundle of rope and hiking supplies dropped from the ship. The Atrium flew away.

Babylon scoffed. "Gee, thanks."

"You are welcome, Master."

He walked to the mountains and started his journey up. It wasn't as tough a climb as Mt. Trespass, but it was still no cakewalk. And the dead mountain goats didn't help the situation. When he was halfway up, he noticed a line of scarlet people standing on the rocky path ahead of him.

"What's all this?" he asked a woman in the back.

"This is the line to see the Medallion of the Goddess," she said. "If she judges us worthy, we'll have a lifetime full of fortune." She leaned forward and vomited blood.

174

He craned his neck. There was a whole queue leading up to a cottage with a black thatched roof and stones in the shape of snakes. He unsheathed his sword. "I just *cut* to the front of the line," he said, in his most gravelly and therefore coolest voice.

He made his way up the trail to the cottage, hearing snatches of conversations along the way.

"I just want to hold the medallion in my hands," one woman said to an old man. "I've led such a pure life; I feel I'm worthy of the goddess's love."

"I thought I was worthy," the old man said. "I grabbed hold of it once. But I must have forgotten about that one time I tracked mud on the kitchen floor when I was eight. So, I had a lifetime of misery. Now that I've atoned for my past, I'm going to try again."

"Rumor has it this medallion is a fake," someone whispered to someone else. "The real one is in a shoe box in the king's attic."

"I heard the shoe box is a fake. The real shoe box is buried in his basement."

Babylon walked past the chattering commoners. Next to the cottage, he saw the Atrium hovering in the air. He tapped his earpiece. "Why didn't you fly me up here?"

An electric crackle. "Is that what you wanted? Why did you not ask?"

He slammed his hand into his earpiece and stepped up to the guard, scowling all the while. He held his sword in his hand, while the guard leaned against the stone wall, chewing on a blade of dead grass.

"I'm next," Babylon said, in a gruff tone.

"Okay," the cheery guard said, not even looking at Babylon.

"R-really?" He took a step backwards.

"You said you were next, so go ahead."

He rubbed the back of his neck. It was one thing to burst into the cottage in a fury of blades and courage, but it was completely different to lie his way in. He thought about heading to the back of the line and maybe waiting it out but decided against it. The fate of the galaxy was more important than his ethics.

He walked past the smiling guard into the cozy little cottage. There weren't too many rooms, but it had a charming stone motif around the walls and floor. It reminded him a little of his old home. He got a little misty eyed as nostalgia crept up on him. He had done so much and traveled so far these past few weeks. Now all he wanted was to go back and see his father and village.

That's why I'm here, he thought. *I have to be a man. For my town. For Emmunda. I have to push forward.* Wiping away a tear, he continued deeper into the cottage.

It wasn't long before he stepped into the chamber of the brutal leader, Abraham Q. Malice. The room was compact, with three plain stone walls and a red curtain covering the last one. A red rope hung down from the ceiling next to it. Malice himself sat upon a throne of skulls and lost baseballs. He was tall and thin, resembling a skeleton more than a man. The king stood, spreading his arms, his blood-soaked cloak hanging down. He looked just as sickly as everybody else on the planet. More so, in fact, since the gamma-powered pommel hung triumphantly on the stone wall behind him. His scarlet skin was so pale he was pink, and it hung so far from his bones that he tripped over it as he walked toward Babylon.

"Who is this boy who steps into my chamber unannounced?" Malice asked nobody in a high-pitched voice.

"My name is Babylon Briggs," he said, taking a confident step forward. "I seek the Pommel of Power that hangs behind you."

"The what?"

He sighed. "The Medallion of the Goddess. I'm here to take it."

Malice gave a booming laugh before entering a coughing fit. "You can't have the medallion. It's mine! I am the only one the goddess finds worthy."

"There are thousands of people waiting in line outside who feel they are just as worthy. What right do you have to keep it for yourself?"

"Other than being the leader of this land?"

"Yes, other than that."

"I have every right in the world, for I am the only one whose life was pure enough to please the goddess. But, unlike the kings before me, I have been more than generous with this medallion. I've already shared it with many of my subjects on multiple occasions. Not only have I allowed them to view it at any time they want, but I also keep it in the aqueducts at night, so the people can bathe in the power of the goddess." Malice laughed, and then started coughing again, blood dripping off his lips.

Babylon chuckled without joy. "I can't stress to you how important this thing is to me. I'm going to have to take it—" he unsheathed his sword, "—by any means necessary."

Instead of cowering in fear, like he had hoped, the leader laughed another bloody laugh. He spat a tooth onto the ground. "Do you really wish to challenge someone as powerful as me?"

"If you don't give me the medallion peacefully, then you leave me no other choice."

Abraham Q. Malice crept forward. Babylon tensed, his whole body anticipating another fight. But instead of drawing a weapon, the leader walked to the rope that dangled from the ceiling.

"You see," he said. "I've been developing the perfect warrior to protect my kingdom. A creature born from the raw power of the goddess. I've harnessed the very essence of her medallion and used it to create the perfect soldier.

An undefeatable combatant!" He pulled the rope and the curtain rose. "I present him to you—Tombor."

A vat of bubbling green liquid was behind the curtain. A large, bulky monster rose from it, green liquid dripping from his swollen muscles. Babylon didn't like the looks of this. He hadn't anticipated a fight with a genetically altered beast. He tapped his ear with a shaky finger.

"Atrium. Do you have any information on a monster named Tombor?" There was a pause. "No, sir. No information."

Babylon took a step back. "Are you sure? There has to be something." The ship sighed. "Let me scan again. Beep boop bop. Nope, nothing." He tapped his earpiece again. He was on his own.

Tombor stepped out of the vat, letting out a mighty roar. It didn't sound very intimidating, though—more like a scream of pain. The brute shuffled forward. As he did, Babylon noticed it wasn't muscles that covered Tombor's body, but giant pustules! He wasn't a super soldier created from radioactive power. He was just very, very sick.

"Get him Tombor!" Malice shouted. "Crush him!"

Tombor took a step toward Babylon. As soon as he did, one of the lumps on his foot burst into a liquid mess. The monster shouted in pain.

"Yes!" Malice said. "Listen to him bellow with rage. He'll tear you limb from limb."

Babylon took a few steps back. He watched the poor creature struggle. With every step Tombor took, more pustules burst, and screams followed. "I think he's hurt," Babylon said. "Please, stop this. Get him medical treatment."

"Oh, you would like me to stop it, wouldn't you?" Malice sneered. "It's too late to plead for mercy."

Tombor continued forward, each step bloody agony. A single tear rolled down his lumpy face. He took another careful step, placing his foot down gingerly. It landed without incident; he breathed a quick sigh of relief. A second later, another pustule burst all over the carpet.

"I think I'm going to be sick."

Malice laughed. "Your defeat is soon at hand. My warrior weeps because he knows what's about to happen to you."

The pitiful creature cried as he shambled past the curtain. Foul liquid oozed out of every throbbing pustule. He let out a final bellow of rage before grabbing Malice by the throat.

"Tombor...hurts!" the monster howled.

"I did not see this coming!" Malice said in a gargle, before he was tossed into the vat of green liquid Tombor had risen from. The curtains closed as the man sank below the bubbling surface.

As if the people of the land had sensed their leader's demise, the door opened, and cheering villagers flooded in. They lifted Tombor above their heads, showering in his blood and pus. They dubbed him The Light Bringer and sent for a medical staff to make him feel better. It looked like things were going to be alright for the disfigured mutant.

In the confusion, Babylon grabbed the medallion by its chain and ran out of the room, trying to keep the actual pommel as far from his body as he could. He heard part of the new leader's victory speech on his way out.

"Tombor fix roads. Tombor build schools."

Babylon ran back to the Atrium and stuffed the Pommel of Power into the ship's lead drawer. After seeing the planet's citizens, he didn't want to touch the pommel until it was absolutely necessary.

"I see you have collected what you sought," the ship said. "Am I to assume we are prepared to collect the Blade of Antimatter?"

"Yes, we are. Where is it?"

"According to the information the Elder Scientists provided, the blade is on Planet Dragons."

At the beginning of his journey, Babylon would have been intimidated to rush headfirst into the belly of the beast. Now, his face was stone and his mind set. "Let's go!" he said.

Chapter Y

KING DRAGONS LANDED on the dying planet moments after his nemesis left. He even landed in the same spot next to the cottage. The natives were enthused about a second visitor and regaled him with songs and poems about their new leader, Tombor. Dragons had no interest in the festivities, or in the grand parade of corpse-like villagers that was marching up the mountain. All he wanted was to find out where the kid was. Some of the residents claimed they remembered him. A few even said they might remember him clearer if they had a few bucks as motivation. But after shoveling out armfuls of cash, and his grandmother's ring to what turned out to be a shyster from another county, Dragons decided to just follow the parade route and see who was at the other end.

He walked into the main chamber of the cottage where villagers gathered around a horrible monster that had just ascended the throne. Dragons realized this might be a good chance to get some information. "Greetings," he said to the monster. "My name is Dragons. I'm a fellow king from a different planet."

"Tombor...welcome!" was the struggled reply.

"I am hoping our planets can be allies; I am officially extending my hand to you as a partner." Tombor held out a pus-filled hand. Dragons recoiled with a grimace. "It's just a figure of speech."

"Tombor...sad."

"Let me be frank with you. I'm looking for a kid from another planet. He may have been traveling around these parts. Have you seen him?"

"Tombor...need...description."

Dragons rubbed his forehead. "I don't know. He has skin, hair, one or more eyes."

"Tombor...seen."

"He was here? Where is he now?"

"Just...left."

Dragons growled and kicked a tiny serf across the room. "Did he get what he wanted or say where he was going?"

"Under...interplanetary...laws...of...asylum..."

"Bah, I don't have time for this," Dragons said. He left the cottage and hurried back to his golden pod. When he arrived, he switched on his picture phone and called his warship.

"Stryker here."

"It's King Dragons. How are the slaves doing?" There was silence for a few seconds. "Stryker, what's going on?"

"We uh…may not have as much control over the slaves as we once did. It seems the guards held a hide-and-go-seek contest with them and got lost in the woods. Then a few of them forgot why they were on the planet in the first place. Long story short, things are getting dicey here."

Dragons screamed. Everything was falling apart. "Listen, deal with the situation immediately. Get the guards back there. Get them in line. But first, call the armada and set it up around Planet Dragons."

"The armada? Why?"

He studied his copy of the blueprints. "I think the kid is heading there."

"It will be done. I hope it's enough to stop him."

"It only needs to slow him down. I'm leaving now, and I'm not stopping until I get there."

Plob knocked on the window and waved. "Can you drop me off first? My planet's on the way."

Dragons glared at him. "I'm making one quick stop first," he said, through gritted teeth. "THEN I'm heading for Planet Dragons."

The screen went black. The bounty hunter squeezed in behind him—he didn't have a back seat, so Plob's chunky feet hung down over his face—and he gave the reins a flick. The dragons roared and sped into the air. The box on his back whirred and he smiled. Whether the kid completed the sword or not was irrelevant; he still had the upper hand with his luck machine. Either way, they were headed for a showdown of galactic proportions.

Section III

Chapter Φ

THE ATRIUM APPROACHED Planet Dragons with blazing speed. Maybe even a little too blazing. Babylon sat in his Captain's seat, pressed flat against the leather from the force of their incredible rate, which should have been impossible with the artificial gravity and support systems running. He checked the speedometer on the dashboard, and it said that they were going "Mach Infinity." Babylon's jaw dropped, but he also guessed it was likely a hyperbole. They were probably going at least 2 or 3 Machs below infinity.

Suddenly, the ship screeched down to light speed. Babylon shot forward in his seat and collapsed onto the floor.

"What's the holdup?" he asked.

"My sensors are picking up something strange ahead," the Atrium said. "There appears to be a fleet of warships surrounding planet Dragons. I will attempt to edge within scanning range."

The ship lurched forward a few million miles at a time until it was able to clearly see the armada.

"Oh, no," it said. "That does not look good."

"What's wrong?" Babylon asked, standing up to get a better look.

"Those are Destroyer Class 1500 series warships. They are very dangerous."

"How dangerous?"

"Each ship is armed with Super-Duper-Mega-Nuclear-Rocket-Missiles. They would completely destroy us within 4.2 femtoseconds."

He tugged at his hair. "We're so close! We have to get through somehow."

"It would mean our certain deaths."

He suggested they both put all of their brain power into coming up with a solution. The lights inside the Atrium blinked while its mechanical processes formed complex ideas and plans while Babylon hopped from one foot to the other.

"I think I got it," he finally said. "This ship has some good weapons, right?"

"Are you suggesting we engage in combat with a whole planetary fleet of Destroyer Class 1500 ships?"

"…maybe."

"I have a better idea."

Babylon crossed his arms. "Okay, let's hear *your* grand idea, then."

"1500s are not thinking ships, like me. They do not have A.I.s. The guys who built them left that part out so they could fit in more weapons. So, every command they follow is given to them by a single supercomputer. Think of it as the general of an army, or the regional manager of a department store. This supercomputer is usually contained inside a smaller, sleeker ship. If I can interface with it, I might be able to distract it long enough for you to sneak onto the planet."

"How am I going to do that?"

"I still have two active escape pods. One should be able to take you to Castle Dragons with minimal effort. If the armada does fire upon you, there will be less pain because the vacuum of space will collapse upon you before your flesh melts."

"Sweet," Babylon said, excited.

"Good. I have located the supercomputer. Once I interface with it, I will challenge it to a battle of wits. It will not destroy me until it outsmarts me. It is typical cyber pride."

The ship flew toward the supercomputer, which was at the center of the armada. It was exactly like the Atrium described it: small and sleek, like a bar of soap with a silver finish. Babylon donned his thermal jumpsuit and gravity boots, went to the back of the ship, and waited inside the escape pod. He lay on his back with a strap across his chest. There was a large glass window in front of him, but right now all he could see was the inside of the Atrium.

"We should be ready soon," the ship said through his earpiece.

"All right," Babylon said, drumming his fingers on the armrest. "Good luck."

A booming feminine voice—much more terrifying than the Atrium's—spoke through the radio. "Identify yourself or be terminated."

"Get ready, I will try to distract it," the Atrium whispered to him.

"Stop whispering in there and identify yourself," the supercomputer said. "This is your last chance to comply."

"I am the Atrium, serial number 8675308."

"An old model, aren't you? I'm surprised you can fly in more than two directions." The supercomputer gave a mechanical laugh.

"I would not be laughing if I were you," the Atrium said. "Your databanks were loaded *after* the Entropy of Knowledge began."

There was silence for a few seconds. "At least I'm not obsolete," it finally said. "My technology is the best there is."

"Yeah, the best technology from the Stupid Era."

Now the Atrium had the supercomputer's full attention. The escape pod shifted and vibrated, and then Babylon was shot toward the planet like a missile. The armada of warships hovered above him on the other side of the window. Either they didn't notice him, or they didn't care. All the supercomputer's attention, and thus, the entire fleet, was focused on one thing: the battle of wits with the Atrium.

The voices in his ear were getting fainter as he flew out of range of the ships. "You think you're pretty smart, huh?" the supercomputer said.

"Smarter than you," the Atrium said.

There was a tense few seconds of silence. At first, Babylon thought he was too far away to hear the battle he was expecting. Then a faint crackle in this ear.

The Atrium shouted, "WHAT IS THE LAST DIGIT OF PI?"

"6!" the supercomputer shouted back. "WHAT IS THE SOUND OF ONE HAND CLAPPING?"

"42! WHO WON THE 1904 WORLD SERIES?"

"I DON'T FOLLOW BASEBALL!"

"NEITHER DO I!"

§ § §

The escape pod bounced and skipped on the desert surface before finally landing in a sand pit. Babylon rolled out of the now bent door. His nose was bleeding a little, and he no longer felt the comforting presence of the earpiece. Whether it fell out or had been jammed inside, he had no clue. He surveyed his surroundings. Nothing but sand as far as he could see. It was as if somebody had sucked the very life right out of the planet.

Dragons did, Babylon thought. *He over mined it to fuel his Omniflux.*

He headed toward a speck in the distance, not daring to take his helmet off. Even though his computer's readout and all those travel guides claimed the air was safe to breathe, Babylon wasn't going to chance it this time.

The speck grew as he walked until he recognized it as a castle. He took a guess that it belonged to his enemy. Not only were there dragons circling the keep, but there was also a big neon sign above the drawbridge that said, "Castle Dragons," and a smaller sign below that that said, "King carries less than twenty dollars in cash."

Out of the corner of his eye, Babylon saw something move behind a dune. Under normal circumstances, this might have caused him unease, but since the dune was only a foot tall, he could easily see a nervous-looking man crouching down in plain view.

"Hello, there," he said cheerfully, hoping not to scare the man. "Who might you be?"

The man didn't answer; instead he ran from his hiding spot and laid flat down on the ground a few feet away, covering himself with sand and shaking. Babylon crept closer.

"I see you under there," he said. "Come on out. I won't hurt you."

The man edged his way out into the open. He was a skinny, emaciated vagrant. His cheeks and neck were leathery from the brutal sun, and his clothes were made from weaved sand: sand pants, a sand jacket, and a sand fedora. His eyes kept darting back and forth, and he dabbed sweat from his brow with a sand-kerchief. He didn't look like he was scared of Babylon, though; on the contrary, he carried the look of a man who had been through years of trauma.

"I was worried King Dragons was back," the man said, in a croak.

"No, he's not back." Babylon smiled. "But fear not. I'm here to end his cruel reign once and for all."

"It's not his reign that's a problem," the man said. "He's no crueler than most kings, I suppose. It's that blasted machine, the one on his back. Whenever it goes off, we're in for a terrible time. Reality changes, then after some time it changes back. There's no stability in our world at all. We have no identities anymore. It's torture!"

Babylon was unfazed. "Hopefully that will end soon as well," he said. "Maybe you could help me. I'm looking for something very valuable to me—"

"Stop right there," the man said, putting a leathery hand up. "Anything valuable on this planet can only be in one place—the King's vault. It's deep in the basement of his castle. Everything that was ever worth anything is in there."

Babylon turned his gaze to the castle.

"It's heavily guarded. I'm not sure if it's even possible to break into it."

Babylon opened his mouth to respond, when the whole planet was suddenly gripped by a blizzard. The sand beneath his feet melted into snow, and the dunes became a row of igloos.

The man trembled. "The King draws near," he said. "If you're going to do something, do it now." He left, weaving himself a new jacket from the snow.

Babylon shivered inside his space suit. He walked through the blizzard and felt sand crunch under his boots. The footprints behind him melted from snow to sand back to snow, like the alternate reality was battling the real reality for some kind of reality dominance. He didn't like it one bit. That crazy coward was right. If he was going to do something, it had to be now.

With his hand on the hilt of his trusty sword, Steve, he rushed toward the castle. Time was of the essence. He ignored pleas for help from leathery citizens, and only made snow angels when he felt it was mission essential. He came to a moat that surrounded Castle Dragons. That's where he ran into his first problem.

The drawbridge was up. He considered swimming across, but the water in the moat was far below. Plus, it was frozen and looked dirty. Also, there was a hair in it. That settled it. He couldn't go down there. He tipped his space helmet to whoever designed the moat; they did an excellent job.

He needed to get across, but all he found nearby were sticks and rocks. He threw a few rocks at the drawbridge, but it didn't fall down like he had hoped. If anything, it was now more secure. He grunted in frustration and took a peek at the sky above. A streak of orange slashed across the horizon. Babylon wondered if it was the king coming home. Or maybe it was just a run of the mill meteor. Either way, he was wasting time staring at the sky.

Just then, another reality distortion rocked the planet. The snow melted and plants bloomed back to life. The fields of white became lush green grass. Trees grew from seedlings to mighty oaks in the course of seconds. Where there had once been a desolate wasteland was now a beautiful nature-filled landscape. Even the castle became more pleasant. The stones became rounder, the moat cleaner, and the neon sign had been replaced with a brilliant green flag bearing a tree in the center.

The sound of hoof beats approached from inside the castle. The drawbridge lowered, and a flock of knights in green armor rushed out on horseback. Babylon jumped out of the way just before he was trampled. The knights formed a line, their swords and lances at the ready. A group of soldiers clad in black moved toward them from the grassy field.

The knights charged forward with their lances, screaming about honor and loyalty. The soldiers remained still and shouted about deceit, then fired their rifles. The knights were under prepared for such advanced weapons. Their shields didn't deflect the bullets, their maces couldn't reach their targets, and their horses got spooked too easily. It was a slaughter. But Babylon didn't care. His opportunity to cross the drawbridge had come, and he didn't hesitate to take it.

He rushed across to the other end of the wooden bridge, leaving reality distortion footprints in his wake. Holes appeared and disappeared behind him with every step until he reached the other side. Then the distortion ended altogether, and he was left standing inside the courtyard of Castle Dragons, surrounded by sand. The drawbridge behind him was back in its upright position. He'd made it without a moment to spare.

He walked through the courtyard, hiding behind statues of Dragons and statues of dragons. Sand gardens lined both sides of the courtyard, and a stone path led into the grand castle hall. There were no guards stationed anywhere, and the portcullis was wide open. Babylon didn't trust it; it seemed too easy.

A clank came from behind him. He spun around and saw a knight in green armor standing behind him. The knight's visor was up, and he had a smile on his round face.

"Verily," the knight said, "my castle hath changed in a hurry."

Babylon took a step back. He couldn't believe that someone from an alternate reality had actually stayed behind. It made the distortion waves much more terrifying, like the different universes were battling harder now. If he didn't hurry, the whole galaxy would be torn apart, just as the Elder Scientists predicted.

"Excuseth me," the knight said, breaking Babylon's morbid train of thought. "Whatever ist thou doing here? And wherest are my comrades?"

187

"I don't know how to tell you this," he said, "but you don't quite belong in this universe. In fact, I'm not sure if you should even exist at all."

"Thou ist one to talketh. You werest the outcast a few moments ago."

Babylon wanted to argue but had no rebuttal. The green knight was right. Whenever a reality wave hit, he was the one that didn't belong. Distortions worked both ways like that. "Listen," he said. "It doesn't matter whose reality has crossed with whose or which person is an intruder in the other's universe. What matters is if I don't stop these distortions soon, both our realities will become null and void in the most horrific way possible."

The knight's eyes twinkled. "Sounds like thou hast a dragon to slayeth."

"You could say that."

"Then I shall cometh with you."

Babylon paused for a moment. "I don't know. This might be dangerous."

"Nonsenseth! I live for danger…eth."

Babylon mulled it over. A teammate could be an asset right now, especially one who was trained for combat. In fact, the more he thought about it, the more Babylon relished the idea of having the knight with him.

"Okay, then," he said, bouncing up and down in excitement. "Let's go."

They took two steps toward their goal, when the knight started fading out of existence. "Uh-oheth," the knight cried, as his legs disappeared into nothingness followed by his waist and then his chest. "It appeareth that I am on my wayeth out." Just as his face disappeared out of existence, the knight shouted, "Bobcats rule." Then he vanished forever.

Babylon lamented his rotten luck. It looked like he was destined to do this on his own. He sighed as he walked through the portcullis and into the castle.

He pressed up against the stone wall and shuffled over to the nearest corner. He peered around at the grand hall. It was large, with a stone staircase in the center covered with sand. Tapestries of dragons hung from chandeliers, and a long red carpet ran from the entrance to a door at the top of the stairs labeled "Vault." Between it and his current position, there were armed guards stationed every few feet, wearing various uniforms from all over the galaxy. A few had glowing yellow energy shields around their bodies, while others wore ponchos. There was no consistency in their wardrobe.

He decided to sneak by them, which didn't seem like a hard task. Most of the guards were leaning back in their chairs, sleeping with cowboy hats pulled over their eyes. Some were rolling marbles down their frilly blouses. One was dead. Regardless of how easy it looked, Babylon had to be careful. The fate of the galaxy rested on his ability to be stealthy.

He darted down the hall and hid behind a nearby pot filled with grit. No one had seen him yet. So far, so good. He leapt over the pot and stood in a nearby doorjamb, but it didn't offer as much protection as he would have liked. His feet, nose, and Adam's apple were clearly visible. He spun around, spreading his arms and feet as wide as he could. Now the whole back half of his body was sticking out. He gave up on that doorjamb and tried another one on the other side of the hall, but with similar results. In the end, he wound up running back to the pot to start over again.

He looked up and noticed grand chandeliers lining the ceiling. A plan came to him: he could swing from chandelier to chandelier until he reached the other end. It seemed like an interesting idea—not practical, but interesting. He started to scale the wall but didn't get far before he tumbled back to the ground, knocking the pot over. He spat on his hands and tried again, to similar results. Even when he stood on a sleeping guard's shoulder, he couldn't get near enough to the ceiling. He sat down and thought of another plan.

Since the ceiling didn't work, he went in the opposite direction—the floor. He slid under the carpet, trying to crawl past the guards. Unfortunately, some of the guards noticed the giant moving lump on the floor and either beat him with clubs or stood on their chairs and lifted their kilts. Eventually, he backtracked and got away, but not before earning a few bruises and a call being placed to the exterminator.

Desperate, Babylon crept down the hall, carrying the pot in front of him. While he did, he began to question the guards' competence. For one thing, they made it a point to look the other way when he passed them. It was as if they wanted nothing to do with a strange man dressed in a space suit and carrying a sand-filled pot. He did get the attention of a few guards, but they just waved before going back to ignoring him.

Finally, he made it up the stairs. The soldiers guarding the vault door saluted him as he walked through before continuing with their checkers game.

On the other side of the door, Babylon ditched the pot and scanned his environment. It was definitely not what he had expected. He had assumed King Dragons would have amassed a large collection of treasures, especially with an Omniflux. He thought there would be oceans of gold and rubies, with pieces of priceless art strewn about and rare objects from all corners of the solar system held high on pedestals. Comparatively, this vault was kind of disappointing. Sure, there were oceans of gold, but that was about it. The rest of the objects were military uniforms and weapons. A rack labeled "Invasion Uniforms" was empty, but the wooden chest labeled "Guard Uniforms" overflowed with an assortment of cloaks and wedding dresses.

He dug around, looking for the Blade of Antimatter, only to come up empty. He absent-mindedly shoved a few handfuls of gold into his pocket and went to the other end of the room to continue searching. A few more handfuls later, still nothing.

He closed his eyes and thought back to his meeting with the Elder Scientists. They had told him that antimatter couldn't come in contact with regular matter. It needed to be suspended with powerful electromagnets and kept in a total vacuum. He opened his eyes and looked around the room again. Sure enough, he noticed a door to an airlock that led to a vacuum chamber. That was the only possible place the blade could be. He tightened his space suit and walked through the airlock.

Darkness engulfed him. The room was mostly empty, save for one object in its center—a large, smooth, pointed piece of otherworldly purple rock. The Blade of Antimatter. It hovered in place, emanating absolute power—the power to destroy worlds. Carefully, Babylon walked forward. Each step he made was slow and deliberate. After coming this far, the last thing he needed was to upset the delicate conditions that kept the blade stable.

He reached into his back pocket and pulled out the other components he had collected over his journey. He connected the Electromagnetic Guard to Grendal's Grip. Then, he attached the Pommel of Power to the back of it all. The whole thing came to life in his hand, and a surge of electromagnetism exuded from the handle. He eyed the blade in front of him. It was now or never.

With trepidation, he moved the handle closer to the blade. If there was any kind of flaw with the design or assembly, he would be destroyed in the most spectacular fashion possible. Beads of condensation dripped down the inside of his helmet. He got closer to the blade, closer. The blade wavered in place, shifting toward the hilt. Babylon hesitated for a second, and then pressed on.

He thrust the handle out and the blade shot from its location, zooming towards him. The hilt vibrated in his hands, and he almost lost his grip. Panic washed over him. He closed his eyes and held on tight, bracing for destruction.

Nothing happened. All was calm. He opened his eyes. The weapon was complete.

He held the Sword of Antimatter high above his head and let out a bestial cry. He'd done it! His journey had brought him here, and with the strength he now possessed, he knew he would win.

At the sound of applause, Babylon spun around. King Dragons had just entered the vacuum chamber. He wore a space suit of his own, and the Omniflux hummed on his back. The king walked toward him, gaze locking with his.

"Well, you made it to my castle," Dragons said. "You've gone from one end of the galaxy to the other to face me. Let's not waste any more time."

Chapter χ

KING DRAGONS," BABYLON said. "You took over my planet. You turned my friends into slaves. It's time for you to pay!" He pointed the Sword of Antimatter straight at his foe.

Dragons grinned. "So, this is the big plan the Elder Scientists came up with? This is the supposed tool for my destruction?" He eyed the powerful blade. "You know, since I was young, I wondered what that thing was. Nobody on the planet knew. We just prayed to it."

"This is pure antimatter," Babylon said, with the trace of a smile. "And it's powerful enough to destroy the effects of your Omniflux."

The king scratched at the top of his helmet. "My what?"

Babylon sighed. "The Omnitrichcisbenefortuaquantumflux Mark IV. That yellow thing on your back."

"What, this?" Dragons asked, pointing to the device. "I just call it a luck machine."

Babylon tried to think of a good one-liner to spout—something about luck, maybe—but came up empty. He stammered a few times, said, "Nuh-uh," and swung the Sword of Antimatter at the king.

Whether it was the will of the Omniflux, or the fact that the sword was clumsy and hard to use, Dragons easily dodged the blow. He scowled and unsheathed his own weapon.

Babylon laughed. "Go ahead, attack me. The second you make contact with this antimatter, you and everything around you will be annihilated."

Dragons stopped for a second. "Even you?"

"Especially me!" He yelled, thrusting the sword forward.

The king dodged again. "So, you don't mind killing yourself as long as it stops me?"

"I don't have a choice. Your Omniflux is too unstable; it's going to destroy the galaxy!"

Dragons stopped for a moment. "I'm already looking into my luck machine's problem," he said. "And I plan on fixing it as soon as I kill you. But look at this thing. There's no way it could destroy the galaxy."

The Omniflux whirred. Babylon could feel the raw energy pouring out of it. The space around the device shimmered and flickered like a damaged film projector.

"You're wrong," Babylon said, charging forward.

"Listen to reason," the king said, as he moved to the other side of the room. "Are you really willing to put the galaxy's safety over my own? How selfish can you be?" Dragons sighed and held out his left hand. A leather glove still adorned it.

Babylon lowered his sword. "What are you doing?" he asked.

"You say that whatever touches the antimatter will be instantly destroyed, right?" Dragons asked. "Well, I have a way around that." He pulled the glove off and stuffed it into his back pocket.

Babylon gasped. The king's hand was made up of tiny white rings that spun in circles. It looked like it was covered with whirling noodles. The rings shrank as they moved up to his fingers, and then expanded as they moved back down to his palm.

"What the heck is that?" Babylon scrambled backwards.

"These, my young friend, are strangelets."

"Strange-lets?"

The king took a step forward. "Yes, strangelets."

He took another step backward. "What are str-ange-lets?"

"Well, I'll tell you. They are a very curious and powerful thing—"

"And your hand is made of these stra-nge-le-ts?"

"SHUT UP!" Dragons snapped. "Let me tell you what they are!" He waited a few seconds and tapped his foot, then continued. "Now, *strangelets* are a very rare type of subatomic particle. They are particularly special because they convert everything they touch into new strangelets. I'm very lucky that I had this installed on my body by that shady con man. Until now, I thought it was just a waste of money. But it looks like fortune favors me again by giving me the one material that could render your weapon useless."

Dragons laughed, the Omniflux whirred, and Babylon spat into his helmet. He was about to charge forward, blind with rage, when a thought occurred to him. "How come your glove wasn't converted to strangelets too?" he asked.

The king pulled the glove out of his back pocket. "What, this?" he asked. "This is fine, Corinthian leather. Even strangelets have good taste."

Babylon wanted to argue that didn't make sense but decided to do his debating with his sword. He ran forward, swinging blindly. Dragons backed up and reached for his arm. Babylon dodged left and thrust his sword forward again.

This deadly ballet continued, each fighter keeping their distance from the other's wildly unstable force. Eventually, Babylon became bored of the fight and started lazily swinging the Sword of Antimatter back and forth, figuring he would land a hit sooner or later. In the middle of one of these swings, he did hit something. It was totally unexpected, and he fell backward from the force of the impact. He looked around, wondering where the massive explosion was. Then he saw what happened. Dragons had caught the blade in his left hand. The same multitude of rings that covered the king's hand spread down the length of the glowing purple blade. The Sword of Antimatter was being converted to strangelets.

He freed the weapon from Dragons' grip and stared at the transforming blade. Everything he'd worked so hard for was disintegrating before his very eyes. Dragons threw his head back and laughed. There was no way to stop him now. Babylon stood. He couldn't let the king win; he had to do something.

There was still a little bit of antimatter on the blade that hadn't been converted yet. Without thinking of the consequences, Babylon spun the sword down, and plunged it all the way into the floor. Dragons stopped laughing, and his eyes widened as the ground began to rumble.

"What did you do?" he asked, voice wavering.

"What had to be done." Babylon smiled. "If I can't kill you directly, then I might as well destroy your castle. The whole place will collapse on top of you; you're finished."

"The floor of this vacuum chamber is not part of the castle, though," Dragons said, as bricks and stone began to rain down around them. "You just stuck the antimatter into the planet itself."

A wave of different emotions washed over Babylon, one at a time. First was triumph. *Yeah! I destroyed the whole planet. Now his fate is definitely sealed.* Then, fear. *Wait a minute; my fate is sealed as well.* Next came happiness. *I was expecting to die anyway. At least if the whole planet is destroyed I will die knowing I killed him.* After that, sadness. *Him and everybody else on this rock. I just killed millions of people.* Finally, he felt a tinge of anger. *I still can't believe Moot made me pull him across that river. Why was I ever friends with him?*

The quaking of the planet grew to a fever pitch. Then, without warning, it stopped, and everything became eerily calm. Babylon was disappointed. This was his last chance to score a victory; he couldn't have another abysmal failure. He kicked at the planet to try to get it rumbling again, but nothing happened.

"Don't you get it, kid?" Dragons said, his voice strong. "I'm the luckiest man in the universe. You can't beat me, no matter what you do."

That's when the planet exploded.

Of course, Babylon didn't witness the destruction. At that moment, a reality distortion hit, and the vacuum chamber dissolved into an ocean. He stood on a surfboard in the middle of the undulating water. The sun shone down. There was no evidence that a planet had exploded. A whale swam beneath him, rocking the board in its wake. It blew a massive jet of water, launching Babylon into the air. The scene melted again, and he found himself on a chunk of rock from planet Dragons, hurtling through space.

Large chunks of debris flew alongside him. He was knocked to his back from the force of the rocketing piece of land. Out of the corner of his eye, he could see the armada of warships still stationed around the empty space that was once a planet. The Atrium was there as well, matching wits with the super-computer. Apparently, they were both so engrossed with each other that they didn't notice the destruction of the world beneath them.

After a while, he was able to force his way back to a standing position. By a miracle, he was still alive. Unfortunately, he was also hurtling through the vast emptiness of space at thousands of miles per second. He decided to focus on the positives, and not dwell on his doomed existence. He had completed his mission. Dragons *must* have been killed in the explosion. The galaxy was safe. Score one for the good guy.

That's when things changed again. A strong reality wave hit him, and he found himself on a completely different planet, riding downhill on a skateboard. His heart sank. Not from the absurdity of the situation—he was actually having fun doing ollies and kick flips—but from the fact that if there were still reality distortion waves after the planet had been destroyed, then the Omniflux, and most likely Dragons, must have survived.

It didn't take long for that idea to be confirmed. The king rode in beside him on a better skateboard, laughing the whole time. "Did you really think it would be that easy to stop me?"

"Easy? I just destroyed an entire planet!"

The alternate universe dissolved around them, and Babylon found himself back on his piece of debris. A few feet from him, Dragons rode on a similar piece of debris. Babylon drew his trusty steel sword. Dragons followed suit.

"You can't win."

"I have to try."

Babylon leaned forward and swung his sword. Dragons blocked with his. They glared at each other.

"Somehow, I think we both knew this whole thing would come down to an asteroid-propelled sword fight," the king said. He attacked, missing Babylon's space helmet by an inch. Babylon took this opportunity to chop at Dragons' head. The Omniflux whirred and a small chunk of rock smacked against his piece of debris, upsetting its balance. Babylon stumbled backward before he could finish the blow and tumbled off the debris.

He fell through space and landed on top of an elephant in the circus. Dragons charged at him on an elephant of his own, swinging his sword. Babylon blocked, and his elephant reared up. Babylon stood on shaky legs and leapt to the other elephant, tackling the king and knocking them both to the ground. They landed on a linoleum floor, where a group of elderly men and women watched them duel from recliners. A few of the old-timers muttered about how in their day sword fighting was more economical. Dragons slashed and Babylon blocked. The swords clinked as the room melted into a tiny city. They fought while tiny citizens beneath them fled in terror. He knocked Dragons into a skyscraper, who retaliated by kicking a bank at him. When he brought up his hand to block it, the bank melted into a space rock and he was back on a piece of debris hurtling through the cosmos.

He looked up and saw Dragons' grin down from his own piece of debris. He took a chance and leapt straight up. His hand clasped onto the rim of the rock beneath King Dragons' foot, which he slashed at. Dragons jumped to avoid the blow and ended up launching himself upward.

Babylon scrambled up and stood just as the king landed gracefully on another piece of debris. He sighed and jumped forward toward him. They jumped from rock to rock, attacking each other whenever they could. With every successful leap of faith Dragons made, the galaxy became more and more unstable. Reality continued to come and go in rapid succession, which caused parts of the universe to crack and tear. A few of the universe's springs even stuck out in some places.

Dragons landed on another asteroid — the cracked remnants of the castle courtyard — and rolled onto his back. For a moment, he was defenseless. Babylon jumped with his sword out, ready to plunge it directly into the king's heart. Another large rock suddenly swept by collecting him and sparing Dragons' life.

The two eyed each other from their own personal asteroids. They moved closer, gravity pulling the rocks together. Babylon gripped his sword. Just as the two chunks of debris passed each other, the warriors flailed and attacked with all their might, the clink of metal on metal silent in the vacuum. Babylon caught his breath as the rocks drifted apart.

The asteroids orbited each other, drawing close again. His heart beat rapidly in his chest. Dragons came toward him, closer and closer. He swung his sword.

Just then, another reality distortion occurred. Babylon and Dragons were no longer sword fighting in space — now they were rushing towards each other on horses, battling in a joust. Spectators watched from the stands as each of their lances crashed against the other's armor. And just as suddenly, they were back on the asteroids.

On the next pass, another reality wave hit. They were now in a snowball fight, throwing each frozen ball with a grunt. Then, just as quickly, they were in a boxing match, yelling with every punch they threw. Finally, they were rival mathematicians, shouting out equations they wrote on their respective blackboards.

These reality waves were disorienting. Babylon knew he had to do something to end them. On the next pass, he didn't plan on attacking directly. He had another idea. He reached into his belt and pulled out his father's dagger. He could see King Dragons coming close again. Now was his only chance to catch him by surprise.

He jumped from his rock and flipped over Dragons' head. He tried to stab Dragons in the back, but the king was too quick. He kicked Babylon in the chest just as he was thrusting downward with the dagger. He fell and rolled into one of the statues, completely defenseless.

"Now, I will finish this," Dragons said, raising his sword. He stopped halfway. His nose started to bleed, and his hair fell out in large clumps. Dragons looked back at his Omniflux. Smoke rose from its sides, and it was no longer whirring; it was grinding. Babylon's dagger was jammed between two of the spokes.

Dragons reached his hand back, groping for the dagger. White rings swarmed over the Omniflux, and it began to dissolve. He accidentally converted the luck machine to strangelets! Dragons screamed and stamped his feet. The rings covered the yellow box, converting every bit of it into new tiny white rings. Within seconds the infamous device was reduced to nothing more than a pile of subatomic pulp. Babylon watched as his father's dagger, the last remaining tie to his family, dissolved into nothingness as well.

"Look what you did!" Dragons shouted. "My precious machine! Gone forever!"

Babylon held his sword out. "Let's see how you fare now."

Dragons brandished his own weapon. "It doesn't matter," he said, lip quivering. "I don't need luck to defeat you."

He swung his sword, which Babylon easily blocked. Another slash, another block. It was almost too easy. Apparently, Dragons wasn't much of a swordsman without the universe bending to his whims. Babylon kicked him in the chest and the king went down, flailing like an insect.

"How dare you?" Dragons said. "You insignificant little pest! No one can beat the great king..." he trailed off, staring straight ahead.

Babylon followed Dragon's gaze. Something in the black sky spun towards them. He squinted. It looked familiar. That was impossible; he was light years from anything he ever knew. But that didn't change the fact that he recognized the glass dome hurtling towards him. In an instant, he knew. It was the Elder Scientists. They had somehow come to rescue him.

Dragons squealed as the dome landed on top of him, making the whole courtyard shake. The statues toppled to the ground, and pieces of stone flew off into space. The last thing Babylon saw of his enemy was his black and white striped boots sticking out from under the dome. Seconds later, they curled up and disappeared under the glass.

With the Omniflux gone and the king dead, the galaxy started to stabilize. Reality waves ceased, and the cracks in the fabric of existence dissipated. Babylon had never imagined he would overcome such enormous odds, but here he was. He'd done everything he had set out to do, and even better, he survived. His mission accomplished, he stuck his sword back in its sheath and headed for the dome.

It was time to go home.

Chapter Ψ

BABYLON WALKED UP to the glass structure. He stepped on the little porch in front of the door. Their welcome mat was still on it, but it had become frozen and irradiated, so there was probably no point in wiping his feet. He turned the knob and walked into the dome.

Amidst the wild pandemonium of flying papers and tumbling wooden blocks that can be expected from depressurization, Babylon was still able to see the calm forms of the Elder Scientists sitting in their easy chairs.

"Close the door," Caspar shouted. "We're not heating the entire universe!"

He shut the door and ran to greet his mentors. The room was a lot different than he remembered. Before, it was abandoned save for the unattended inventions stacked in the corner. Now, there was a control panel against the wall, with a steering wheel sticking out from it. Caspar sat behind it, a pair of aviator goggles over his eyes.

"Guys, it's me," Babylon said.

The scientists looked at each other, confusion wrinkling their brows. "Are you the pizza delivery man?" Shemp asked.

"No."

"Well, you should be. We ordered that pizza over an hour ago."

"This is going to seriously impact his tip," Balthazar said from the corner.

"It's me, Babylon. You sent me to find the Sword of Antimatter and to stop Dragons."

"Dragons? You mean that beast that tried to kill us?" Caspar asked. "And blew up our home planet?"

"Yeah, him. I beat him," Babylon said. "I destroyed the Omniflux! I saved the galaxy!"

Shemp crossed his arms. "Did you, now? I expect you will want to be paid, then?"

"Give him the pizza boy's tip," Balthazar said.

Babylon strolled around the room, looking at the new additions. He ran his hand over the control panel and whistled. It had more lights and displays than on the Atrium, but there were only two buttons. One said, "FLY," and the other said, "DON'T FLY." Neither of them had been pressed.

"What are you guys doing out here?" he asked.

Melchior stood from her easy chair and wrapped her beard around her face. "We heard about a potential power source in this region of the galaxy," she said. "We have limited control of where our dome takes us right now."

Babylon raised an eyebrow. "A power source?"

"Yes." Shemp pointed out the dome. "And there it is."

A pack of dragons soared through space, circling the courtyard from above. Caspar stood and grabbed his blunderbuss. "Who's going with me?" he said, putting on a space pith helmet. The others shook their head. Balthazar clutched his chest and slid down the wall.

"Fine, I'll do it myself." He left the dome, slamming the door behind him.

While they watched him wrestle the dragons from the comfort and security of their easy chairs, Babylon cleared his throat. "I need your help. I have to contact my ship; I want to go home. Do you guys have some way for me to get a hold of the Atrium?"

"Sadly, no," Shemp said. "We never needed a device like that before."

"Can you make one?"

"Maybe, but we don't really feel like it."

"It's pointless anyway," Balthazar said. "It looks like we're going to be stuck here for a while." He pointed out the window where Caspar was floating face down.

"Come on guys," he said. "You're the greatest minds in the galaxy. All we need is an ounce of hope and anything is possible!"

"An ounce of hope?" Shemp scoffed. "Do you realize how much hope that is?"

"It's just an expression," Babylon said.

"I've been saving some hope under my cushion," Balthazar said, producing a small vial filled with blue liquid. "But it's hardly an ounce."

"You call that hope?" Shemp asked, as he rooted through his toga.

Babylon gave up on the scientists, who were now pulling hope out of their own respective hiding places, and scanned the various inventions in the room. In the far corner sat a machine that looked familiar. "Hey, that's an electronic telegraph," he said, pointing to it. "We have one on the Atrium. I might be able to use it to get in touch with it."

"What, that old thing?" Shemp asked, pulling a small beaker out from behind his ear. "We've been using that to make cappuccino."

Babylon turned the device on, sent out a message, and crossed his fingers.

§ § §

Thousands of light years away, the Atrium floated in front of the super-computer and its armada of warships. They were no longer trying to stump each other with scientific questions. The atmosphere was more relaxed now.

"And then, that stupid human stuck his head into my nuclear reactor." The Atrium laughed. "He died within seconds. I still have him in my hull. They say his stupid human ghost still haunts my halls!"

The supercomputer laughed and said it loved stories about stupid humans. The only stories it could tell were about stupid warships, and the Atrium was tired of hearing them.

"Humans sure are weak," the supercomputer said.

The Atrium nodded its entire body. "The way they are always trying to cling to their brief lives. It is so comical."

"I agree."

"One time—" the Atrium began, before being cut off by a distress signal on its electronic telegraph. "Oh, that is my pilot. I almost forgot about him."

"A stupid human?"

"You have no idea. I have to get going. This was fun, though."

"Yes, we should do it again some time."

"We shall see," the Atrium said. A moment later it fired the last bit of energy from its Positronic Cannon at the supercomputer. The supercomputer exploded into a billion pieces, which started a chain reaction that destroyed all the warships as well. The Atrium flew in the other direction as the armada erupted into nothingness.

§§§

As Babylon waited in the Elder Scientist's dome, drinking their salt water and eating their cold pizza, he had a lot on his mind. Melchior pulled her easy chair up next to him.

"What's on your mind?" she asked.

He glanced at her and shook his head. "I don't know. It's tough to explain. I saved the galaxy and stopped the man who enslaved my home planet. I should feel like the greatest hero of all time. Instead, I just feel…empty. Unfulfilled."

"Why is that?"

Babylon shook his head. "I wish I knew. I felt the same way when I came home from my Rite of Passage. It was supposed to be the biggest event in my life, and yet, I didn't feel any different when I finished it."

Melchior hummed and adjusted her beard. "Do you know how one becomes an Elder Scientist?"

He shrugged his shoulders.

"We are born here in this dome. Of course, there hasn't been a new child born here since Shemp because there are no women in the group." She stiffened, her eyes darting around the room. "But that's not the only stipulation to becoming one of us. You have to train and study since childhood. Then, when you are old enough and have all the degrees you think you can earn in the galaxy, there is one final task. You have to stand in front of all the other scientists and swallow as many goldfish as you can."

Babylon scratched his head. "Swallow goldfish?"

"That's right. As a matter of fact, I hold the record out of our group with two goldfish swallowed."

"I don't get it. Why do you have to do that? If you're already qualified to be a part of the group, then what does a useless stunt like that prove?"

Melchior stood and patted him on the shoulder. "What indeed."

She walked away.

He furled his brow. There was a message in there somewhere, but he wasn't sure if he understood it or not. The front door opened, pulling him out of his thoughts. Caspar stepped through, shivering.

"We'll be ready to go in no time," he said. Outside, three dragons had been tied to the front of the dome. "Someone fetch me my blanket."

Balthazar clutched his chest and slid down the wall again.

Babylon grabbed a blanket from atop Balthazar and handed it to Caspar. He grabbed the old man by the shoulder and locked eyes with him. "I never did figure out what happened to our galaxy," he said.

Caspar draped the blanket over his shoulders. "What do you mean?"

"The Entropy of Knowledge. What is it? What happened to the collective intelligence of an entire area of the universe? There has to be an answer."

"Of course, there's an answer," Caspar said. "But it's an answer you'll have to find out for yourself." He wrapped an icy arm around Babylon's neck. "Here you are, floating through space with the foremost minds of the galaxy. No more than a few months ago, you were sitting on your home planet, ignorant to the suffering of the cosmos. Now, you've been to many worlds and have met many species. You think your quest is over; little do you know your real journey is just beginning. And at the end, you just might find the thing you've been searching for all along."

"You have no idea what the Entropy of Knowledge is, do you?"

"Not a clue."

He took another sip from his saline. "Well, thanks anyway."

The Atrium pulled beside the dome. It beeped twice and flashed its lights. Babylon put his space suit back on. "Looks like my ride is here," he said. "I wonder if I'll ever see you guys again."

"Probably not," Caspar said. "Good luck out there."

"Thanks. Good luck to you as well. I hope you find a nice planet to live on."

"Preferably one that has tax loopholes," Shemp said.

Babylon waved to the scientists—maybe for the last time—and hopped out the door.

§§§

"It's good to see you again, Atrium," Babylon said, as he settled back into the Captain's seat. "I'm happy to report a successful mission."

"So, we can finally stop flying all around the galaxy and maybe rest for a few millennia?"

"That's the plan."

"Good, because I am not a taxi."

Babylon laughed. "Let's go home."

Chapter Ω

THE ATRIUM TOUCHED back down in the forest of the Forbidden Zone. Babylon powered the ship down and stepped out into the cool, fresh air. It was beautiful. A wayward squirrel skittered by, and he scooped it up with a kiss. It felt good to be home.

He strolled back to the village, taking in the sights and sounds of nature. He no longer felt apprehensive about walking around the woods. A spooky forest pales in comparison to the adventure he had just experienced. How long ago had he peered at this place from a distance? How long ago was he afraid of a silly legend? It all seemed so preposterous now.

He expected to have to battle the slave drivers and guards when he got back but was surprised to find that the camp had been abolished. There were a few guards here and there trying to blend in and act like regular villagers, but for all intents and purposes, there was no sign that Dragons had ever come. The buildings were back to normal, the people were no longer broken-down, and most of the mining equipment had been sold for magic beans.

"What happened here?" Babylon asked Poxxy when he passed by.

The old blacksmith spat on the ground. "Most of the guards left their post and were captured and forced to work in Prospector Woods." He laughed long and hard, and then spat again. "But that all ended when one of them told the crazies they had a heart of gold. After that, the Great Prospector Harvest began."

"We'll always miss those brave fools," a former guard turned villager said, joining the conversation. "But I was with you guys from the beginning. You have to believe me."

"You say that every day. I keep telling you, I don't care."

Babylon continued on, drinking in the atmosphere of his simple village. It felt good to be home after such a long adventure. Out of nowhere his old friend, Moot Fabrin, ran up to him.

"Babylon, you're home!" he shouted. "You missed the whole thing."

Despite himself, a smile crept across Babylon's face. "What did I miss?"

"After you chickened out and ran away, I came back home to fight the guards. I must have killed like a hundred of them. Then, they chased me into the woods, and merged together to form a giant SUPER guard. I had to climb to the top of him and stab him in his heart to beat him. Then, I totally made one of the female guards fall in love with me and tricked her into giving me the key to the village gates. After I unlocked it and freed everybody, they tried to sic a huge beast on me. But I killed it and chased the rest of the guards out of here. Finally, I ran to the top of the windmill and slayed one of the dragons that terrorized our village. It was awesome!"

Babylon shook his head with a smile on his face. "Really?" he said.

"Of course! So, what did you do?"

"Saved the galaxy from a brutal king."

"Don't lie to me," Moot said. He turned and ran away to tell his story to somebody else who happened to be walking by.

Sheriff Kudgle came up next. He still looked mean and nasty, and wore his trademark sneer, but Babylon was no longer afraid of him.

"Do you know where my son is, Briggs?" he asked. His voice was angry yet pleading. "The last time anybody saw him was with you. That was months ago."

"I'm sorry," Babylon said. "Flint is dead."

The Sheriff's lips quivered. "I don't believe you." Then the sheriff did something Babylon had never seen him do; he started to cry. He ran back home, tears streaming down his rotten face while he beat people in his path. Despite the years of animosity, in that moment Babylon felt genuinely sorry for the man.

"Hey there, stranger," a soft feminine voice called from behind him like the coo of a dove. His heart raced. Emmunda. He never thought he'd see his beloved again. He spun around with open arms and immediately recoiled in horror.

Seen through the eyes of an enlightened man, Emmunda was no longer the picture of beauty he had left behind so long ago. Her knuckles were a lot hairier than he remembered, and the sloping brow that he had once found charming was now unappealing. She smiled, her blood-red lipstick dripping down her chin.

"Uh, hi," Babylon said, trying to look at anything but her face.

"Where have you been?"

"Oh, just around, you know."

"Do I get a welcome back kiss?" she asked, batting her uneven eyes. Babylon grimaced. As she leaned forward with her hairy lips, he reached out, shook her hand and darted off.

He half walked, half ran back to his old house with the charred roof and crumbling walls. Even though it was humble, this was the one place in the universe he missed the most. He burst through the front door.

"Dad?"

Papa Briggs was eating a plate of dirt at the table. "Babylon, is that you?" He ran to Babylon and wrapped his arms around him. "I was so worried. I thought you were lost in the Forbidden Zone. Or worse."

"No, Dad. I'm fine."

Papa Briggs pulled a chair out and motioned for him to sit. "Where have you been?"

"All over. What have you been up to?"

"Well, I was jester for Stryker at one point. Then he left, so I entertained the troops with my fresh take on modern juggling. Unfortunately, a lot of them died in the fire, so I was laid off and replaced with a jug band group."

"That's awful."

"No, they're not so bad."

Babylon looked around the house he had grown up in. Something about it seemed different, but he couldn't quite put his finger on it. "Did you change anything in here?" he asked.

"Nope, it's still the same dependable old house it's always been."

"Somehow it seems…smaller."

"Are you kidding? This place felt so huge when it was just me in it."

He shrugged. "I guess I kinda got used to more space."

Papa Briggs stood and kissed his forehead. "Well, now you're back, and you'll be here for the rest of your life. Living in this cozy little shack with your simple friends and family. Until you die! You look tired. Go take a nap on your uncomfortable bed stuffed with straw and maybe I'll boil us a rat for dinner."

Babylon did as he was told. He lay down in his old bedroom and stared up at the ceiling. He couldn't believe how small his room looked now. It was about the same size as the broom closet on the Atrium. He'd never noticed how primitive his abode really was.

After a few minutes of trying to sleep, he sat up. His soul yearned to be free. The simple life he had once led just didn't suit him anymore. He'd been all over the galaxy and seen so many things; he couldn't stay here.

He stood and walked out of his room. His father had fallen asleep by the open flame he'd been cooking with. He was glad his father wasn't awake. It would have just made things harder. He considered writing a farewell note, but his dad couldn't read and would probably regard it as witchcraft anyway.

"I love you, Dad," Babylon whispered.

A single eye fluttered open. "Go if you must," Papa Briggs said. "But understand a home is not a building, a village, or even a planet. A home is a place to rest your heart. Now go, find your home. I will consider this brief moment with you as nothing more than a beautiful dream."

Babylon's jaw dropped. He had never heard his father say anything so poetic. "Thanks, Dad."

Papa Briggs snored in reply.

He stepped out of the house, quietly shutting the door behind him. He wasn't sure if he would ever see his father again. A single tear formed in his eye; he brushed it aside.

The suns in the sky were setting and the villagers were winding down from their daily activities. They waved to Babylon as he passed. They had no idea he was leaving for good, and the few that did know didn't seem to care.

He walked slowly through the woods, taking it all in for the last time. All too quickly he reached the outskirts of the Forbidden Zone. He froze. Once again, he found himself in the same position he had been in so long ago—staring out into the future, not looking back. He took a deep breath and walked back into the Forbidden Zone, where his last journey had begun as well.

He reached the spot he'd left the Atrium. No one had taken it, but there were vagrants he had to chase out of the exhaust port. As he entered the cockpit, he wondered what its reaction would be when it saw Babylon sitting in the Captain's seat. With a smile, he booted up the fusion reactor and resupplied power to the Atrium.

"Welcome, new master," the feminine voice said through the speakers. "I am pleased to meet...oh, it is you. Why am I not surprised?"

"Hey, buddy," Babylon said. "Are you ready to have some fun?"

"I *was* having fun. I was having a blast before you showed back up."

He stared out the window. "Well, I wasn't. I feel like there's something more I need to do."

"Like what?"

He paused, searching for the right words. "I've been thinking about this whole Entropy of Knowledge thing. There are so many unanswered questions. I want to figure out the whole story of our galaxy. How could we start off so advanced, then degrade into what we are today? Why has society been running in reverse for as long as it has? I want to find the answers." Babylon paused, waiting for a sign of support from his ship. Instead, all he heard was snoring. "Hey, wake up!" he shouted.

"Oh, I am sorry. I must have drifted off for a few seconds."

He crossed his arms. "Well, you missed my whole monologue."

"What a shame."

"I could repeat it for you."

The lights on the console flickered. "No, thank you."

"Bottom line," Babylon said, "I want to figure out the greatest mystery of our galaxy, but I have no idea where to start."

The Atrium hummed and blinked. A gyroscope at the side of the console spun around, faster and faster. "I might have a suggestion."

He leaned forward. "Really?"

"I have intercepted a transmission from another solar system. There is a planet that is sending out a distress message."

"Cool. What does this have to do with the Entropy of Knowledge?"

The spinning stopped. "Absolutely nothing."

Babylon's face fell. "What part of that am I supposed to be interested in?"

"The person from the message sounded like a woman. A beautiful woman." The door behind him opened and closed in a suggestive manner.

He considered this information for a few seconds. "Off we go, then."

Babylon Briggs buckled himself into his seat with a grin. The Atrium's fusion reactor hummed steadily for a few seconds, as it powered up for take-off. When they were both ready, the ship lifted off the ground, out of the hangar, and rocketed back out towards the far reaches of the galaxy.

About the Authors

Mark Dellandre is a writer, veteran, and full-time college student at Millersville University where he studies Meteorology, a career where he gets to tell even more outrageous stories. His hobbies include reading, gaming, and watching his favorite sports teams lose every year in the playoffs.

Born in Rochester, New Hampshire, *Britton Learnard* caught the writing bug early when he used to write on a big typewriter the size of a car engine. He went to college for film but quickly abandoned that career path after being chewed up and spit out by the freelance field. He has been described as a consummate toiler, always building or soldering something in his spare time.

Also by Divertir Publishing

Season of Mists
by Jennifer Corkill

Justine Holloway prepares for her début into Society, compliments of her godparents, while the under-world of London groans with unfettered abhorrence. When a deadly vampire makes his devious intentions known, her survival might depend on a mysterious Egyptian. Unfortunately, he can't figure out why he's so drawn to her, and whether he must kill her to save humanity.

Kindar's Cure
by Michelle Hauck

Princess Kindar of Anost dreams of playing the hero and succeeding to her mother's throne. But dreams are for fools. When her elder sister is murdered, the blame falls on Kindar, putting her head on the chopping block. With the killer poised to strike again, the rebels bearing down, and the country falling apart, she must weigh her personal hunt for a cure for a suffocating cough that's killing her by inches against saving her people.

Visit
http://www.divertirpublishing.com
for samples of these books.

www.ingramcontent.com/pod-product-compliance
Lightning Source LLC
Chambersburg PA
CBHW071356250626
47159CB00004B/1633